VORTEX: BERLIN

LEE JACKSON

SEVERN ⚓ RIVER
PUBLISHING

Severn River Publishing
www.SevernRiverBooks.com

ISBN: 978-1-64875-571-2 (Paperback)

ALSO BY LEE JACKSON

The Reluctant Assassin Series

The Reluctant Assassin

Rasputin's Legacy

Vortex: Berlin

Fahrenheit Kuwait

Target: New York

The After Dunkirk Series

After Dunkirk

Eagles Over Britain

Turning the Storm

The Giant Awakens

Riding the Tempest

Driving the Tide

Never miss a new release! Sign up to receive exclusive updates from author Lee Jackson.

severnriverbooks.com

In Honor of my Great Friend
&
Brother-in-Arms

Jim Skopek
We Had One Hell'uv a Ride!

Corinne and Krista are Proud of You
Well Done. Be Thou At Peace.

MAJOR CHARACTERS

Atcho: Protagonist
Antagonist: The Russian
Sofia Stahl: Atcho's Wife
Burly: Retired CIA Officer
Tony Collins: Investigative Reporter
Ivan: Ex-Soviet KGB Officer
Rafael: Atcho's Friend
Major Joe Horton: US Army Intel Officer
Wolfgang Sacher: East German Politburo
Johann Baumann: Director of the Stasi
Veniamin Krivkov: Nuclear Engineer
Klaus aka Sahab Kadyrov: KGB Deserter
Ranulf: Stasi Officer

PROLOGUE

August 13, 1961 – Berlin.

A car with US diplomatic license plates pulled to the side of the street across from a home in a residential neighborhood. A father and two small girls emerged. The girls smiled at each other and hugged, then one started across the street under the watchful eye of the father. The other girl held his hand.

They heard the roar of an engine and glanced down the street. A military vehicle traveling in the opposite direction slowed and parked on the other side. An East German soldier emerged, carrying a paint can.

The first girl crossed the street safely and skipped to the front door of the house. She turned and waved. "Bye, Cousin. Bye, Uncle. See you soon." Her eyes shifted to the soldier. Her uncle followed her gaze.

The soldier walked to the middle of the street and crouched, fumbling with the paint can. He pried open the lid, produced a brush from his pocket, and dipped it.

Sounds of trucks from both directions broke the peaceful quiet of the neighborhood. The vehicles stopped at intervals, and East German soldiers climbed out. They spread themselves along a line in the middle of the street.

Standing next to her father, the other girl took in the activity but quickly dismissed it and waved back. "Bye. See you soon."

The man felt a pit form in his stomach. He stood in the American Sector of Berlin. The soldiers stood in the Soviet Sector—and so did his little niece, who watched the unfolding scene with innocent fascination.

The soldier lifted the brush out of the can. The paint was white. He reached down and swiped it across the rough surface, indelibly marking the boundary that separated East from West on the streets of Berlin. Germany was now a divided country, and Berlin a divided city.

* * *

December 1988 – In the Atlantic, Over the Horizon from the Coast of the Azores.

Gonçalo, a fisherman, glanced from his net to the sky. His kindly eyes squinted in the shimmer of sun on rippling water. A roar out of the northwest descended to the waves and bounded toward him, increasing in intensity. He knew what it was: a military cargo jet bound for Lajes Air Base on the main island. He cupped his hands over his brow and searched in the direction of the roar. Soon he saw it, enlarging as it approached on a flight path that would go directly over his head. As he made out the detail, he gaped in wonder at the enormous aircraft, pulled through the air by six jet engines and held in steady flight by giant twin stabilizers.

Gonçalo recognized the markings of a Soviet aircraft. He never paid much attention to world affairs but was sufficiently informed to know of the bitter East–West rivalry between the US and the Soviet Union. He found it curious that both superpowers used the landing facilities at Lajes.

The jet thundered overhead, and Gonçalo watched until it disappeared beyond the horizon. Today, he was alone on the sea. He looked about in all directions, but not another ship, fishing vessel, or object of any sort that he could see floated on the deep blue waters. When the smell of the jet's exhaust was blown away by the breeze, he adjusted his nets and settled back to take in the sounds and fresh air of the vast Atlantic Ocean. He felt at peace here. His eyes closed and he snoozed.

An hour later, a peculiar vibration strumming the wispy clouds awakened him, but he could not immediately place it. He thought he had heard a rhythmic whirring, a sound he knew belonged to the US Navy helicopters that frequently crossed the skies. Sometimes he was close enough to their mother ships that he could watch liftoff or landing, and he marveled at the enormous size of the vessels and the engineering genius that made flight possible for a machine as ungainly as a helicopter.

He heard whirring again and tried to spot the aircraft, but as he searched, the sound halted momentarily, like a cough. When it resumed, it was choppy, sputtering. Then he saw the it. A plume of black smoke marked its location against the blue sky, trailing after what appeared to be a mechanical beast in distress.

The main rotor flopped about out of control, striking the boom. The body gyrated chaotically. Even from his position a half mile away, Gonçalo knew it to be, without a doubt, one of the big US Marine helicopters. As he watched in alarm, its forward motion altered sharply, and it plunged toward the sea. Its descent accelerated as its nose dropped. It rose again, as if in a desperate attempt to save itself, and then it smacked the water.

A column of sparkling droplets sprayed into the air. When the water cleared, all Gonçalo could see was the tail of the chopper. It jutted from the water at an angle, its rear rotor still spinning. Then the boom rotated perpendicular to the horizon, and the helicopter slid into its watery grave. Calm descended once again on the ocean.

Horrified, Gonçalo could only stare. Then, as if rousing himself from a dream, he stumbled in the rocking boat to the tiny cabin at its center and fumbled with the ignition. He glanced over his shoulder to keep a bearing on where the aircraft had gone down. The motor kicked in. He angled the boat toward the crash.

He knew when he had reached the site because small bits of debris floated in an expanding circle among the waves, but he saw no sign of human life. Circling about the center of the flotsam in a tightening spiral so as not to miss anything, he was sure that rescue teams would soon descend from the sky. For survivors, seconds counted.

He spotted a globular piece of flotsam on the surface and guided the boat toward it. As he approached, the object rotated in the water, exposing a man's face, mouth open, gasping for air. Gonçalo pushed the throttle for greater speed, and then cut it as he coaxed his boat alongside the man. He reversed the engine slightly to stop forward movement, and then doused it. Snatching a pole with a crook at one end, he leaned over the vessel's side.

The man seemed oblivious to the boat's presence at first. Then as awareness dawned, he clutched at the side.

"Easy, easy. I'll get you out," Gonçalo called in Portuguese. "Grab the rod."

The man's arms came out of the water together. He flailed at the pole without securing a firm grasp.

"Don't worry," the fisherman called. "I'll do the work." He maneuvered the crook of the pole behind the man's back and under one arm and pulled gently. When the floundering man was within reach, Gonçalo leaned down and grabbed a shoulder. He struggled to draw the man closer to the boat, and then grasped him under his arms and pulled until he had his upper body over the side. With great effort, he pulled the man's torso over, and finally his legs. The unlikely guest tumbled to the floor of the boat, barely conscious.

The fisherman rushed to his cabin. He rummaged for a blanket and then hurried back out to the deck and covered the stranger.

The western horizon had grown dark with a brewing storm. They were too far out to sea to be caught alone in a squall, and he still had heard no sounds of an approaching search-and-rescue party.

He noticed a scarlet stain growing through the blanket on the man's left thigh. Pulling back the cover, he saw a round hole in the trousers. Blood seeped out. He tried to inspect the wound, but his ward stirred and cried out in pain.

Gonçalo pulled the blanket completely off and looked over the man's frame. He drew back in alarm at what he saw.

1

November 3, 1989 – West Berlin, Federal Republic of Germany – Late Evening.

Atcho whirled and struck. He acted on instinct. He had no idea why he had been attacked. He knew only that two assailants had come at him from an alley on Budapest Strasse, near the bombed-out hulk and spire of Kaiser Wilhelm Memorial Church in West Berlin. It served as a reminder of the horrors of a world at war. In the center of this brightly lit part of the city, few places offered darkness. The attackers had positioned their ambush well.

With no warning, they had come from the recesses of a construction site, seemingly intent on pushing Atcho back into those deep shadows. Two men had already grasped his arms. As he struggled against them, a third came from his rear. He heard the screech of tires in the direction he was being pushed. A van appeared ahead of him.

He dropped his head, slumped his shoulders, planted his feet, and shoved backward. He felt his arms sliding free. Then he spun around and saw the man from behind start to raise a pistol.

Atcho kicked hard. The man's groin took the full impact of the stiff toe of Atcho's leather shoe. The thug yelped in pain. His gun clattered to the concrete.

Atcho spun again. The two men who had held his shoulders had no time to stop their forward momentum.

Ahead of them, the van accelerated. Atcho heard the ascending whine of its engine above the street noise. Its lights flicked on as it sped straight toward them.

Two men crouched on the edge of the open sliding door, ready to grab Atcho and force him inside. He shoved hard against the attacker nearest to the front of the van and tripped him into its path.

Tortured brakes screamed to a halt over the *th-thump* of the van running over the man's body. Atcho whirled on his third assailant. This man was big and ponderous and had not yet grasped what had happened. He stared at the van.

The two male passengers inside had been thrown out. They sprawled on the ground, stunned.

Atcho hurled himself at the third man's knees. He heard a crack of bone and a cry of pain as his weight connected, forcing the brute's knees to buckle in the wrong direction.

Atcho rolled to the side and came to his feet. The dropped pistol lay a few feet away, its surface glinting in the half-light. He scooped it up.

The two gunmen by the van shook their heads, blinking, still stunned from the impact. They raised themselves onto their elbows, groggy, glaring at Atcho. Both were lean and fit and carried H&K MP5 submachine guns strapped across their chests. They trained their weapons on him.

Atcho ran for the nearest cover—a stack of bricks—the pistol still in his hand. His chest heaved. He dove behind the bricks. The ballistic *thwt* of bullets breaking air sounded inches from his face. He glanced around for better protection. Finding none, he looked across the street. Pedestrians had vacated the sidewalk.

Then, from three blocks away, the peculiar high-pitched waxing and waning of a Federal Republic of Germany police car sounded, its ascending timbre signaling that it was speeding Atcho's way. He crept to the opposite end of the bricks where shadows were deepest and peered around them.

The man who had gone under the van was now a bloody corpse lying just behind the back wheels. The thug Atcho had kicked still held his groin while he staggered toward the vehicle. The big, slow ruffian rolled on the ground holding both knees.

The two gunmen by the van heard the sirens too and jumped to their feet. Without warning, they turned their weapons on their two live companions and opened fire. The staggering man dropped to the ground.

Atcho pulled back, stupefied. He heard one of the gunmen yell orders to the driver. The engine revved up.

Atcho peered around the bricks again. With tires squealing and the smell of burnt rubber, the van sped back into shadows. The heavyset man clutched his wounds. He twitched uncontrollably as blood poured onto the ground. Then he was still. The third assailant did not move.

* * *

Atcho glared into the muzzles of an array of police automatic weapons aimed at him, the red dots from their lasers dancing on his chest. The acrid smell of gun smoke hung in the air. A spotlight blinded him. Brilliant strobes pulsed white and blue from the roofs of green and white patrol cars. He held his arms high over his head. In his right hand, he still held the pistol. He lowered it to the ground. Slowly.

Immediately, two burly Polizei forced his arms behind him and cuffed him. One patted him down and took his wallet and passport. Minutes later, he watched from the back seat of a police car as West Berlin night scenes flashed by. Sirens blared.

On arrival at the station, he tolerated being fingerprinted, photographed, and booked. Then he sat alone in an interrogation room.

2

Sofia Stahl basked in the big bathtub in her suite at the Mövenpick Hotel, one of the great historic establishments in Berlin, not far from the Brandenburg Gate and the Berlin Wall. She knew Atcho was not comfortable with the luxury of their suite, but they had paid the difference between the cost of the room and the government allowance for themselves and their security detail.

In her view, Atcho deserved everything good that could come his way. He had been tortured in Cuba's prisons. Then the Soviets had coerced him to become an unwilling sleeper agent inside the US.

An image formed in her mind of Atcho's muscular physique and finely sculpted face. She had kidded him on his way out the door that the silver in his hair was overtaking the dark brown. She smiled.

Tony Collins, an investigative news reporter for the *Washington Herald*, had once described Atcho as akin to Gary Cooper's character in *High Noon*, a man who "carried the weight of the world on his shoulders but could unleash holy hell at any moment."

Momentarily, she thought about her mission and tensed. *If Atcho really knew…*

Twelve years younger than he, Sofia was ostensibly an analyst with the US State Department. Her elegant looks, with a softly sculpted face and dark hair over brilliant green eyes and an easy smile, belied the lethality of her toned figure. Strangers found her warm and friendly. Friends saw her that way too, and also knew her to be loyal and competent. Enemies of the US who encountered her learned to beware.

The phone rang. Sofia reached for the extension on a table beside the tub.

"Is this Ms. Xiquez?" A man spoke, his voice low, ominous. He enunciated slowly, deliberately, with a heavy German accent. When Sofia hesitated, he repeated, "Is this Ms. Xiquez?"

"This is Mrs. Sofia Stahl-Xiquez. Who's calling?"

"Listen carefully, Ms. Stahl. You're an official of the US State Department. You're here to watch the Wall come down. Am I right?"

Sofia stepped out of the tub and reached for her towel. "Who are you?"

"Shut up and listen."

Sofia sucked in her breath at the brutality of the voice. She pulled the towel around her.

"We have your husband," the speaker continued, and then paused. "Are you ready to listen?"

Sofia cleared her mind and focused on the moment. "How did you get this call through screening? You're playing with fire. The idea that you have Atcho—"

"Yeah, yeah. We know you're both tough, and you have CIA connections, and Atcho saved the Soviet Union and the planet." The man mocked her. "We also know about the great security your state department put around you at the hotel.

"Now listen to me. Atcho visited the Kaiser Wilhelm Church ruins the last three nights. He's there now, but six strong men met him. He won't be returning to you tonight. Do I have your attention?"

Sofia muscles tightened. "All right. You think you know something. What do you want?"

The man laughed. "Not much. Just stick with your official state department duties and stay away from whatever else you're doing."

"What are you talking about?"

"Just do as I say. In a week, if all goes well, you'll get your darling husband back." The line went dead.

Sofia reached for her robe. Slipping her arms into the sleeves and yanking the belt tight, she crossed the suite and threw the door open. The state department security specialist positioned there heard the sound and turned his head toward her.

"Get Stan Brown in here quick," she told him. "We've got a situation."

The agent hurried into an open room across the hall. Moments later, Brown emerged. He was sinewy and in his late forties. "What's wrong?"

"Atcho's been kidnapped." Sofia re-entered the suite.

Brown followed. "What happened?" His frustration showed. "Atcho keeps ditching our security. He says he can take care of himself."

"That's not helping," Sofia retorted. She told him about the call. "The man didn't demand a ransom. He told me to stick to my state department business and to stay away from doing anything else."

Brown peered at her. "Are you doing something I don't know about?"

Sofia stopped pacing. "Not really. Well, yes, but it doesn't involve the state department."

Brown arched his eyebrows. "You'd better tell me. Everything."

"I'm doing my job," Sofia snapped. "You know why I'm here. To observe these street demonstrations and see where they lead. To be ready to lend assistance if there's an opening in the Wall. And to gather intelligence."

Brown raised his eyebrows. "Gathering intelligence." Skepticism laced his tone. "Is that for us or your other employer?"

Sofia bristled. "Do you have a need to know?"

"Maybe now I do. What could the kidnappers know to pressure you?"

"I don't know. My only other activity is trying to contact family members in the East. That shouldn't spark this type of response."

"I see. Your maiden name is Stahl." He studied her expression. "Are you sure that's all?"

"Yes, I'm sure." She was clearly annoyed. "We're wasting time. What about Atcho?"

"I'm trying to figure out a direction to go. Tell me about your family in the East, and anything else that could be helpful."

"What's to tell? They're a normal family. Well, as normal as they can be living behind the Iron Curtain."

"Have you ever seen them?"

Sofia's eyes misted. "Yes. When we were children. My father was posted at the US Consulate here. In those days, they could come across to the American Sector, and we could go over there. I was ten when the Wall went up."

Her voice broke. "I remember it. My cousin, Miriam, spent the night on the consulate compound. We took her home that morning. When we let her out of the car, an East German soldier drove up. He painted a white line in the middle of the street. In my childish mind, I didn't think anything of it —it was just a curiosity. I watched him. Miriam did too. Then she waved goodbye. She called to me, 'I'll see you soon.' That was twenty-eight years ago.

"By the next day, tanks guarded the streets, and workmen cemented the first bricks in place. After that, we could still drive into the East, but meeting with us was too dangerous for my relatives. The East German guards were already threatening to shoot people who tried to escape into West Berlin."

Brown's voice softened. "Are you trying to see your cousin now?"

Sofia glared at him. "That Wall is coming down," she said flatly. "I want to see my family. I want to bring them to the West. That's the other thing I'm doing."

Momentarily speechless, Brown responded kindly. "I get that. I'm trying to figure out who grabbed Atcho, why, and where they took him." He paused in thought. "You seem awfully sure the Wall is coming down. I don't know anything that makes that certain. In fact, the mayor of West Berlin contacted a member of the politburo in East Berlin directly, a Mr. Wolfgang Sacher—they had lunch together in the East without US approval. That violates the treaty that governs Berlin. Our state department is not happy about it. Do you know something I don't?"

"No," Sofia answered, a little too quickly.

Brown seemed unconvinced. "OK. You told me the man on the phone said Atcho had been going to see the Kaiser Wilhelm Church every night since your arrival. Why would he do that?"

Sofia shrugged. "Why shouldn't he go see it? He likes history. He came along to keep me company. The church is a short distance away. It's one of the most iconic relics of World War II. Obviously, he was being watched."

"Well, he should pay attention to his security," Brown said, clearly agitated. "If you can't tell him that, I will. Now my officers will have to risk their lives to rescue him. And there's one other factor you should consider. Your cover is blown. Whatever you're doing, you'll have to withdraw."

Sofia looked thunderstruck. The phone rang. She grabbed it and listened for a moment. "I understand," she said, and hung up. She turned to Brown, her face pale.

Brown had worked with her for years and knew her to be cool and steady under the worst pressure. "Who was that?"

"An officer at our consulate." Her eyes showed strain. "The police took Atcho into custody. They suspect him of taking part in a shooting. Three men were killed."

3

Five minutes after the assault on Atcho, the van with his attackers pulled into a public parking garage two blocks from the Kaiser Wilhelm Church ruins. They halted next to a small, nondescript car. Moments later, they departed in it and drove through back alleys until they had traveled a safe distance.

The driver, Uri, spoke first. He was young, barely an adult, but tough looking, as though raised on the streets. "Ranulf won't be happy," he said in German.

"Ranulf can shove it," the younger of the two gunmen, Etzel, retorted. A few years older than Uri, he bore an air of experience. A scraggly mustache and beard framed his mouth over dark, piercing eyes. "This Atcho is an experienced fighter. No one warned us."

"Ranulf sent six of us to get him. That should have told us something."

The other gunman, Etzel's older brother Klaus, stared grimly out the window. In addition to resembling Etzel, albeit without the beard, he carried an air of authority. Both brothers were of medium height and in superb physical condition. "Get your ID ready," Klaus ordered. "We're nearly at the border."

They rounded a bend on a cobblestone street and entered the well-lighted area of Checkpoint Bravo at Dreilinden, one of several heavily armed crossing points into East Berlin. An American soldier waved them through. Then the narrow lanes took them to barriers guarded by East German soldiers with machine guns. As they approached, a uniformed member of the East German passport control stepped out and raised his arm for them to stop. After checking their papers and scrutinizing their faces, he signaled for the barricade arm to be lifted and waved them through.

They drove past thick, graffiti-covered concrete walls with tube-like, horizontal tops that prevented scaling. On the other side lay a wide sweep of ground with sentry towers spaced intermittently and continuing as far as could be seen in both directions. The towers were manned by guards armed with machine guns. Another identical wall stood on the far side of the wide area. It was stark white, with no graffiti. Lights as bright as day illuminated strung-out barbed wire, barring safe crossing of the ground between the two walls. Minefields magnified the chilling effect.

On the other side of the double walls, the streets resembled those of decades earlier. They were dark and dirty, with scattered, dim streetlights. The few cars about were old and clunky. Buildings showed signs of decay.

The men headed for their headquarters. "What are we going to tell Ranulf?" Uri asked.

"What *can* we say?" Klaus answered. "We didn't get Atcho, and we left three men dead. By now, the news is being broadcast. Ranulf might have already heard. Let's hope he hasn't called Atcho's wife yet. I let him know just before we attacked that we had spotted Atcho. He said he would make the call immediately."

Uri shook his head. "Why wouldn't he wait to be sure we had him?"

Klaus grunted. "He likes to gloat."

Uri let out a long breath. "Maybe we should have defected while we were still on the west side."

"Don't be stupid. We would have been suspects in the shooting. Our contingency plan was in case we couldn't grab Atcho. We didn't count on leaving three dead agents."

"Why did we?"

Klaus grunted, clearly annoyed. "Because one was already dead under the van. We didn't have time to help the other two—the Polizei were on their way, remember? We couldn't leave them to be interrogated."

"What are we going to do?" Etzel asked.

Klaus was quiet a moment. "We're almost there. Keep your trigger fingers ready."

Uri suddenly swerved the car to the curb and stopped. "I'm not going back." His voice shook. Moisture formed on his brow. "Ranulf will kill us." The other two stared at him. "Think about it. He's crazy. Besides, this mission was ordered by the Stasi director himself, with Ranulf in charge. We failed. Three men are dead. It'll be in the news, and Ranulf will look bad. Heads will roll."

Klaus and Etzel exchanged glances. "He's right," Etzel said. "If we go to headquarters, we're dead." He turned back to Uri. "What are you going to do?"

"I'll go east and south. Hungary is letting people from East Germany through the border there. Ranulf won't know right away whether the West Berlin police captured us or not." His voice took on a pleading quality. "Come with me. The Stasi is preoccupied with the street demonstrations. They can't spare men to look for us. We could take a train through Czecho-slovakia to Hungary. We might be out by the time anyone looks for us."

"Our government already closed that route."

"Yes, for tourists," Uri persisted. "We're Stasi. We can intimidate our way through."

The brothers swapped another uneasy look. "If we're caught, we're dead."

"If we go back, we're dead. But, if we get to Hungary, we can go to the US Embassy for asylum. I have information they would pay for. All I want is to stay alive."

The brothers turned to each other. "What do you think?" Etzel asked.

"I don't know," Klaus replied. "There's something going on with this Atcho we don't know about. The Russian wants him. Ranulf knows that." He turned back to Uri. "What's your information?"

The driver eyed him, reluctant to speak. Klaus shrugged, his impatience obvious. "We're not going without knowing what we're staking our lives on."

Uri still hesitated. "All right," he said at last. "I know who's selling weapons-grade plutonium on the black market. I know where it's coming from, and who's buying it."

Surprised, Klaus raised his eyebrows. He sat a moment, contemplating. "That would be valuable." He cast a sidelong glance at Etzel, who returned it with a worried expression. "How do you know this? The Americans will ask."

"It's good intelligence," Uri blurted, his voice insistent. "I was outside Ranulf's office a few nights ago. He must have thought no one else was around. The door was open. Two other men were in his office. I saw one of them come in a little earlier. He limps and looks like death come alive. He said he had heard from his cousin that the bomb is ready. That's what he said. He spoke with a Russian accent. He said he's waiting for the plutonium."

Klaus sucked in his breath. "He said that?"

Uri nodded. "Those were his exact words."

Klaus rubbed his chin. Uri and Etzel watched him. "All right," he said at last. "That's good. The Americans will love it. Any idea who the two men were with Ranulf?"

Uri sighed. "No. I only knew the second man was there because I saw his shadow next to the door. I got out fast and didn't hear any more."

"But you said you know where it's coming from and who's buying it."

Uri grimaced. "Putting two and two together isn't difficult," he retorted. "Obviously, Ranulf is on the buying side, and that means the Stasi, or at least elements of it. Whoever he was speaking with seemed to be getting it for him. I didn't hear much of the conversation. The Americans could easily put surveillance on Ranulf to track down the other men. They might already have them on tape from listening to their calls."

Klaus stared at Uri. "Good thing you got out of there," he said. "Ranulf would have carved you up on the spot." He thought a moment longer. "You're right," he said finally. "I think we have something to trade, and a plan." He turned to his brother. "Etzel, let's go to Hungary." When Etzel nodded, Klaus turned to the driver. "Let's go."

Uri looked relieved. He shifted to face the front and reached down to start the engine. As he did, he heard a sharp metallic noise, and felt the cold nose of an MP5 behind his ear.

Klaus pulled the trigger. The MP5 spat. Uri slumped. The sharp smell of gunpowder spread through the van.

"Did you have to do that?" Etzel reproached his brother. "Now we have four dead bodies to explain to Ranulf, instead of three."

"Leave Ranulf to me. I was the other man in that office. All the Russian cares about is making sure the Wall doesn't come down. You and I have bigger plans far east of here. We're just letting the East Germans pay for them."

Etzel sat in thought. "I don't understand this urgency to get Atcho. Why were we doing it? If he's a problem, why not kill him?"

Klaus shrugged. "That was the Russian's bargain. He knew Atcho would be in town. He told the director that if Atcho caught wind of their plans, he would be hell to deal with."

"Great. So, we've alerted Atcho, the Polizei, and all the Americans, not to mention the Soviets. Ranulf could be the least of our problems. Someone should have told us that Atcho could be so difficult. We would have planned better."

Klaus nodded distantly.

"So, what now?"

Klaus explained his plan. "Uri did have one good idea," he said as he finished. "Getting out of the country through Hungary would work. Let's hide this vehicle before we see Ranulf."

"Why do we need to see him?"

"We still want the bomb. If we don't show, that will kill the deal. But before we go to his office, we'd better know how we're getting out."

4

Jerry Fenns, a US State Department consular officer, met Sofia and Brown at the police station. He bore the appearance and demeanor of a bureaucrat's bureaucrat: middle-aged, dumpy, with a worried face and wearing a thick overcoat against Berlin's icy temperature. "You can't see Atcho now," he said. "Not until they're done interrogating him. One of our guys is in there to protect his rights."

"What happened? I got a call saying that six men kidnapped Atcho."

"What?" Fenns grimaced. "I hadn't heard that."

"I got that call first. Then the one from you about the shooting."

"What happened?"

Sofia turned to Brown. "Fill him in."

While the two men talked, Sofia looked around for the interrogation rooms. A bay of uniformed police officers sat studiously at their desks or otherwise bustled about their duties. Beyond them, she saw a short hall with a set of doors, each with an embedded window. "Is that where they're holding Atcho?" she asked.

Fenns replied. "Yes, but you can't go in yet."

As he spoke, a man in a business suit approached Sofia. "Mrs. Xiquez? I'm Detective Berger. Please follow me." He turned to Fenns, his manner brusque. "You can join, but don't speak during questioning." He faced Brown. "Who are you?"

"I'm the security officer for a delegation from the US State Department." He produced his credentials.

"Were you with her this evening?"

"For a short time. She came to tell me about a kidnapping."

If Berger was startled by the revelation, he did not show it. Tall and lean, his demeanor was that of someone thoughtful and deliberate. "Who was taken?"

"Atcho—uh, Mr. Xiquez. People call him Atcho. Her husband."

Berger studied Brown. "Don't leave. We'll be asking you questions too."

Fenns stepped forward. "You know that Ms. Xiquez, her husband, and Mr. Brown are covered by diplomatic immunity?"

The detective eyed him coldly. "Yes," he retorted. "But is pushing that point a good idea?" His English was flawless, albeit gruff and with a German accent that made him sound almost British. "There was a shooting in a public place. Three men are dead. Do you want reports to say that this Atcho was involved, and that the US State Department refused to cooperate? We need to find out what happened. If I need to request cooperation at a higher level, tell me now."

Before Fenns could respond, the glass door of the front entrance swung open. A middle-aged man wearing a wrinkled overcoat walked through. He had a balding head and wore horn-rimmed glasses. As he ascended the three steps into the foyer, he glanced up and made eye contact with Sofia.

Her heart dropped.

"Sofia!" The man was ebullient. "How great to see you. Are you here about that shooting?" He scanned the trio of US State Department officials. He knew them all. "Was an American involved?"

Sofia struggled to remain placid. "Collins? What are you doing here?" She was fond of him, but he was an investigative reporter, and relentless.

"Digging out news," he said. "With the demonstrations in Leipzig last month and Gorbachev's statement the other day, anything could happen. Where are you staying?"

"Mr. Gorbachev does seem to have opened up possibilities," Sofia replied, ignoring his question. "I think he surprised the world." *Collins always gets into the middle of things.* Last year, he had pursued a story to Paris and Moscow that uncovered a coup attempt against the Soviet general secretary. Collins was a good man, though—he had subdued the story in the interest of national security, and he had even helped bring about a favorable conclusion and kept his participation quiet. "We're staying at the Mövenpick Hotel."

From the corner of her eye, she saw Berger scrutinizing the newsman. She turned to the detective quickly. "This is Mr. Tony Collins. He writes for the *Washington Herald.*" She watched as Berger, still studying the reporter, changed his expression to mild skepticism. She turned back to Collins. "You must be referring to whatever happens with the Wall? Are you here to cover it?"

"Yes. Isn't it exciting? Do you think it'll come down, or at least open up?"

Berger interrupted, stepping between Collins and Sofia. "Nice to meet you. We have business to do." He took Sofia's arm and indicated for Brown and Fenns to walk ahead of him, leaving Collins behind.

"We don't need the press involved now," Berger murmured. He directed them into a conference room and then addressed Sofia. "We require statements from you and Mr. Brown. We'll question you separately. I'm finished with Atcho. The gun he was holding wasn't fired—he says he took it from one of his attackers. Fingerprints on it matched those on one of the dead men. We need to find the three who got away. Now, tell me about the kidnap call."

* * *

In the early morning hours, Berger finished with Brown and Sofia. She and Atcho reunited in a conference room. Amid their embrace, Brown barged in. "They have a lead," he announced. "A van that fits the description of the ambush vehicle was found close by in a parking garage. The kidnapping attempt looks like a Stasi operation. That brings in the West German federal government and German intelligence."

"I hate to show my ignorance," Atcho commented, "but I'm not familiar with the term 'Stasi.'"

"That's the East German State Security Service," Brown explained.

"Everyone refers to them as 'Stasi,' the most dreaded secret police in any Iron Curtain country. They've recruited over three hundred thousand internal spies and filled prisons with men, women, even children. Ya don't like the quality of bread? Don't mention it unless you don't mind torture or execution.

"Their formal job is internal security. Their real job is keeping the population docile. The Wall and the armed fence on the border prevent people from escaping. The Stasi discourages them from making any attempt. They quell uprisings before they start.

"They'll shoot you as fast as look at you, but first they want to torture whatever information they can get out of you. Does that answer your question?"

Atcho nodded. "Sounds like Castro's secret police."

"Yep. The Stasi. That's whose bell you rang."

5

Tony Collins had watched with curiosity as Detective Berger, Sofia, Brown, and Fenns disappeared down a corridor. He surveyed the work bay, noticing the short hall on the opposite side with regularly spaced doors and embedded small windows. *The interrogation rooms.*

He went to speak with the desk sergeant. "Excuse me." The policeman looked up with a tolerant, disinterested expression. Collins presented his credentials. "I heard about the shooting this evening. An American was arrested? Who is he?"

The man looked at him blankly. "There's no information we can release. If you want to stay, please have a seat."

"But he *was* an American?" Collins persisted. "The man you arrested."

The officer bristled. "I told you there is no information to release. When Detective Berger is ready to brief the press, ask him."

Collins sat down in the foyer and watched. After a while, one of the interrogation room doors opened. An officer stepped out. Another man followed, athletic, above medium height, striking good looks, and dark hair peppered with silver. Collins sucked in his breath. *Atcho!*

Collins knew Atcho well. He had done background stories on him when Atcho was released from Cuba into Miami. Several years later, Collins had watched with interest when President Ronald Reagan honored Atcho in his

State of the Union Address. The reporter had followed Atcho's career ever since.

"What have you got into this time?" Collins muttered. He obscured his face with a magazine and sank lower in his seat. Atcho followed the officer down the same hall where Berger had led Sofia and her colleagues.

Hours passed. Then, the officer who had escorted Atcho re-emerged, this time with Brown and Fenns. He walked them to the foyer.

Brown stopped in front of Collins. "How did you get this story so soon?"

Collins stood. "Just lucky, I suppose. What can you tell me?"

"Nothing, really. There was a shooting. Three men dead. Unidentified. You'll get the specifics from Detective Berger."

"I saw Atcho coming out of one of the interrogation rooms. Is he involved?"

The two state department men stared at him coldly. "You'll get details from Berger," Fenns replied.

While Fenns spoke, Brown glanced back down the hall. He caught a high sign from Berger. Then he nodded almost imperceptibly at Fenns. "We have to be going."

Collins watched them leave the building.

Their officer-escort went back to his duties.

"Wait," Collins called after him. "Can you tell me how your suspect is involved?"

"We have no suspect," the officer called over his shoulder.

"But I saw you lead him from the interrogation room."

"You mean Mr. Xiquez? He's not a suspect. He's been cleared. He's gone."

Collins fought down rising frustration. Obviously, Atcho and Sofia had been let out through a back way. He hurried out the glass door and into the street.

A major hotel occupied the opposite side. Collins bobbed and weaved his way through traffic to safety and entered the lobby. He spotted a bank of telephones. At this hour, no one else was using them. He called his editor, Tom Jakes, in DC.

"We heard about the shooting," Jakes said in response to Collins' greeting, "but no specifics yet. What have you got?"

"It's sketchy," Collins told him. "The Polizei haven't released details, and the state department is keeping mum, at least for the moment." He filled Jakes in on what he had witnessed.

"How did Atcho get in the middle of this?" Jakes exclaimed when Collins finished.

"Good question, but we have enough for a semblance of a scoop. There was a shooting, leaving three men dead, and that's confirmed, but we don't know who did the shooting or why. Before going to the police station, I got eyewitness descriptions of a man handcuffed and taken away in the back seat of a police car. Atcho fits the description. I saw him, his wife, and three state department officials there."

"We can report all of that," Jakes broke in, "and that we conclude without confirmation that state department officials intervened for Atcho. Initial reports are that he's been cleared of wrongdoing. We don't know how he became involved."

"That's it. Have the story ready to run but hold it until right after the police press meeting. Don't wait to hear back from me. The briefing will be televised. If Berger doesn't contradict anything I've said, run with it. Throw in a couple of side stories about the political situation over here and the hope that the Wall is about to come down."

"Got it."

* * *

Dawn was only two hours away by the time Atcho and Sofia reached their suite at the Mövenpick Hotel. "Tony Collins saw me," Sofia said. "He heard about the shooting and came to investigate. He saw me with Brown and Fenns and figured out that an American was involved in the shooting."

"Then he probably saw me too," Atcho replied. "He'll conclude that I'm the American." He groaned. "He's on the story, and he won't get off."

Both were exhausted, but neither felt like going to bed. Atcho made drinks, and they sat on a sofa in the bedroom.

"We have to talk about all this," Atcho said after a few minutes.

"I know, but this isn't a secure location. Almost anything we say would be classified, or at least fall under operational security."

"Didn't Brown have his guys sweep this room?"

"That was hours ago."

"This can't wait. Let's go in the bathroom."

They did, and turned on the faucets, the fan, and a blow-dryer, and they spoke with their heads close together.

"All right," Sofia said, "tell me what you're doing."

"What *I'm* doing? How about you tell me about your real reason for being here."

"I told you, the police, and Brown: I want to get my family out."

"Nope. There's more to it than that. The man who called knew which hotel room you're in. He knew our names, that you're a state department official, and that you're involved with the CIA. And all he wanted was for you to stop doing whatever you're doing? If it were simply that you're helping your family, the East Germans would haul them away. Something else is up. How did he get that call past the security intercept anyway?"

"We don't know for sure. He must have had inside help and called into a location that could detour around the intercept and place the call directly. But what about you?" Sofia's voice became prickly. "You take a walk by those church ruins every night, and then tonight you almost get kidnapped, or worse. So much for being able to take care of yourself. Brown's on my case about it."

"I'm a tourist." Atcho's exasperation showed. "I should be able to move about freely like a normal person.

"The church is three and a half kilometers from here. That's my normal distance for a walk, and there are three routes to get there. I'm in Berlin for the first time. I like history. Do you think I'm not going to get out and see the sights? I don't need or want the entourage. I've also taken a walk by the Brandenburg Gate and Checkpoint Charlie. Not everything I do is secret squirrel. But that kidnapping attempt was to stop you. So, what are you doing?"

Chastened, Sofia wrapped her arms around his neck. "I can't say, darling. You know that. It's classified." She reached up and kissed him lightly.

"Forget that," Atcho retorted angrily. He reached behind his neck and unclasped her hands. "You know my clearance is high enough. Under the circumstances, I have a need to know."

"You're not working for any agency needing a clearance, so technically, your clearance is void."

"You forget that I'm an officer and a major stockholder involved in daily operations of a company that produces classified technology. I'm cleared, and those were real bullets they shot at me. I need to know. Now tell me."

Sofia stared at him. "All right. You know about the demonstrations last month in Leipzig, and the video that appeared all over the world. Lots of people say that footage will bring about the end of the Wall, maybe of East Germany."

Atcho nodded. "Particularly after Gorbachev's statement."

"Exactly. But there's huge hard-line opposition to allowing such radical change. If the Wall comes down, their power is over. Some elements will do anything to stop it."

"I see that."

"The East German government is drafting a change to its travel law. They have attorneys working on it now. The leader is a young guy. We know him. He'll only make two changes in the wording, but the effect will be to open the gates for free passage between East and West Germany. We don't know when it will be enacted."

"It's good that they're working on it."

"Yes, but the law can be sabotaged, delayed, not signed, not implemented, discarded. I'm here to make sure that it goes into effect. A press release will announce it regardless of what the hard-liners do. That will at least create the illusion of law, and once acted upon, it will be almost impossible to retract."

Atcho looked at her, speechless. "How are you supposed to do that?" he said skeptically.

Sofia sighed. "You lived under Communism." Atcho nodded. Sofia went on. "Family and friends don't forget each other, even when some live in captivity. You find ways to communicate to the other side."

Atcho nodded again. "Are you telling me that your family in East Berlin is helping with this?"

"No, but don't forget, my father was stationed here with the state department when the Wall went up. He had close contacts stranded on the wrong side. He maintained some of them. A few rose in government without losing their desire to be free. You had friends like that in Cuba."

"Yeah. I knew a guy whose family owned the Bank of Havana. When Castro took over, the bank was confiscated. My friend went to selling ice-cream cones on the streets. A few weeks after the coup, Castro's officials came looking for him because they didn't know anything about banking, international finance, or foreign exchange. They were losing millions of dollars on lost sugarcane contracts. They wanted him to fix the situation.

"He did, and Castro kept him there on the board of the bank. His office was right next to Che Guevara's, and Fidel had one across the hall. Despite that, the banker's old friends came in and begged for help to get out of Cuba. That was dangerous for him. He did what he could. After a few months, Castro and Che felt confident enough to send him to Canada on a trade mission. As soon as he stepped off the plane, he took a taxi to the US Embassy and requested asylum."

"That's the same situation," Sofia exclaimed. "People do what they must to survive until they can do something better. There are people like that in the East German government, some of them very high up. And some of them knew my father."

Atcho looked keenly into her eyes. "How high?"

"One of the men helped force Erich Honecker out of power last month. He's a politburo member of the Social Unity Party."

Atcho whistled. "That's who's supposed to read that press release?" He looked around as if to assure himself that no one could overhear their conversation. "And what are you supposed to do?"

"Make sure it happens. Once those crowds start tromping across that border, the East German government will be powerless to stop them."

6

Ranulf slammed his hand down on his desk. He turned off the ancient black-and-white television on a table close to him. "How could they screw this up so bad?" He was alone, his eyes dark and hard, his lips drawn taut. "I sent six of them."

He had just watched a news report from the American Sector about a shooting in which three men had been killed. A US citizen was being questioned. Ranulf knew the description of the van was accurate. Nothing was said about those who had escaped.

The phone rang. He answered sharply. "I saw the report. I haven't heard from them yet." He listened. "Don't push me," he growled, and hung up. He was a brute of a man with a thick neck and a heavy rounded jaw. He was nearly bald at the top of his head, with long dark hair on the sides that hung over his ears.

He rose from his desk, tramped to the door, and called out, "Sergeant, have you seen Klaus and his brother?" He received a negative reply. "Send them to me as soon as they come in." He thought a moment longer. "Send in Uri too."

He closed the door and took his seat, lit a cigarette, and leaned back in his chair. Then, as if resolved, he snuffed out the cigarette and made another phone call. He spoke briefly and hung up.

Moments later, a small, oily man with wicked eyes entered. "Do you know Klaus, Etzel, and Uri?" The man nodded. Ranulf continued. "They'll be in my office soon. When they leave, take them out. Let me know when it's done. Any questions?"

Oily shook his head.

"Uri will be easy but be careful with Klaus and Etzel. Get it done tonight."

Oily nodded and left.

* * *

Klaus and Etzel walked into Ranulf's office and stood in front of his desk. Both managed to look outwardly calm. They had left their MP5s in the car, hidden several blocks away in the ruins of an abandoned war-era building.

Ranulf smoked another cigarette. For a time, he sat, his eyes shifting alternately between the brothers, looking them up and down. "Where's Uri?" he rumbled at last.

Klaus drew himself up. "Dead."

Ranulf's expression did not change. He puffed on his cigarette. "How did that happen?"

"I shot him. He blew the mission and turned on us."

Ranulf inhaled another puff and watched the smoke as it circled overhead. "How did he blow the mission? I sent six of you."

"Uri came too fast," Klaus said. "The other three men had Atcho. Uri drove in fast and too close. Geiss had Atcho's right arm. Uri mashed the brakes but couldn't stop. Geiss went under." Klaus shrugged. "Etzel and I were thrown out. The other two comrades lost their hold on Atcho. He ran for cover and I shot them."

Ranulf contemplated. "Why?"

"Someone must have called the police. They came our way almost instantly. Atcho put your goons on the ground. We couldn't leave them to be interrogated."

Ranulf bristled at the jabbing remark. "So Atcho was the only one who could run or walk?" His eyes glowered. "How did Uri turn on you? Where is he?"

"He was a coward," Etzel broke in. "We took him to the morgue."

Klaus nudged Etzel, a cautionary gesture. "Uri was terrified of you," he said. "He wanted us to escape to Hungary with him. He pulled a pistol on us," he lied. "I shot him."

Ranulf grunted. He appeared mollified. "All right. I'll need a full written report. Use one of the desks out front. Do it now."

Klaus stood his ground. "Did you talk to the Russian?"

Ranulf bristled. "I don't know whose organization you came from, but on this mission, you report to me." He indicated Etzel with a thrust of his chin. "Does he know everything?"

"Of course. I couldn't pull off this job by myself."

Ranulf studied their faces. "I spoke with the Russian. He's not happy. He says Atcho is a greater risk now, thanks to this screwed-up mission. Now get me that report."

Klaus did not move. "One more question."

Ranulf glared at him.

"What about the job? Where does it go from here?" When Ranulf only stared, Klaus commented, "If you like, I can ask the Russian, or the Stasi director."

Ranulf glared. He rose from his desk and stood inches from Klaus. He leaned down to look him in the eye. "Crossing me is the worst thing you could do," he breathed. "The job is still on, but you're both out of it. Now get me that report."

The brothers left. They walked down a hall toward an open bay where officers worked at their desks. On the other side was the main exit.

"He didn't believe anything we told him," Klaus muttered. "He's probably ordered a hit on us already. Keep heading out the door and get to the vehicle."

As they crossed the bay, the officers paid them little heed. The brothers glanced toward the door. It was down a set of stairs in a foyer with a low ceiling, casting shadows. Two officers lounged there, effectively blocking passage. Each had a hand near his pistol. They looked up and made eye contact with the brothers.

Klaus nodded to them and turned to Etzel with an easy smile as though conducting small talk. "Take the one on the right. You know what to do."

Etzel smiled. They kept a casual pace as they started down the stairs.

"Comrades," Klaus called to them. "Do you know if it's raining? When we came in, the weather was looking bad."

One officer turned to glance through the door. The other shifted his view to see outside.

Klaus and Etzel pounced. They jammed their forearms into the two hapless men's throats, ramming their skulls against the hard edges of the doorframe. The men crumpled. The brothers caught them below their chins as they fell and twisted their necks until they heard sharp cracks.

Klaus peered up the dark stairs into the bay. No one had seen them. They dragged the bodies into the night.

On the other side of the Wall, Sofia and Brown had just arrived at the police station.

* * *

At that moment, Ranulf placed a call on the ancient rotary phone. "The brothers are here," he said without greeting. "There's another man dead. We were lucky he was shot on our side of the Wall." He listened impatiently. When he spoke again, his voice rose. "This changes nothing. You'll get what you want, and so will we. We don't need the brothers. You just be sure you deliver."

He listened. When he hung up, he had a sinking feeling. In his final comment, the Russian had insisted the brothers attempt again to kidnap Atcho.

Ranulf felt sweat beading on his brow. This project had been assigned by the Stasi director himself, with those two damnable brothers.

Ranulf dialed Oily's number. "Find Klaus and Etzel. Send them to me. And call off the hit, at least for tonight."

"Too late," Oily replied.

Ranulf's agitation reached new heights. "What?"

"They escaped. When they left your office, they kept walking out the front door. They killed two men I posted there and took their pistols. They dumped the bodies outside the door. By the time anyone saw the corpses, the brothers were gone."

Ranulf felt his chest tighten. "Get in here."

He dropped his forehead into his hands. He was a classic bully, using his physical size and position to push his way around, but becoming unnerved when a challenge threatened his objectives or, in this case, his life.

He had been twenty-two when the Wall went up in 1961. He was a guard in the East German Army then, at the frontier between the Russian and American Sectors created under the Four Power Agreement that governed post–World War II Berlin. A source of pride for Ranulf was that he had shot a celebrated casualty of the Wall a year after the start of construction. His target had been a boy in his late teens who had tried to scale it and had become entangled in the barbed wire.

That had been an easy shot. Ranulf had watched the boy writhing in agony, begging for help. East Berliners who had seen the horror were frozen to the spot. On the other side of the Wall, people had heard the agonized cries, and they wept. The boy's pleas became muted. Then, silence. The boy had bled out

At the end of Ranulf's enlistment, the Stasi had recruited him, confirming that brutality provided a path to promotion and a lethal deterrent against further escapes. His mediocre intellect had curtailed promotion above mid-levels, but his proven willingness to inflict pain had provided access to higher circles. He was the go-to guy for illicit actions. He had overseen countless off-the-books operations on behalf of senior Stasi individuals with personal aims. He never involved himself in the politics; he did not understand them anyway.

Over the years, Ranulf had gathered a cohort of shadowy operators, all as ruthless as he. He had rewarded them with favors for successful clandestine actions. None felt allegiance to the country, the Party, the Stasi, or each other. Given sufficient provocation or reward, they would turn on him and Oily, who coordinated their actions.

Ranulf had felt rising angst for weeks. It resulted from unrest spreading through the country. Nearly a month ago, on the fortieth anniversary of the founding of East Germany, Soviet Communist Party General Secretary Mikhail Gorbachev had said, "I believe danger awaits those who do not react to the real world. If you pick up on the currents ... moving society, if you use them to shape your policies, you have no reason to fear difficulties."

Gorbachev's statement, made in the context of protests in Leipzig for more liberty, seemed to signal that the Soviets would not intervene to maintain East Germany's iron grip. To Ranulf and many others, the statement had felt like the death knell for the East German regime. *He might as well have marched to the Brandenburg Gate and breached the Wall himself.*

Three consecutive days of massive street demonstrations in Leipzig followed, and were emulated in other major East German cities. Infuriating senior Stasi officials, a videographer had sneaked into the bell tower of an old church in Leipzig and filmed the demonstration of over one hundred thousand people.

A West German journalist had smuggled the video to the West. It had aired to a worldwide audience. Those who saw it were awed by the sheer size of the crowd openly defying the East German terror machine. The clip showed confused Stasi officers standing around, helpless.

Ranulf shook his head. *The Stasi!* The same organization had injected fear in every citizen and had tortured masses. No one had been safe from the Stasi. And now they stood by meekly while citizens mocked them.

Ranulf's predictable life, along with that of the country, seemed to be spiraling out of control. His superiors whispered their fears. Some talked of escape if the Wall came down. Some feared that escape was no longer possible, that there was no sanctuary from the courts in The Hague.

Others were determined to protect the status quo. No other alternative existed that preserved the Party, its members, and their privileged way of life. Fear of enraged citizens suffused the lines of authority. Furtive conversations centered on desperate measures outside the control of the Soviet Union, to forestall an opening of the Wall.

The Stasi director, Johann Baumann, had called Ranulf into his office on the day of the pivotal Leipzig demonstration. There, Ranulf had met Klaus, who lounged next to a window near Baumann's desk.

Baumann was an old man in his eighties and a proud one, the last of the original hard-liners that had lowered the Iron Curtain on East Germany at the end of World War II. He had executed purges and survived more purges, the most recent being the one that cleared out his hard-line colleagues—all but him.

Only the sides of Baumann's head had any strands of hair remaining, neatly combed to the back. He wore thick glasses, and his formerly robust physique had been reduced to that of a slight figure. Nevertheless, he stood erect. As the years had taken their toll, he had come to realize that one of his most potent attributes was that of being underestimated.

Also present in his office when Ranulf had arrived was a Russian. He was lean and hard, but gaunt, as though he had been through physical trials. His eyes had seemed to burn from an angular, leathery face, and he walked with a limp. He bore the air of a man with sharpened survival instincts, one ready to kill for what he wanted. He could be dangerous to anyone, including the other men in the office. They sensed it.

Baumann introduced the Russian. "He can bring us a small nuclear bomb. We'll funnel money to him through one of the front companies doing business with the West. The Soviets don't know about this." He had turned to speak directly to Ranulf. "Take charge of the details and keep me informed."

Ranulf had been startled at the mention of a nuclear bomb. Even more so, he was shocked that the information would be withheld from Moscow. He knew better than to show concern. "What's it for?"

"Blackmail, if need be. Detonation, if we must. Preserving the Wall is imperative. I'll tell you more later. Right now, our Russian comrade has another mission for you. There's a man coming to West Berlin in a few days. He is called Atcho. His wife is a US State Department senior analyst." He had gestured toward Klaus, still lounging by the window. "Klaus will fill you in on details. Atcho must be seized and brought back to Stasi head-quarters."

Ranulf had been disconcerted. On impulse, he asked, "Why?"

Baumann glared at him and gestured toward the Russian. "Because he wants him here."

Ranulf gulped, angry with himself for asking the question. "Yes, sir." He had turned his attention to Klaus, made eye contact, and knew in an instant that he was very dangerous. Neither man had liked the other.

The next day, Klaus had come to Ranulf's office with the information that Atcho and Sofia would be staying at the Mövenpick Hotel in West Berlin. He had supplied the specific dates. Ranulf had assigned Uri and three men to the effort. Two days later, Etzel had joined the group. Together, they had planned and rehearsed the mission to abduct Atcho.

* * *

Ranulf regretted his call to Sofia. He tended to impulsive action. On hearing that Atcho was in his men's sights, he had reveled in the drama he pictured resulting from that call.

That Atcho could be such a hard target had never crossed Ranulf's mind. Now he had to clean up the mess and develop a good story for Baumann.

He heard a knock on the door. Oily came in. "Find Klaus and Etzel," Ranulf told him. "Use all the hit teams. I'll double their normal pay, but it's got to be done quickly."

* * *

"Now what?" Etzel's impatience surfaced, but he held it in check. An hour had passed since they had eluded execution at the Stasi station.

Klaus stared out the back window of the car, hidden deep inside a vacant building. "Ranulf will expect us to run, but he'll have his hands full with the demonstrations. We have to get to the Russian."

"How? By now Ranulf must have told him that the mission failed. He probably saw it on television."

Klaus' brow furrowed. "Baumann wants the Wall to stay in place. The Russian can get him a nuclear bomb. We don't care what Baumann plans to do with it. We also don't know what the Russian wants, except this Atcho. No other American will do. It has to be that one, and he has to be alive."

"Why?"

"Doesn't matter why. If we deliver this Atcho, we can get what we want."

"Which is a second bomb."

"Exactly. Since we know Atcho is a hard target, we can plan better. Ranulf's three hoodlums were incompetent. Better they're dead. We can do this ourselves."

"Are you crazy? With everyone looking for us? They might expect a second try."

"We can do it. We'll steal new Stasi ID and go to our own network."

Etzel looked doubtful. "The only way we'll get Stasi ID now is to kill someone."

Klaus grinned. "We know how to do that."

7

The next day, Atcho and Sofia drove to the US Consulate for a long meeting with Brown, Fenns, and other US State Department security officials. The CIA station chief, Sean Shelby, also attended. The intent was to discern why Atcho had been a target.

Shelby was a rising star in the intelligence community, a taller than average officer with dirty blond hair. His reputation was sterling within the agency for a keen mind and tactical know-how. He had a bookish personality but maintained an athletic regimen, and he knew how to take a joke. He listened closely, analyzed quickly, and arrived at sound decisions without delay. Further, he was known to support his field officers fiercely but allowed little slack if an error resulted from poor planning, analysis, or execution. For this mission, he was Sofia's boss.

"Fill me in," he said as the meeting commenced.

"Things are not adding up," Stan Brown began. "I could understand if the kidnappers had tried to take Sofia." He switched his attention to her. "But as far as anyone knows officially, you're a senior intelligence analyst with no diplomatic portfolio. You should hardly be anyone's target." He paused in reflection. "But to try to kidnap Atcho to pressure you?" He exhaled. "I'd sure like to know what you're really doing here." He looked her directly in the eyes. "Before you answer—I hate to do this, Sofia, but we have to address the fact that your cover is blown. The caller said straight out that he knew about your connections to the CIA."

Sofia rolled her eyes.

"Brown makes a good point," Shelby said. "Someone found out your status and maybe has a good guess why you're here. I've known you a long time. No one doubts your capability, but prudence and policy say to take you off the mission."

Sofia felt a rush of adrenaline. "Don't do that, Sean. We're too close. If you pull me out ..." She looked around, recalling that not everyone in the room was cleared to know her mission. "If you pull me out, the principal is likely to balk. You can't shove in a substitute. You know why. We'd have to go on a wing and a prayer."

The room had gone quiet. Shelby looked perplexed.

"Please," Sofia implored. "You know the stakes. My mission is already on a deniable basis."

Shelby sat in silent contemplation. "Go on with the meeting," he said at last. He directed his attention to Sofia. "You and I will have to talk."

"My job would be a lot easier if I knew what the hell was going on," Brown said pointedly.

"My apologies," Shelby replied. "This is close hold. We won't talk about it further."

Atcho broke in. "Has anyone contacted the Stasi?"

"The US made a formal complaint through diplomatic channels," Fenns said. "Obviously, the East German government disavowed knowledge and issued another harangue about violent crime in the West. They won't claim the three dead bodies."

"What about West German intelligence?" Atcho pursued.

"Nothing," Fenns replied. He thrust his chin toward Shelby. "CIA and FBI are in the loop, but so far the van is our only lead. It's registered in West Berlin to a bakery that had reported it stolen. That's a dead end too."

"KGB?"

"Same."

"That brings us back to where we started," Brown stated flatly, frustration straining his voice. He turned to Shelby. "The wannabe kidnapper said that Sofia needed to stick to official duties and stay away from whatever else she's doing."

Shelby and Sofia met him with blank stares. Brown became visibly irate. "We're trying to help." He directed his outburst at Shelby. "You know the rules. If we have the required level of clearance and a need to know, we're allowed to know. The person who originally classified the information can make the determination. That's either you or Sofia. Now, help us help you. Please."

Sofia stared at him coldly. "If I think you need to know," she said evenly, "you'll know. Meanwhile, I suggest you beef up security at the hotel."

Shelby stood. "I said we would not discuss the mission further. I have to go." He caught Sofia's eye. "See me when this is over." He left the room.

Brown grunted his irritation. "All right." He turned to Atcho. "You might need this." He handed him a Glock, Atcho's preferred pistol. Atcho put it in his jacket.

"Your permit to carry is done," Brown added. "Sofia, you have yours?" Sofia nodded. "Good," he went on, "we'll tighten security, but we're already spread thin."

* * *

The group left the meeting tired and disgruntled, with nothing resolved. Sofia had a short session with Shelby, then she and Atcho returned to the hotel.

When they arrived back in their room, fatigue had set in. They intended to retire early but sat on the sofa in the bedroom to talk. Atcho flipped on the television and turned up the volume to disrupt any listening devices.

"Why won't you tell anyone what you're doing?" he asked.

"Because too much is at risk, too many lives affected, too many people could be killed. You saw Shelby. He backed me on that."

"Then tell me precisely what you're supposed to do."

Sofia sighed. "OK. That declaration about opening the Wall to free travel is imminent. Just the fact that the date hasn't been set shows how tenuous it is. We're going to preempt the formal announcement by reading it publicly as soon as we can, as if it's a done deal, effective immediately.

"People are already crowding in front of the crossing points expecting an announcement any day. The longer this goes without one, the more likely it will die from neglect. Or, if the crowd keeps pressing, it could lead to violent retaliation by the East German government. If the declaration is read out publicly by a known official, the government won't be able to stop it. We're forcing their hand."

Atcho stared at her. "We?" he queried brusquely. "Who's we? Who is doing the preempting? Not you, obviously."

Sofia forced a laugh. "No, not me." Her expression became somber. "That representative of the Social Unity Party I told you about, Wolfgang Sacher. He'll read the press release, but it's dangerous for him. He won't do it unless he has security around him, and safe passage out of East Berlin immediately."

"So, what are you supposed to do?"

"He was a friend of my father's," Sofia said. "I knew him when I was a child. We've met in various places over the years." She saw Atcho's questioning expression. "I'll tell you about it another time. You know I was a covert operator." He nodded. She continued. "We'll put undercover security around him right after he makes the announcement. My face at the press conference is the signal. When he sees me, he'll know the plan is in place, and he'll read the announcement."

Atcho gaped. "You're supposed to be inside East Berlin at the site? At the time the press announcement is made? But it's not the official announcement, it's a preempted one?" His brow creased with anger. "Are you crazy? Do you know what the Stasi will do to you if this goes wrong and you're caught? What about that security team? Get real. They'll be regarded as spies. *You'll* be treated as a spy. You know what they do to spies? Especially those caught trying to bring down a totalitarian regime?" He glared. "They shoot them. Or worse."

"Which is why we're volunteers. Our government officially knows nothing about it." She regarded him stubbornly. "We're all big girls and boys. We've known the risks of our jobs for a long, long time." She reached up and held Atcho's face in her hands. "We're expecting large crowds when

Wolfgang reads the announcement. It includes an order for the border guards and passport officers to stand down. With that, we think the crowds will press through the gates immediately.

"After Wolfgang reads the announcement, we'll work him into the crowd. His family will be there too, and we'll escort them through the gates into West Berlin. To freedom." Her voice broke. She caught herself. Then her eyes glinted with determination. "My family too."

Atcho was speechless. He took her in his arms. "Your family will be there?"

Sofia nodded into his chest and pulled back. "The East German government shot and killed a hundred and forty people escaping over the Wall since it was built—and who knows how many others along the border?" Anger shook her voice. "All the people ever wanted was to live their own lives..." Her voice broke again. "This is my only chance to make sure that doesn't happen to my family."

"I know," Atcho said softly. "You don't have to explain." He thought of the hundreds of Cubans lost at sea attempting to reach Key West. He recalled the desperate action his friend, former KGB Major Ivan Chekov, had taken to rescue his own family from Soviet clutches the year before. "Why didn't you come to me? I could have put another team together."

"The operation was planned and dropped on me before I knew about it. The CIA knows about my family connections and decided to use them. I was happy to accept the assignment. It's all set. The team is here, we're rehearsed, we know what we're doing."

Atcho continued to hold Sofia, but a discomforting thought entered his mind. "Sofia," he said after a few moments, "who would know why you're here? How did they find out?"

"I don't know." She wrapped her arms around his neck. "Whoever it is knows some of your background too."

"What did Shelby have to say?"

Sofia sighed. "He's concerned. I told him I would lie low until mission execution. The heavy lifting is on my teammates, and they're already on the other side of the Wall."

She fell silent, not meeting his eyes. She felt badly for still deceiving him. Completing the mission would require two forays into the East. Her private discussion with Shelby had been heated. He wanted to scrub her participation. She had persuaded him that expecting Wolfgang to trust a substitute on short notice was unrealistic.

"We're all at risk," she had told the CIA station chief. "We can't trust the East German government to do the right thing. It's taken them nearly three decades to get to this point. If we don't do the mission, more decades could pass. If I pull out because I'm compromised, Wolfgang will worry about making things more dangerous for his family. He'll balk. Count on it."

Shelby had acquiesced to her continued participation in the mission with the proviso that Sofia report on her next trip into East Berlin. "I'll make a final decision then."

With that conversation fresh in her mind, Sofia now held Atcho close. Exhausted, they finally fell asleep, still wearing their street clothes.

Sometime later, while Sofia slept, Atcho left the sofa and crept into the living room, closing the bedroom door quietly. He took the phone to the length of its extension cord and placed a call. He spoke almost in a whisper for a few moments, then hung up and went back to the bedroom.

He contemplated waking Sofia, so they could change into pajamas and move from the sofa to the bed, but she seemed so peaceful. Instead, he took his place next to her once more.

8

While Atcho and Sofia slept, Klaus and Etzel studied the layout of the Mövenpick one more time. They had spent the day since the first kidnapping attempt poring over sketches and the security arrangements around Atcho and Sofia. In particular, they had induced hotel staff members to provide key information for their new plan.

They paid particular attention to the floor where the state department delegation and its security team were housed. They had studied methods used for protecting American diplomats on foreign travel. They also learned that a security operations cell had been established in a room across the hall, that the door remained open around the clock, and that an agent was always posted in front of the couple's door.

Before dawn they entered the hotel through a back entrance, dressed in workmen's coveralls. They took a freight elevator to a floor two levels above their target. Klaus had a towel thrown over one shoulder. They moved swiftly to a set of stairs that descended within a short distance of the room. When they spotted a surveillance camera in the stairwell, they slowed their pace to one indicating nonchalance.

On reaching the floor, they engaged in light conversation and entered the hall. Down the corridor, a state department security agent watched them. As they drew near, he spoke into a handset and stepped into their path. The brothers raised their hands as if to submit to a search. The agent reached out to pat down Etzel.

In a flash, Etzel grabbed the man's wrist, jerked him forward, swung him around, and tightened his other arm around the agent's neck in a chokehold. Then, he held a cloth with a liquid substance close to the man's nose. Seconds later, the agent slumped to the floor, unconscious.

At the same time, Klaus moved to the open door of the security operations cell. He reached into his coveralls and pulled out a pressurized canister. It contained dry, siliconized micro-pulverized CS2—an aerosol version of tear gas. He peered quickly into the room, prepared to release the fine incapacitating cloud. An agent stared into a surveillance monitor. Another started for the door, his hand already on his pistol.

Klaus tossed the canister deep into the room, grabbed the door handle, and slammed the door shut. He drew a gas mask and goggles from another pocket and donned them. Reaching into a third pocket, he brought out a steel device bent ninety degrees at the center. One of the arms was tubular. He slid that end over the handle and wedged it against the door, preventing the handle from rotating down. Then he snatched the towel from his shoulder and pushed it against the bottom to prevent gas from escaping. From inside the security cell, he heard coughing and gagging.

Etzel threw on his own protective gear. He located two surveillance cameras and fired muffled shots into them. Then he fired additional shots into the lock of the suite.

He looked at his watch. Thirty seconds had passed since they had entered the hall. He broke the door open into Atcho's and Sofia's suite. Crouching low, he stepped inside and positioned himself in the doorway to keep watch.

Klaus entered, sizing up the suite. Seconds later, he stole into the bedroom. Atcho and Sofia were still curled together on the sofa. Klaus put the nose of his MP5 next to Atcho's head and nudged him. Atcho awoke with a start.

"Don't move."

Atcho turned his head to look at Klaus through sleepy eyes.

"Wake up your wife. I need you both in the living room. Quickly. I won't hesitate to shoot first if necessary." He pointed his weapon across at Sofia.

The commotion had already awakened her. "Who are you?" Her voice was hoarse. "What do you want?"

"Get up." Klaus fired a bullet into the sofa between Atcho and Sofia. Then, he herded them into the living room at gunpoint.

"We're in a hurry," Klaus snapped. He gestured toward Atcho. "You're coming with us." He tossed Atcho a set of goggles and a gas mask. "Put these on."

Atcho did as ordered while watching Klaus. Atcho's eyes shifted briefly to Sofia. She stood with a calm, composed face. He turned back to Klaus. "You were the gunmen in the van. You shot your own men."

"Shut up." Klaus indicated Etzel still keeping vigil by the door. "My brother will cover us on the way out," he told Sofia. He tapped his MP5. "Don't follow. Go back to the bedroom. Open a window."

While he spoke, Etzel pulled two more CS2 canisters from his coveralls. He held one ready to activate.

"I planted a bomb in this room," Klaus told Sofia. "I have the remote. If I have any trouble on the way out, I'll blow it." He jabbed Atcho in the ribs. "Keep that in mind." Grabbing Atcho by the scruff of the neck, he shoved him toward the door. "Let's go."

Etzel uncapped the canister and tossed it into the living room. Sofia hesitated, and then ran into the bedroom. Etzel prepared the second canister as Klaus and Atcho moved past. Then he closed the door.

Etzel had fitted the last canister with a tube. He crossed the hall, stooped to one side of the security cell door, fed the tube under it, and opened the valve. When he heard the sound of more gas spilling into the room, he moved on.

Atcho peered at the security agent lying unconscious on the floor in the hall. He had no time to see if the man still breathed.

Klaus pushed Atcho along the corridor the way he and Etzel had come. Behind them, his brother tossed a smoke grenade. Within moments, the stench of it filled the air. Alarms clanged, and water poured out of the ceiling's fire suppressors.

Klaus pulled Atcho into the stairwell and down one level. They emerged on the next floor. Already, people rushed from their rooms in panic. "Don't try anything here," Klaus told Atcho in a low voice. He pulled an electronic device from his pocket. "Remember, I have the remote. Etzel has one too."

They pulled off their gas masks and headed to the back of the hotel. The numbers of running people thinned. They took the freight elevator down.

They emerged on the bottom level of a parking garage and headed toward a dark corner. A steel-mesh door leading into a utility room stood open. A dim bulb cast faint light inside. Klaus shoved Atcho through.

They moved behind some machinery. While Etzel kept watch, Klaus moved a grate on the floor. Below it a set of steps led into the ground. "Go," he ordered.

At the bottom, he stopped. "Put this on." He handed Atcho a blindfold. "These are the tunnels that Hitler built. If you don't know where to make the turns, you're dead. If you want to see your sweet Sofia again, don't make trouble."

"Where are we going?"

"You'll know soon enough."

"Why are you doing this?"

"Simple. I deliver you, I get something."

They proceeded at a fast pace, with Klaus pushing Atcho along. The air stank from decades of moisture and decay. Klaus used a flashlight to avoid debris and water puddles, and to find crude route markers. Sometimes, they walked straight a good distance. Then they made several turns. A few times, they crawled on their knees through even smaller tunnels.

Atcho could not tell if all the turns were necessary, or if Klaus had spun him around to confuse him. One thing was certain: without a guide, he would be lost in this maze, possibly never to emerge.

When they had walked for roughly ten minutes, they heard running footsteps. Soon, Etzel caught up with them, panting.

"We're safe," he told Klaus, switching to a language the brothers had in common—one that Atcho did not understand. "The door into the utility room is locked," Etzel continued. "I have the only key. The light is turned off, and the machinery is pulled back over the grate. If they find that entrance, they'll still have to make their way through these tunnels. We'll be long gone." He watched Atcho carefully and was satisfied that the man did not understand what they were discussing.

"What do you want with me?" Atcho interrupted with undisguised anger.

"I told you," Klaus snapped. "I deliver you, I get what I want."

"What do those people want? The ones you're delivering me to."

"I don't know. I don't care. All I care about is getting what I want."

"And that is?"

"Keep going," Klaus growled. "Etzel, lead off. Fast."

They continued their trek through the dark, Etzel forging ahead. The stench made breathing nearly unbearable.

Atcho steeled himself against distress. "Etzel," he called, "how much farther?"

"Shut up," Klaus grunted from behind. He jabbed the MP5 into Atcho's back. He called ahead to his brother in the language they had used before. "Etzel, he thinks he knows your real name." They laughed.

Atcho understood nothing of the exchange.

After more time trudging in darkness, they came to a set of stairs. At the top, Atcho caught a breath of clean air. His spirit buoyed momentarily. Then he heard the low rumbling of distant traffic and felt wind on his face. He was outside. One of the brothers shoved him forward a few steps. He heard a door creak and close. He was indoors again. Faint light shone through the blindfold.

"You can take off that scarf," Klaus said. "You're not going anywhere."

Atcho removed it. He was in a dimly lit room with high walls and a single door. An open window high above his reach provided ventilation. It also let in a late-autumn chill. There was no heat. A table and chair were set in the middle of the room, and a cot with some blankets was placed along a wall. Etzel was not in the room.

"Sit down, get comfortable," Klaus said amiably. "Welcome to East Berlin. I don't know how long you'll be here. It shouldn't be long." Atcho sat on the cot.

"A few things for you to know," Klaus continued. "I won't hesitate to kill you. Don't give me a reason. I saw what you can do. I won't take chances."

Atcho rubbed his hands together to warm them. "You just created a sensation. Do you think the US will let that pass?"

Klaus chuckled. "I don't care. I don't exist, and neither does my brother. No one knows who we are or where to look for us."

"I've seen your face."

Klaus grinned. "Yes, and my brother's too." He laughed. "So, what?" His eyes bored into Atcho. "I want you to hear a phone call. If you make a sound, it will be your last." He tapped the MP5 still slung over his shoulder. "Am I clear?"

Atcho nodded and leaned his back against the wall.

Klaus went to the door and knocked. Etzel entered carrying a rotary phone on a long extension. His omnipresent submachine gun pointed in Atcho's general direction.

Klaus dialed the phone and waited. "I have what you want," he said into the receiver. "It's here. In the East." He listened. "The price went up," he broke in. "I want two of them. One for Baumann, and one for me." His face showed no expression as he listened again. "Understand this," he retorted into the receiver, "I took a lot of risk. That's my price. Tell Baumann he has twenty-four hours. Then he gets what he wants, you get what you want, and I get what I want. I'll call you. If the deal falls through, I'll tell you where to pick up your package. Expired."

9

As soon as Sofia saw Klaus throw the canister, she knew what it was. Momentarily, she was undecided about what action to take. *I can't help Atcho if I'm dead.* She ran into the bedroom and threw the door closed while flipping on the light. Then she grabbed the pillows from the bed and jammed them across the bottom of the door. She scooped up her purse with her pistol and ran into the bathroom. There she used towels to seal off airflow below the closed door.

She looked around the walls. A small vent was embedded above the mirror over the sinks, its louvers lifeless. She flipped a switch by the door, activating a ceiling fan. The louvers opened to circulate air. Then she called the hotel main desk.

"Security is aware of an incident on your floor," the operator said. "The police have been notified. Help is on the way."

Within a minute, Sofia heard movement in the bedroom and then a knock on the door. "Ms. Stahl. This is the hotel security duty officer. May I come in?"

Sofia did not immediately answer. She grabbed her gun, aimed it at the door, and crouched against the wall in the far corner behind the bathtub. "I'm armed," she called. "Open the door slowly. If I see a weapon, you're dead."

The handle rotated down. The door swung open. A man stepped through, hands raised to his chest. "You're in no danger from me," he said. "We have the halls secured. The tear gas has dissipated. We've opened the windows and removed the canister. You're safe."

"And my husband?"

"We're still learning what happened. Your security detail is in bad shape. Our team downstairs is reviewing surveillance videos."

"Kidnappers took my husband. They said they planted a bomb in the living room."

The duty officer raised his eyebrows. "We haven't found one. They might have bluffed to keep you in here. We'll intensify the search. Tell me what happened."

Sofia told him. The officer placed a call. When he hung up, he said, "All exits are sealed. No one is being allowed to leave. The police arrived a few minutes ago. Detective Berger left a message requesting that you wait for him. He'll be here shortly. We have a team to provide security until Mr. Brown and the others have recovered. Is that agreeable?"

Sofia had begun to pace. She stopped and stared at the officer as if only half understanding. "Sure. That's fine."

A few minutes later, the hotel security officer posted at the door escorted Detective Berger into the suite. The detective was as professional as he had been at the station, but his manner now had an empathetic touch. "I know you've told the story already," he said. "Please tell me again. Don't leave out any details."

They sat on the sofa and Sofia began to speak.

"Our units have the hotel secured," Berger said when she was finished. "Your state department and the US military headquarters are notified. They'll have people here soon. We'll find your husband."

"I'm fine. But I'm furious." She looked at Berger fiercely. "Those two have no idea who they're holding."

"Maybe. The trouble is, we don't know who we're dealing with either. If they were Stasi, they've gone rogue. We don't know what they want." He told Sofia that his officers and hotel security personnel had already done a quick sweep of the building and would do another one, more thoroughly. Guards were stationed at all exits. The hotel security director was screening the surveillance videos. "This is an early conclusion, but either the abductors are still in the hotel, or there's another way out we don't know about."

Brown stumbled through the door, pale and crestfallen, his breathing labored. "I'm sorry," he coughed. "I let you down."

Sofia rushed to support him. "No one's blaming you. Sit down."

He waved her away. "Our military police will go over every square inch of this hotel." He smiled sardonically. "The US Army still runs the American sector of West Berlin." His expression changed, determined. "We'll bring in the full force of the US government to get him back."

"The kidnappers were in and out fast," Sofia cut in. "They're brothers. They must have scoped out our security. I don't see how they could have done it without help from inside the hotel."

"We'll be questioning everyone," Berger interjected. He took note of Sofia's composure and her analytical mind. "Are you sure there's nothing else?"

She looked at her watch. "I'm sure. I have things I have to do. Can I go?"

Berger searched her expression and saw only professional neutrality. "Yes, but one favor before you go." He gestured to a woman waiting behind him. "This is our sketch artist. Give her a description of the kidnappers."

Brown watched Berger leave, then waved the artist away. "I need to speak with Ms. Stahl." When they were alone, he turned to Sofia. "Where are you going?"

"I can't say."

Despite his weak state, Brown bristled. "How am I supposed to protect you if you won't tell me what's going on?"

"I can't." Sofia softened her tone. "I have to step outside of your security for a while."

Brown's exasperation showed.

"Don't worry," she said, without emotion. "I'll be covered by US assets the whole time. Right now, I have to help Berger's police artist with her sketch. Then I have to go."

10

When Collins had arrived in Berlin on the evening of the assault, he had checked into his hotel and then strolled on a sightseeing jaunt toward the iconic Kaiser Wilhelm Church ruins, a few blocks away. As he took in the flavor of Berlin's streets, his news reporter's instincts spiked when several police cars suddenly screamed by. He had hurried after them.

Reaching the site too late to see any arrests, he had observed the dead bodies and had been fortunate to speak with several eyewitnesses. From there, he had made his way to the police station.

Astonished to see Sofia there and to learn that Atcho had been briefly detained, he had remained at the station for several hours until he had exhausted the information the police would divulge. After his call to Jakes to lodge his probable scoop on Atcho's arrest and release, he had gone back to his own hotel to rest.

The following day, he had felt frustrated that he could learn no more about the attack. He had spent his time gathering background information on events that precipitated building the Wall and those that might bring rapprochement between the two halves of Germany. *After all, that's the story I was sent here to cover.* He had retired early that evening, fatigued from having been up for most the previous night.

Before dawn, the phone interrupted the reporter's sleep.

"I just watched Berger's briefing," Jakes said. "He doesn't mess around. He gave a full account, including that the Stasi might be involved, and that therefore German intelligence would be in the mix. And, since the shooting happened in the American Sector, US Army criminal investigators and intelligence officers would actively participate."

"Did he identify Atcho?"

"No. He said the Polizei had detained an American as a person of interest, but the man had been cleared. Therefore, he saw no reason to release the name. But get this: Berger said that the American was the intended victim in the shooting."

"What?" Collins was astounded. "I can think of plenty of people who might take a shot at Atcho in the US, and even in Moscow or Siberia, but here in Berlin?" He was quiet as he put his thoughts together. "All right, run with the story as we discussed. There's no reason not to identify Atcho. I'm going to the police station. Maybe I'll pick up more information." He thought about what the hour must be in DC. "Jakes, what are you doing at the office this time of night? It's just turning daylight here."

Jakes laughed. "I'm at home. I had one of our monitors call me when the report came in. If you don't need me for anything else right now, I'm going back to bed."

An hour later, Collins presented himself at the front desk of the police station. He was surprised at the lack of officers in the bay. The sergeant manning the desk had stepped away, so Collins looked around. Movement caught his eye through the glass front, and as he watched, one police car after another sped by, all headed in the same direction with sirens blaring and lights flashing. The sergeant returned.

"Good morning," Collins said pleasantly. "There's a lot of excitement going on out there." The sergeant glared at him, clearly bored. Collins tried another approach. "Is Detective Berger in? I'd like to speak with him."

The sergeant scoffed. "You can try the Mövenpick Hotel, if you can get through all of that." He gestured toward three more police cars rushing by on the street outside.

"What's going on?" Collins presented his press credentials.

"I don't know. The call came in a few minutes ago." He turned his attention to other matters. "Anyway, that's where you'll find Detective Berger."

Collins took a taxi to the Mövenpick, which was ringed with a throng of green and white police cars. In the foyer, he saw men in US military uniforms moving about the luxurious lobby, joined in some cases by colleagues in civilian clothes. Anxious guests scurried past them with furtive looks.

Being as unobtrusive as possible, Collins listened to the whisperings and low-toned conversations. He picked up that there had been an attack—an abduction maybe—a short while before his arrival. *Probably while I was speaking with Jakes.*

He sat near a huddle of serious-faced men, but they eyed him sullenly and moved away. Finally, he walked up to the check-in counter. "Would someone please tell me what's going on?" he demanded of the clerk. "I'm supposed to check in today, but with all these police cars around, I might go somewhere else."

The clerk assured him that he had no need to do that. "What am I supposed to think?" Collins responded. "At least tell me why the police are here so I can make an intelligent decision. Was somebody murdered?"

"Oh no, nothing like that."

"Then what? Do I need to call the manager?"

"No sir," the clerk said in a low tone. "A man was kidnapped this morning. That's all I know."

Another story? Collins went back to the foyer and sat where he could see as much as possible. After he had been there a while, Detective Berger emerged from an elevator and strode toward the main entrance. Collins rose to intercept, but Berger recognized him and waved him off. "No time, Mr. Collins. I'm busy."

"Just one question."

"No." Berger continued on his way.

In frustration, Collins sat back down. A short while later, he saw Sofia come out of another elevator. Her face had "mission" written all over it—a set jaw and distant stare. She wore dark slacks and a winter jacket.

Collins called to her, but she did not hear. She hurried out the door and climbed into the back of an olive-drab-colored sedan. Collins hailed a taxi and followed.

On the other side of the Wall, Atcho and the brothers had just exited the tunnels in East Berlin.

* * *

Sofia felt rattled, an uncommon state for her. The simple recognition of her anxiety unnerved her more. She took deep breaths and forced herself to think calmly.

Her errand had been pre-planned. The ramifications of missing it were formidable. She must meet with Wolfgang in East Berlin one final time. Disruption of this part of her mission could doom the plan and put people's lives in danger.

Maybe the Wall would come down anyway. Maybe not. Her action team was already on the Communist side of the divided city. The sedan she rode in belonged to the US Army's Flag Tour, an elite intelligence group that had free access into East Berlin per the Four Power Agreement. Each team consisted of a senior intelligence officer and an expert driver. Both were intimately familiar with the streets of East Berlin.

The sedan crossed through Checkpoint Charlie without stopping. Almost immediately, the driver called back, "We've picked up a tail. It's a Stasi car. I'll ditch him. That might take a few minutes."

"I don't have time. Take me around the corner and drop me. My team is nearby to pick me up."

"All right. I'll get fifteen seconds ahead and make some turns. When I holler, bail out fast and get out of sight." The driver made a quick turn, and then another. "Get ready." He made another turn and halted next to a van. "The street's clear. Duck in front of that delivery truck. Go."

Sofia jerked the handle and shoved the door open. She rolled out of the car and slammed the door. The sedan speeded away. Sofia moved rapidly to the front of the van and crouched. The sedan turned at the next street. Ten seconds later, the Stasi car sped by.

Sofia waited until it had made the turn, and then stood. A big man with unkempt hair and a grizzled beard blocked her way.

"You like my van?" He spoke in German, lascivious intent gleaming from his eyes. "Maybe you'd like to see inside."

Sofia tried to shove past him. He grabbed her wrist. She glared at him. "Don't do this." She spoke in German. Her voice carried a deadly undertone.

The man tightened his grip and jerked her arm. Sofia used her forward momentum, kicked high, and struck under his chin. He crumpled, unconscious.

She looked about. Seeing no one, she hurried to her rendezvous. Five minutes later, she saw Checkpoint Charlie. She paused under a tree to catch her breath.

Across the street, she saw her destination, a café. She reached into her purse for a pack of cigarettes and lit one. Then she pulled a brown knit cap from her coat pocket and pulled it over her ears, protection against Berlin's late autumn gusts.

She crossed the street and entered the café. It was Spartan, the shelves in the bakery almost bare. She stopped at the counter to order a cup of brackish coffee. A listless attendant looked up vacantly and waved her to a table. She had barely sat down when a female voice addressed her. "Do you have a spare cigarette?"

Sofia turned to face a young woman, perhaps in her late twenties. "I'm in a hurry," she replied.

"Oh, I'm sorry. It's just that I haven't had one in a long time."

Sofia regarded the young woman with barely concealed hostile skepticism. The woman continued to stand there with bright, hopeful eyes. "My name is Nina. I could buy you another cup of coffee."

Sofia scowled, reached into her purse, and handed her the pack. "Keep it."

Nina thanked her and joined a young man at another table deeper in the café. After a few minutes, Sofia called to the café attendant. "Don't take my coffee away. I'll be right back."

She headed toward the coffee shop's rear and found the restroom. Inside, she locked the door and began to undress. A minute later, she heard a soft knock on the door. She opened it a crack. Nina stood there.

Sofia opened the door enough for her to enter. Neither said a word. Immediately, Nina removed a wig from her head. Sofia put it on. Nina undressed. They exchanged clothes. Once fully dressed, Sofia checked the hall and left the restroom. Back in the café, she joined the young man at the table. Moments later, Nina re-entered and took the seat at the table previously occupied by Sofia. She wore the brown knit cap.

Several minutes passed. Nina finished the coffee and left through the front door.

The young man rose from his seat. He led Sofia out the back into a narrow cobblestone alley. "Good to see you got here safely," he muttered. "So far."

"Good job, Jeff," Sofia replied. "What's the rest of the plan for Nina?"

"A pickup team will meet her a block down from the café and take her to the embassy. You'll meet her there later." He pointed ahead. "A car will meet us at the end of the alley." It arrived just as they reached the street, a boxy, lime-green Wartburg that spewed exhaust into the choked East Berlin air.

* * *

Collins watched the olive-drab sedan carrying Sofia disappear around a corner on the other side of Checkpoint Charlie. His frustration deepened. His taxi could not follow.

He mixed with pedestrians crossing into the East through the checkpoint, and presented his press credentials, passport, and permit to travel inside the Soviet Sector. *I might as well pick up on local flavor. Maybe I'll find another story.*

A few minutes passed before he entered the east side. The immigration control officer studied his face and compared it to his documents several times before grunting approval for Collins to proceed.

He had been in East Berlin before. Then as now, he was struck by the obvious differences in quality of life, expressed in despair written on the faces of those he passed. Nevertheless, he felt a change in the air demonstrated by a larger number of people in the streets, many of them standing near the checkpoint and gazing into the West. They seemed less concerned than on previous visits with the intimidating glances thrown their way by border patrol officers.

Collins looked at his watch. More than ten minutes had passed since he had seen the dark sedan with Sofia navigate the checkpoint. He reached the intersection where he had seen it disappear around a corner. He turned in the same direction and ambled along, taking in the bleak feel of the city. His attention was drawn to a solitary woman standing under a tree across the thoroughfare looking along the street ahead of him. She seemed familiar, and she wore clothes similar to what he had seen on Sofia.

That *was* Sofia. His pulse quickened.

As he watched, she lit a cigarette and drew a brown knit cap over her head. Then she crossed the street and entered a small café.

Collins held his excitement in check. He strolled down the street and looked through the café window.

Sofia sat alone. A young woman approached, apparently asking for a cigarette. *I've never seen Sofia smoke before.* He backed away from the window to a place where he could observe unobtrusively. He saw Sofia go down the hall, followed momentarily by the young woman. He used the opportunity to enter the establishment and take a seat by the door. A few minutes later, the young woman returned, and then Sofia.

Somehow, Sofia seemed different, her face more roundish. Startled that she did not recognize him as she passed him on leaving the café, Collins stared after her.

He cast his attention back to the young couple at the table. They headed out the rear door, and Collins was positive he recognized Sofia's figure—that the girl who had gone out the front in the guise of Sofia was a diversion. He hurried to follow the couple and hung back as they walked down a cobblestone alley. Then, he saw them enter a waiting car, a lime-green Wartburg.

Collins knew of Sofia's CIA associations. He had learned of them last year while ferreting out the story of a Soviet coup attempt. *Did I just see an operation in progress?*

* * *

"Most of the people in the café were our own," Jeff said as he and Sofia rode away in the Wartburg. He rode in the front. "But a man came in just before you and Nina got back from the restroom. He wasn't ours, but he looked like a Westerner. He was definitely alert and looking around. He noticed when you came back."

"What did he look like?"

"I'm sure one of our guys got a picture of him, but it still has to be developed." He described the man.

Sofia's heart sank. "Collins."

"You know him?"

"A *Washington Herald* investigative reporter. One that won't let go."

The driver, who had not yet spoken, turned partway in his seat. "We're almost there. I'll let you out up ahead. Jeff, you know what to do?"

"Yeah. We'll be out in ninety minutes. Meet us at the next corner."

The driver nodded and pulled to the curb in front of a grocery store. A long, thick line of shoppers hung close to the edifice, waiting their turns to purchase scarce merchandise. Other pedestrians walked past in both directions, peering through the store window at the nearly empty shelves.

Jeff led Sofia through the crowded walkway and entered a five-story apartment building. It looked to have been built pre-war. The walls were a dreary pastel and peeling, the stairwell dark. On each landing were two apartments that faced each other. Sofia and Jeff climbed to the top of the stairs and entered one of the flats. "We occupy the top three floors," Jeff muttered. "They're cleared. We can talk here."

The shallow foyer opened into a medium-sized living room with a dining area. Two men observed the street through the windows.

"Has he arrived yet?" Sofia asked.

"He's running late," one of the men replied. "He'll be here in an hour."

Sofia quashed her frustration. There was nothing to do but wait and fidget.

* * *

Collins' annoyance mounted. He had no way to pursue, but that was the nature of his job. He shook off his irritation while he thought through his next step. Nothing more was to be gained by remaining on the east side of the Wall, and there was that fresh police situation at the Mövenpick. *What a coincidence that the event happened in the same place where Atcho and Isabel stayed. I wonder what Atcho is doing now.* He returned through the check-point into West Berlin and took a cab to the hotel. He had been gone less than an hour.

The police had set up a perimeter around the Mövenpick and were tightly controlling access. Collins gained entry with his press pass. A crowd of serious-looking officials swarmed the lobby. He returned to the check-in counter. The same clerk was still there and peered at him nervously. "I have friends staying here," Collins told him. "Would you mind ringing the room? The guest's name is Eduardo Xiquez."

The clerk stared, befuddled. "Sir, I can't ring that room." He looked over his shoulder as if for help.

"Why not? They're here. I saw his wife just a little while ago. Her name is Sofia Stahl-Xiquez."

"But sir, I can't." He looked back and forth. "That's the room. That's where the attack...the kidnapping..." He stopped talking.

Stunned, Collins stared at the clerk. "You mean Mr. Xiquez? He was..."

The clerk backed off. "I can't say any more, sir. The police..." He looked about again. "I have to go."

Collins ambled back through the lobby, his mind in overdrive. To one side, a loose group of reporters focused attention eagerly toward an empty podium bedecked with microphones. *My competition, waiting for a statement.*

Nearby was a knot of serious-faced men deep in conversation. A younger man stood close by. He appeared to be part of the group, but junior to the extent that he was not yet allowed into the inner sanctum. Collins approached him.

"Quite a bit of excitement," he said conversationally.

The man looked at him and nodded without reply.

"Are you with those detectives? That must be a complicated job in West Berlin."

The young detective held back a smile, seemingly pleased with the implied compliment. "It has its challenges."

"Will you be able to find him?"

"Who?"

"Mr. Xiquez, the kidnap victim."

The man stared coldly. "We made no statement. Who told you that?"

Collins hurried away to call Jakes. "Have you heard about some kind of attack at the Mövenpick?"

"It came through on the wire about half an hour ago, but no details. We're waiting for a statement now."

"Get ready to copy." In rapid time, Collins told him what he had learned, and about what he had seen with Sofia. "Get the story out that we believe Atcho has been kidnapped. Throw in that the motive is unknown. He had no known enemies in this area. Run with the fact that he's married to the state department's Sofia Stahl-Xiquez but leave out that I saw her in East Berlin. Hurry. I'm in the hotel, and the press briefing will start at any moment."

Collins was about to hang up when he had a sudden thought. "Jakes, what did they do with Borya Yermolov last year? You remember, the rogue Russian general who tried to take over the Soviet Union. Atcho stopped him."

"How could I forget, with you holed up there at Camp David posting stories in *Pravda* and *Izvestia* about fake Rasputin descendants? Anyway, I don't know where they put the general. Are you thinking he's involved?"

"Not necessarily. My mind was just running through Atcho's possible enemies, and Yermolov popped to the top of the list."

"Last I heard, the Marines took him into custody. I'll get a researcher to check it out. Is that all? If I'm going to scoop this story on Atcho's kidnapping, I'd better run."

* * *

Sofia and Jeff continued to wait in the flat with other team members. Finally, the door opened, and a man walked in. He was husky, with blond hair tending to gray. Despite his furtive expression, he had a rugged air. When he saw Sofia, his face broke into a smile. "Sofia! How great to see you again."

Sofia crossed the room, hugged him warmly, and then stood back. "Mr. Sacher. We don't have much time. I'm happy you could make it."

He drew away. "Please call me Wolfgang. We've known each other too long to be formal."

Sofia smiled. "Wolfgang it is. Are you all set?"

Wolfgang's expression turned to one of sadness. "A bit afraid, I'm afraid," he quipped, "but I'm ready." He gestured toward the other men in the room. "My biggest concern is getting my family out. Your team explained the plan in a previous meeting." He peered at her. "What about your family?"

"I'm still working on that. The main thing is to be sure the press release is read, and the stand-down order gets issued to the border guards and passport control officers. If that works, we'll have no worries."

"And if it doesn't," Wolfgang said softly, "we could all wind up dead. Our families too."

Sofia shot him a determined look. "That's not going to happen. The crowds at Alexanderplatz are growing every night." She eyed him roguishly. "They haven't been very nice to you lately. I've seen the footage of them booing you."

Wolfgang shrugged. "They see me as part of the ruling class."

Sofia shook her head. "If they only knew. What date do you think will be set for the press release?"

"There's been talk of November tenth."

"So, you'll preempt on the evening of the ninth? How will you bring that about?"

"The general secretary gives me notes with things to talk about before I go to each press conference. I've been holding one every night for a while, so that one won't be out of the ordinary. On that evening, I'll pretend I just got the release, and read it."

"What if he doesn't give you the announcement?"

Wolfgang drew in a deep breath. He smiled as though in a faraway place. "I have one made up."

"How big are the press conferences?"

"Very large. I think every news outlet in the world sends a reporter. Tom Brokaw is there, and other leaders in the Western press." He rolled back on his heels and indicated with his jaw the operatives in the room. "I understand they can assure the right questions are asked, with immediate transmission to the West."

Sofia nodded. Then she hugged him spontaneously. "I'm glad this monstrosity of a government is about to end." She stood back. "Remember, don't do anything until you see me. If I don't show up, it means something's gone wrong." She locked her eyes on his. "In that case, pull back. We'll have to wait to see if the declaration is executed at the scheduled time."

"I understand." He held her gaze, his fondness inescapable. "Your father must be so proud."

"My father doesn't know," Sofia cautioned, "and you can never tell him."

Wolfgang nodded sadly. "What a world we live in." He sighed, and then another, sharper expression of concern crossed his face. "I heard the reports of the shooting two nights ago. The police questioned an American, and then he was abducted this morning. Was that your husband?"

Sofia's mental warnings blared. "How did you know that?"

"I'm on the politburo." Wolfgang chuckled. "I helped force Honecker out, remember. I sit in meetings with the director of the Stasi, Johann Baumann."

"Oh, right. Sorry." She felt a pang of guilt at the rush of suspicion that had overtaken her.

"Besides," Wolfgang added, "Atcho has already been identified in the Western press. The *Washington Herald* ran the story just before I came over here. It was picked up by the newswires. I'm surprised you hadn't heard."

Sofia stared, stunned, recalling that Jeff had seen someone looking like Collins in the café. Then she gathered her wits, and once again forced calm on herself. "As you say," she murmured, "what a world we live in."

She focused back on the mission. "Yes, that's my husband, but your concern is to be ready with that press release on the ninth. Let me worry about Atcho." She looked at her watch. "Okay, you've seen me, you know the operation is legitimate. Unless you have questions, we'd better be going. The next time you see my face will be the signal to read the announcement." She turned to Jeff. "Get me to the embassy, and then back to the hotel."

Wolfgang tapped her. "To better times," he said brusquely. He held her by the shoulders and kissed her lightly on the forehead. "I'll be ready."

* * *

Collins sat in the foyer of the Mövenpick, reflecting on the events that had entangled him with Atcho last year. The reporter had gone to New York to cover the last meeting between President Ronald Reagan and the General Secretary of the Soviet Communist Party, Mikhail Gorbachev. He had had no great expectations for the story, just routine coverage of the two leaders' last official visit while both were still in office.

Then, as Collins had trailed behind them with the press gaggle at the Long Island estate, a door had opened, and Atcho had stepped through. He had stood there only momentarily with a Secret Service agent, and then had stepped back and closed the door. However, in that brief moment, Collins had seen Ronald Reagan make deliberate eye contact with Atcho, and then nudge Gorbachev. The Soviet leader had also made eye contact, nodded slightly, and moved on.

His curiosity piqued, Collins had pursued the lead and had subsequently become embroiled in one of the most intriguing episodes of his career. One piece of information Collins still did not know was what had happened with Yermolov, the rogue Soviet general who had mounted a coup attempt against Gorbachev. The newsman had followed up lightly and had been told that the information was classified. That had not been surprising. Other stories had taken his attention, so he had let the matter drop. Now he wondered. He hoped Jakes would turn up some answers.

Twelve hours later, Jakes called again. "Bull's-eye!"

"Calm down," Collins replied. "What are you talking about?"

"Your hunch. It was a good one."

"That's great to hear. Which one? Start over and explain slowly."

"Sorry. I did as you asked and checked with Pentagon sources on the whereabouts of Yermolov. Recall that he spied for the Soviet Union as a US Air Force officer for thirty years."

"I know all that. He was a lieutenant general, aka Paul Clary. What did they do with him?"

"Atcho turned him over to two US generals, one a Marine and one Air Force. In the Azores."

"I remember that. Then what?"

"The helicopter that picked Yermolov up never made it to the *USS Enterprise*. It crashed on the way, with no survivors."

Collins sat back, stunned. "So he's dead? I guess that closes that possibility."

"Wait. I had our researchers scan through any sources they could find about the crash. One of our bright guys found an article about it in the *Air Force Times* from nearly a year ago. It's short." He read it to Collins. "Here's the important part: 'A US Marine helicopter on a routine training mission crashed in the Atlantic Ocean four days ago near the Azores. No survivors were found. The identities of those missing are being withheld pending notification of the families. In a rare coincidence, a local fisherman identified as Gonçalo Alvarenga went missing. His dinghy was found listing in shallow waters off the east coast of Terceira, the main island in the same archipelago. He is overdue by four days. A search is underway but will soon turn into a recovery mission.'"

Collins sucked in his breath. "Are we saying that Yermolov could be alive?"

"That's a possibility, and he could be free. The fisherman was in the area where the helicopter went down. We don't know what happened to him."

Both men were quiet, thinking. Then Collins broke in. "Jakes, get your assistant to order me a ticket for the fastest way to the Azores. I'll head to my hotel to get my things and then go to the airport."

11

Borya Yermolov stood in Stasi Director Johann Baumann's office. He rubbed a scar on his chest under his shirt. It instantly refreshed a memory of hand-to-hand combat in Havana two years ago. He remembered vividly the searing pain when Atcho had turned his own knife on him and plunged it deep between his ribs. Those scars still ached occasionally, particularly in the bitterly cold weather of East Berlin, as did the scars on his leg. Atcho had shot him there last year, bringing to a dismal end Yermolov's ambition of ruling over the Soviet Union with its nuclear arsenal.

They thought they were done with me. He had thought so too. The huge Antonov An-225 Mriya, the flying six-engine beast designed to ferry the Soviet space orbiter, was to have provided his triumphal passage to Moscow. Instead, it had become his mammoth detainment cell as Atcho and his team had commandeered the aircraft, subdued him, and flown him to Lajes Air Base in the Azores. They had not seen the fishing dinghy below where Gonçalo had watched the aircraft on its final descent.

Yermolov remembered being in a drugged state when he was taken from the Mriya on a gurney, his leg still swollen from where Atcho had shot him. Marine MPs had transferred him to a waiting helicopter. He did not remember much of the next several minutes except that he had heard a loud clanging noise, felt the sensation of dropping through the air, and then had been immersed in water. The next thing he remembered was lying in the bottom of a boat under a blanket.

The morphine must have been wearing off, because the agony had started up again. Then he had seen the fisherman staring at his handcuffed wrists, his bloody leg, and his Soviet uniform. His instincts had told him he had to act.

He did not wait. Ignoring pain and the effects of drugs, and when Gonçalo's back was turned, Yermolov had struggled to his feet, lunged with the same pole used to save his life, and beat the fisherman's head in with it. Then he had wrestled the lifeless body over the side and watched it disappear into the waves.

Yermolov had then checked the boat's wake. It was straight, but a storm was moving in. His head had cleared from the adrenaline generated by his brief struggle. Surmising that the fisherman had been cruising toward shore and out of the way of the storm, he had stumbled to the cabin and checked the heading.

He had made landfall and beached in a secluded cove, sheltered from the wind. Then the storm had rolled in, bringing torrential rain.

That night had seemed endless. Throwing a blanket over his shoulders in the wheelhouse, he had worked by the light of a dim lantern to nurse his wounds with a first-aid kit rummaged from a cabinet. Then, he had filed off his handcuffs using a tool he found in Gonçalo's toolbox.

* * *

"Comrade Yermolov." Stasi Director Baumann indicated another man entering the office. "You wanted to see Ranulf?"

Yermolov's brow immediately creased with anger. "Yes." His mood was dark. He turned to Ranulf. "How did you screw up this operation so royally?"

Ranulf's anxiety took a leap. His options were limited. He could not blame someone else now, here in the office of the Stasi director. Baumann had issued the order. "My fault," he said at last. His stomach churned. Making such an admission could invite his own demise. "I should have sent more men and planned more carefully."

Yermolov's fury was obvious in the bulging muscle between his eyes.

"Klaus called," Baumann interceded. "He has Atcho. Here. In the East."

Ranulf stared, dumbfounded. "Where?" That was all he could manage.

"He won't say. He's positive that you sent a hit squad after him and his brother."

"I did," Ranulf blurted. "They're crazy. They killed eight of our men in one night."

"Listen to me." Yermolov moved between Ranulf and Baumann, his tone venomous. "I should shoot you myself. But we don't have much time."

Ranulf swallowed. Baumann threw a hard look at Yermolov. "I'll deal with my men," he said tersely.

Yermolov whirled on him. "The Wall is coming down. Unless we stop it. Do you understand? We're talking days, not weeks." He read Baumann's anger. "You let Erik Honecker be driven from office. Your Stasi lost control of the people. *Your men* hovered around the demonstrators without lifting a finger." Rage sparked in his eyes. "A million people marched in East Berlin, and *your men* stood by and watched." Perspiration beaded on his forehead. "Why didn't *your men* use their guns? You let the genie out. Only extreme measures can put it back."

He stepped closer to the director. "Do you wish to continue your life under Soviet security?"

The director moved not an inch. His nostrils flared. The two men stood toe to toe, eye to eye.

"You'd better listen," Yermolov said through pursed lips, his voice steely. "With epic disruption comes opportunity, if you know how to exploit it. That opportunity is now." He turned from Baumann to Ranulf. "Can you communicate with your hit squad?"

Containing his anger, Baumann crossed to the window and stared out.

Ranulf looked on silently, surprised at this strange Russian's blatant exercise of authority and the director's acquiescence. Baumann had imprisoned hundreds of thousands of people, subjecting them to torture and starvation. He had signed off on the death warrants of a staggering number of unfortunates. Now he deferred to this Russian with only a bleat.

In that moment came comprehension. The director of the fearsome

Stasi was in a state of paralysis. *East Germany really is on the brink of extinction. It's every man for himself.*

"Can you communicate with your hit squad?" Yermolov repeated, his voice impatient.

Ranulf nodded in response.

"Good. Tell your men to find out where Klaus is holding Atcho but do nothing more until I give the word."

Ranulf looked to Baumann for approval. The director consented. Ranulf started to leave. "One more thing," Yermolov said. Ranulf stopped. "Tell your men if things go wrong and you can't bring Atcho here, kill him."

After Ranulf left, the director turned to Yermolov, furious. "Why is this Atcho so important? Why do you want him?"

Yermolov scoffed. "He's a nit, of no importance, but he gets into the middle of things and messes them up. His wife is doing something. We don't know what. By abducting him, we've taken him out of play, and we'll use him to pressure her. It was supposed to happen quietly."

The director looked puzzled. "I don't understand his wife's position."

"I told you, she's a CIA operator." Yermolov scowled. "Why didn't you know that? Her state department job is a cover. She has no diplomatic portfolio, so what's she doing here? Her father was a US diplomat in Berlin when the Wall went up. My guess is she has contacts in the East she's trying to exploit to make sure the Wall comes down. We're only days away from all hell breaking loose."

"Why not take her out?"

Yermolov saw that the question was genuine. "Because that could cause the US to intervene directly, which would ensure the end of the Wall and East Germany."

Baumann pondered that. "I suppose, but the US is known for backing down these days. Can your cousin deliver the bombs in time?"

"He can, but Klaus' demand for two bombs complicates things."

"What will he do with the second bomb?"

Yermolov rubbed the back of his neck. "I can only guess. Selling it on the black market is a possibility, but he's not motivated by money. He's a zealot. He sees the United States as the 'Great Satan,' and he's happy to help bring it down."

"Where did you get him?"

Yermolov stared at the director. "You're asking a lot of questions. Is this an interrogation?"

Baumann stared back. "I've cooperated, per the KGB chairman's direction. I see things the same way you do. That doesn't mean surrender. If I'm going to be of use to you, I need to understand. I still command the Stasi."

Yermolov was silent a few moments. He masked his anger at Baumann's comment. "Klaus and his brother were in a KGB group organized by a Soviet colonel in deep cover. He was my executive officer in last year's coup attempt. You heard about it. The brothers deserted after the coup failed. They work independently."

"Can you get help from the colonel? Can he reorganize the group?"

"No. He was promoted to major general and has his own ambitions. I'll have to deal with him when the full plan is executed. As it turns out, he was also working undercover. His last name is Putin. Gorbachev dispersed the group, with members going back to their units. That's when the brothers deserted. But, as you know, I have the ear of the chairman of the KGB.

"Klaus and Etzel are Chechen Muslims, recruited and trained by the Soviet *Spetsnaz*. They hate the Soviet Union as much the US. They want to see both powers brought down."

Baumann looked incredulous. "Why on earth would you allow Chechen Muslims in the *Spetsnaz*?"

Yermolov sighed. "Another example of Soviet stupidity in high places. The thought was that a multinational army would not be loyal to a particular region and could be deployed to control people anywhere. Anyone who studies Chechen history knows they hate Russia, and why. The region will be a future cauldron."

"What happens if we don't meet Klaus' demand?"

Yermolov took his time to respond. "Worst case, he turns Atcho loose. Best case, he kills him. He won't take the first option, and he probably won't take the second one unless he runs out of alternatives. Right now, he sees Atcho as a bargaining chip. He has his own target in mind. We need to make sure his objective serves our purpose."

"I still don't understand why Atcho is such a threat."

Yermolov's impatience surfaced. "He's an amateur, a rank amateur, but he stopped two conspiracies, including Gorbachev's assassination. He's a Don Quixote, taking on what should be lost causes. But he wins." Yermolov's exasperation showed. "He graduated from West Point and went to Ranger and Airborne schools, but he never served in the US Army because he was an exchange cadet from Cuba. His only combat experience was that American disaster at the Bay of Pigs. Castro captured him and kept him in prison for nineteen years. The fool should be dead, but he keeps going."

The director observed Yermolov curiously. "You're afraid of him."

Yermolov whirled on him. "You should know better than that. I'm a survivor, but ready to meet death at a moment's notice. While I'm alive, I intend to live life to its fullest, which for me means the top of national power."

The director responded, his voice grave. "I'm not clear on how you intend to accomplish that."

"I'll go over the plan again. Maybe you should take notes." Yermolov struggled to contain his disgust. *Careful, don't make an enemy of him.* "You're an old man, but you are East Germany's last hope to remain intact as a sovereign power. Honecker's replacement is too weak. We need a Stasi director who will not hesitate to shoot into crowds of protesters, someone who doesn't mind seeing bloody corpses on the streets, who will face down the US without flinching. You've been held back by your new, softer East German political masters. When we execute the plan, you'll be the power. You'll appoint your own Stasi director and open the way for my plans inside the Soviet Union."

Baumann rubbed his chin. "I see. And you intend to take power in Moscow."

"That will happen quickly. We'll set the bomb to explode inside the US Embassy here in East Berlin. I'll cut a deal with Klaus to detonate another one in Chechnya. He wants one for his own purposes. I'll get him a third one. He can do with it whatever he likes, as long as his target is outside of Soviet interests."

Baumann's eyes opened wide. "A third bomb? You intend to have three bombs?"

Yermolov nodded. "They're small, but nuclear. They'll take out anything within a mile of the blast. The devastation will boggle the mind." His eyes gleamed. "The East German Army will have to impose martial law, and the West won't interfere. The Soviet Union will be forced to provide support. Gorbachev will be discredited beyond repair. He's already unpopular with anyone opposed to *glasnost* and *perestroika*. Those policies encourage independent thinking, which spells the end of the Soviet Union."

Baumann's face was a mask of consternation. "What will Klaus do with a third bomb?"

Yermolov read his concern. "Don't worry. Klaus' aims are in the Middle East. *Jihad*. Hitler cultivated ties in that part of the world. When we get what we want, we won't care about blowing up a few camels and sand dunes out in the desert."

The director looked unconvinced. "What about the KGB? You need them."

"I do," Yermolov agreed. "The chairman, Nestor Murin, is on thin ice. He crossed Gorbachev and let a KGB general take the fall when the coup failed." He grimaced as he recalled his own capture. "The Soviet Union is ripe for takeover. Last year, we had one-third of the senior generals ready to move. Another bunch are still in prison for participating in the first coup attempt. Their troops would welcome them back. Even the Soviet politburo sent a member to our planning meetings. Gorbachev's days are numbered."

The director stroked his chin. "So, your plan is to create chaos here and in the Soviet Union at the same time, discredit the general secretary, and replace him."

"Exactly." Yermolov was unusually effusive. "When the US Embassy blows up here, East Germany's national leader will be lost. You'll step in and act in East Germany's best interests by ordering martial law. You'll request Soviet military intervention to re-establish order. A day later, the second explosion will take place in Chechnya. That will arouse the population in the Soviet Union and seal Gorbachev's fate. He'll be seen as incapable of keeping his country secure. Even world opinion will be against him."

"And you'll ride in to take over."

"It's more complex than that, but essentially yes."

"And you think you can handle the KGB chairman? He's a tough old bird. I've known him for years." Baumann subdued his skepticism, but his expression gave away his doubt. "Your plan sounds like one hatched in desperation."

Now Yermolov was angry, and he did not care that Baumann saw it. "Any plan to forcibly replace any government is desperate. What are your choices? The East German government is sinking. The Soviet Union is not far behind. You're the last of East Germany's hard-liners still in senior position. What do you think will happen to you if East and West reunite? You'll be tried for crimes against humanity in The Hague. You'll be hung by your nails. That's if the people don't get to you first. Think of what the Italians did to Benito Mussolini."

"I know, I know." The director deflected with his hand. "I want to make sure I understand completely. We've already had too many slipups."

"Because of the crew you sent after Atcho."

Now Baumann's anger flared. "Seriously? What would have happened if we'd just left Atcho alone?"

"I'll answer that when we know what his wife is doing. Now, he's out of the picture, and she's preoccupied with finding him."

"Are you sure you didn't go after Atcho for revenge?"

Yermolov almost laughed. "I'm a sociopath. I couldn't care less about revenge. I care about survival and pursuing my own ambition. Atcho got in my way twice. I won't give him a third chance."

The director condescended. "I'll buy that. But what about Murin, the KGB chairman? What will you do about him?"

"He has many enemies. His allies are bought. He's insulated himself, but he can't stop the bullet of a determined killer. If I need to, I'll deliver it myself."

12

Director Baumann sat alone in his office, his anger simmering. He had been with the East German state since its inception. *How did things get this way?* He remembered the days when Joseph Stalin had ruled all of Eastern Europe with an iron fist. No one would have dared speak to "Uncle Joe" the way that Yermolov had spoken to Baumann in his own office.

For that matter, no one would have dared speak to Baumann that way, period. He was one of the triggermen who had murdered two policemen in Berlin in 1931 and escaped prosecution. He had executed the Great Purge in the Soviet Union on behalf of Stalin. After the war, he had returned to Soviet-occupied Germany and helped organize it into a totalitarian Marxist-Leninist state.

He, Johann Baumann, had converted historic castles into full-capacity dungeons, built more prisons, and filled them. He had overseen construction of the Wall and the eight-hundred-mile fortified border. On his orders, anyone attempting escape was shot.

From 1957 until now, he had been the longest-serving and most-feared secret police chief in the Soviet bloc. He had developed chummy enough relations with the KGB that the Soviet government had invited him to establish Stasi offices inside its borders to monitor East German travelers.

So great was Soviet confidence in him that the Stasi had been afforded autonomy for the last thirty-two years. In return, he granted KBG officers the same authorities and privileges inside East Germany that they enjoyed at home. So close were KGB and Stasi operations that the KGB still maintained offices in East Berlin in each of the Stasi directorates.

Baumann was nothing if not a survivor. When Erich Honecker and the rest of the hard-line East German leaders had been driven from office, only he, Baumann, had survived the political purge. Nevertheless, he had seen an escalating diminution of his power, and not because of his advancing age. It had first been demonstrated on a large scale at the damnable protest in Leipzig. The Stasi had been rendered helpless, and thanks to that videographer, the world had watched Baumann become impotent. His face contorted with rage at the thought.

His isolation had increased when he had found himself left out of key politburo meetings. Every day brought new challenges to the regime and to Baumann. His thoughts turned to the ranch he had built in Argentina with millions of dollars grafted over decades.

When Yermolov had shown up, he had claimed to be a KGB general and told Baumann to call Nestor Murin himself, chairman of the KGB, to confirm his *bona fides*. Baumann knew Murin. They were each other's counterpart. In effect, he reported to Murin. The director reflected on the conversation about Yermolov.

"He's in Berlin?" Murin had been amazed. "The last I knew, he was either dead or under military arrest in the United States. Do you know how he escaped?"

"No. What should I do with him? He says he can bring me a nuclear bomb."

Murin sighed. "He's done it before." He gave one of the deep, guttural guffaws for which he was known among associates. It signaled that the machinations of his mind were engaged. "Keep him there. Patronize him. See where he goes with this. He has a brilliant mind." He paused. "Take his direction but keep his presence quiet. Who knows? He might be able to save East Germany. You need an ally. Our village idiot Gorbachev will not lift a finger to save you. Keep me informed."

Baumann's fury boiled. *The Soviet Union is on its way down. East Germany is near its end. I'm supposed to sit and watch it happen? These people ordering me around were playing with nursery toys when I sent senior Soviet officials to the gulags.*

* * *

Ranulf did his best to hide his anger as he left the director's office. For a bully who frequently acted on impulse, he found constraint difficult. *Why did Baumann drop this on me? That Russian underestimated Atcho.* If the matter could not be cleaned up, Ranulf would be the fall guy.

He worried about Yermolov's statements on the future of East Germany. The Russian sounded so sure, as if East Germany's fall were a certainty unless his plan succeeded. *A plan I don't understand, except that they're going to give that crazy Klaus a nuclear bomb.*

In the director's office, he had exercised rare discipline against his urge to ram his fist down Yermolov's throat. *What fool notion did he have to kidnap this Atcho?*

Whatever Yermolov's grander scheme, the Russian had increased the risk by immeasurable degrees. *And they won't tell me the plan because they think I'm dumb.* His thoughts turned to exasperation. *I'm the guy who has to get the money.*

In times past, getting cash had been no issue. With fear of the Stasi to back him, Ranulf had developed contacts and pressure points within agencies to bypass controls.

The amount would be a challenge, but he felt confident he could deliver. However, given the palpable fear of East Germany's imminent demise, Ranulf's mind went in a different direction. *Can I escape with it to the West?*

He dismissed the thought as soon as it entered his head, but as he walked the street, it persisted. He could not shake the idea. As soon as he was back in his office, he sent for Oily. "Have you located the brothers?"

Oily shook his head. "We'll find them. We have our best agents looking for them. Any change in orders?"

"Yes. Don't do anything to them until you hear from me. There is one exception. They've taken a captive. The director wants him alive." He gave Oily a photo of Atcho. "But, if you can't capture him, kill him."

13

As soon as Atcho had taken off his blindfold, he looked for some means to escape. They were scant.

He guessed that several hours had passed since his abduction and wondered what Sofia was doing now. She had mentioned something about a meeting that was critical to her mission, but she had not divulged details and he had not pressed. He hoped that she would have presence of mind to continue with her plan.

While Klaus spoke on the phone, Atcho studied the door. It had been reinforced with steel. Breaking through was not an option. He took note of other elements in the room, and slowly a plan formed in his mind. If he failed, hiding his attempt would be impossible. His next cell and treatment would likely be much worse.

Klaus hung up the phone. The *plunk* of the receiver on its base jerked Atcho back to attention.

Klaus stared at him. "Aren't you curious about the other side of the conversation?"

"Are you going to tell me?"

Klaus chuckled. "No. I just thought you might like to know."

"I'm curious about how long I have to stay here. What's so important about me that you came after me twice?"

Klaus stretched like a man with time on his hands. He grinned. "Honestly, I don't know. My job was to get you. Now, I wait for payment."

"You messed up the first time."

Klaus shrugged. "Not me. The crew they gave me were bunglers. If I'd been better informed, we'd have planned better." He gestured toward Etzel. "When we know the lay of the land, we're pretty good."

"Who's 'they'?"

Klaus grinned. "I'm not the talkative type." He rubbed his stomach and glanced at Etzel. "I'm hungry. Let's go eat."

Etzel nodded. Klaus turned back to Atcho. "We'll bring back food. If you're good, we might let you have it." He laughed, and then looked up at the window. It was the kind that leaned into the room along a hinge at its base. No sill to hang on to. It was high on the wall, above where a tall man could reach, even standing on the table. "Don't get any ideas. We won't be gone long." They left, locking the door behind them.

Atcho stayed in place until their footsteps receded. He heard an outside door close. Then he jumped to his feet.

He shoved the table, deliberately making it screech across the floor. He stopped to listen. No returning footsteps.

He set the chair on the table and stood on it. The window was still too high. He moved the table against the opposite wall and set a chair on it. Next, he upended the cot, bracing one end against the back of the seat and the other at the window's horizontal hinge along its bottom. Then he wedged the flimsy structure in place. He tested it with his weight a few times.

He stopped again to listen. No sound.

He spread a blanket under the window, wrapped a shoe in a second blanket, and clambered onto the tabletop.

He tried crawling up the surface of the cot. It was too slippery.

He shinnied by wrapping his legs around each side of the cot. That worked, but the chair fell forward slightly. The cot buckled.

Atcho's breath caught. The chair and cot held. He exhaled slowly. Sweat poured from his forehead and down his neck. He climbed until his hands reached midway up the open window, then he pushed against the glass.

The window stuck in place. He shoved harder. It creaked. He almost fell off the contraption.

He pushed again. The window gave, but still did not close. He stopped to listen. Nothing.

He reached as high as he could and delivered a blow with the shoe to the side of frame. The window closed a few inches, but still leaned into the room. He banged it a few more times, with the same result.

His legs perspired. He felt himself slipping. He squeezed his legs against the side of the cot for more traction but knew he could not hold the position much longer.

The cot sagged. Furiously, Atcho reached with both hands and pushed on the window as hard as he dared without losing his balance. By slow degrees, the window closed into its upright position. Sweat poured from every one of Atcho's pores.

He found that by wedging his feet against the crossbar under the cot, he could hold himself in position. He stretched farther up the cot. Then, holding the blanket-wrapped shoe tightly, he struck the pane, hard.

The glass was ancient and brittle. It shattered easily. Most of the pieces tumbled outside the window. A few fell inside and landed on the blanket below. A hole appeared in the glass, framed by jagged shards. Atcho knocked them outside.

When the window was sufficiently clear, he dropped the shoe and threw the blanket over the bottom edge of the sill. Then he slid down and put his shoes back on.

He heard the outside door open and then the voices of Klaus and Etzel. They conversed easily, seeming in no hurry, headed his way.

Atcho sucked in his breath. He thought of jumping up to the window. That was impossible. The angle was too steep, the distance too great, and he might slice his hands shards of glass protruding through the blanket put there to protect them.

The brothers continued to approach. Atcho heard their footsteps above their voices. He wrapped his legs around the open cot and struggled up the incline again, his hands reaching the window frame.

He tried to pull himself up. The blanket prevented a solid grip. He shinnied furiously, his legs weakening their hold. Finally, his arms slipped over the window's edge to his armpits. He lifted one leg through the window.

As he struggled to pull himself up, the brothers' conversation stopped. Then Klaus spoke from just outside the door. Etzel mumbled something. Keys jangled.

With a herculean effort, Atcho pulled himself astride the window frame. Without time to see where he would land, he slipped his other leg through, and dropped. To his surprise, he fell just a few inches, onto the roof of a shed attached to the building.

He heard the door open and then Klaus' yell of alarm. Running footsteps followed.

Atcho crouched. When he heard the outer door slam shut, he stood and lifted himself back over the window frame. No one was in the room. The door was open. Both men had gone in pursuit.

He climbed down the way he had come. *They'll look everywhere but here.* He lowered himself to the floor, then crept to the door and peered around the frame. It opened into a foyer, empty except for a few old pieces of broken office furniture and trash strewn about. The only light came through windows coated with the dust of ages. On either side of the main entrance, halls led into darkness in both directions.

Atcho moved to the center of the foyer. In the distance at either end, he saw what looked like balustrades for staircases. He chose the corridor to his right and ran. As he reached the end of the hall, the telephone in the foyer rang. He darted into the shadows and started up the stairs.

The ringing continued, and then stopped. Atcho hugged the shadows. He reached the second floor. Another hall traversed the building. Near the center, he saw a break, and then a continuation of the corridor.

He stole through the half-light filtering from the windows of offices lining the corridor. He reached the break, a second-story mezzanine that overlooked the foyer.

The phone rang again, interrupting the ghostly silence. It kept ringing.

* * *

Staring around the empty room, Klaus fumed. Atcho was gone. A glance at the broken window, the blanket over its edge, and the cot propped against the wall atop the chair and table told him how the escape had been engineered. True to his word, Klaus had brought a bag of food. In his rush to pursue, he tossed it onto a chair in the foyer.

Klaus and Etzel raced out the front doors. The building was a large relic of wartime Germany, a bureaucratic headquarters left to decay. Several minutes elapsed before they arrived under the broken window at its rear. They stared at the gaping hole.

Around them more old structures decayed, some with crumbling walls and caved-in roofs, all abandoned. East Berlin did not tolerate vagrants, squatters, or the homeless, declaring that in a socialist state, such people did not exist. Hidden as it was by other development, this small area stood empty, inhabited sporadically by only the criminally minded.

Etzel's lungs heaved from running. "Where could he have gone?"

Klaus leaned over, hands on knees, catching his breath. Sweat poured from his brow. "He could be anywhere."

They examined the ground for footprints. Finding none, Etzel climbed atop the low shed under the window. Broken shards of glass lay scattered about. Nothing indicated Atcho's direction. Etzel jumped down and they looked farther afield. Finding no clue, they trudged back around to the front of the building.

When they reached the entrance, they heard the phone ringing. It was an old phone, dating back to wartime. Finding one that could be repaired to working condition and then stringing a hidden line had been difficult, but they had managed. Although never anticipating the current turn of events, they had long ago scouted for a place like this, intending to develop their own organization here.

Despite the building's age and poor maintenance, it was strong, having been spared most of the bombs that had hit Berlin near the end of the war. It was roomy, with numerous inside structures capable of hiding groups of men.

"The *jihad* is coming," Klaus had told Etzel, "maybe sooner than we think. East Germany is near its end. The Soviet Union is creaking. All it needs is a push. When that happens, the *jihad* will rise."

He hurried to the phone, grunted a greeting, and listened. The conversation was in English. "That's good." He listened some more. "We can do that. Have them at that location tomorrow at this time." More listening. "Three days?" He exhaled into the receiver. "All right, but hear me on this. If there is another delay, we'll deliver Atcho ready for burial. Then we're gone. You won't find us." He hung up.

"You heard?" he said, turning to Etzel and neglecting to switch languages.

"How are we going to deliver?" his brother responded impatiently.

Klaus chuckled. "We don't have to. If Atcho is too much of a problem, my instructions are to kill him."

"Why didn't they kill him to begin with?"

"Who knows? Anyway, they want to triple the assignment. Three bombs."

Etzel stared at him in shock. "Three? Three nuclear bombs?" His face broke into an amazed smile, his eyes wide open. "I thought they would be furious with us. You were right—*jihad* will come soon!"

Klaus ignored the last part of his comment. "Why are we speaking in English?" he said, as if suddenly realizing that is what he was doing.

Etzel shrugged. "You got off the phone using English. That's what comes from using so many languages."

Klaus switched to their native tongue. "Who else can do the job? By now, most of the Stasi operators already hear the roar of the Wall coming down. They're running for cover. Yermolov knows we were *Spetsnaz*. By bringing Atcho here, we regained credibility."

Etzel nodded glumly. "And now Atcho's gone."

Klaus laughed out loud. "They don't know that. All we have to do is kill him—or not—and say we did." He laughed again and slapped Etzel on the shoulder. Etzel joined in. "We'll watch for Atcho," Klaus went on. "He still has to escape East Berlin."

Etzel mulled over what Klaus had said. "What are the targets for the bombs?" he asked at length.

"The US Embassy is still the first. They'll tell me the second target later. Our price for kidnapping Atcho and setting their bombs is a third bomb for our own use.

"I agreed *not* to hit anywhere in the Soviet Union. I can live with that if it means taking a nuclear bomb into the Middle East." He let the notion sink in.

"You said something is happening in three days. What was that?"

"We get the bombs then." Klaus started toward the door. "Come on, we need to find Atcho."

"I thought we didn't have to deliver him."

Klaus rolled his eyes. "Etzel, if we tell them Atcho's dead, we can't have him showing up. Our goal is to get those bombs. After that, who cares? Meanwhile, we have to make sure Atcho stays silent." He headed out at a fast pace. Etzel followed.

"He's got to be hiding in one of these empty buildings," Klaus said, closing the door behind him. "We'll come back at dusk. He'll go for the embassy. If he tries to get out any other way, he'll be treated like everyone else attempting to escape East Germany. He'll be shot."

They walked to a smaller adjacent building. Inside was the entrance to their tunnel. Forty-five minutes later, they emerged in West Berlin. They made their way to an apartment building in Little Istanbul, a section of the city inhabited by a community of Muslims. After climbing several stories, they entered one of the units.

Soft strands of Eastern music met them, at once merry and doleful, its quarter-note chords alluding to an ancient struggle. The aroma of mint tea floated on the air.

A group of men sat cross-legged in a circle on the floor. The music ceased. In terse words, Klaus told them what he needed. He spat out orders. Several men jumped to their feet and headed out to go back through the tunnel and keep watch around Klaus' building. Four more left to alert their network to set up surveillance on the eastern side of the Wall.

When all were gone, Klaus and Etzel sat alone on the floor. "Will they find him?" Etzel asked.

"I don't know. They're not trained or armed."

"They're not good for much."

Klaus regarded him irritably. "Those Turks were good enough to keep working until they broke through the tunnels. They're good enough to have jobs at the major hotels, and they helped get us through security at the

Mövenpick. They don't love Germany. They came for work. The population here was decimated after the war. They helped rebuild West Germany. The country needed them but treated them like vermin. They're happy to help us."

Surprised at Klaus' passion, Etzel drew back. "Sorry, brother. I just meant that they won't do us much good in a fight." He arched his eyebrows. "They're not really good Muslims. They like their women and their drink and other Western depravities."

Klaus held his brother's gaze with an expression at once faraway and fierce. "That will change." He sat another moment, wrapped in thought. Then his expression reverted to normal. "They aren't fighters. I want them to keep Atcho from escaping until we get those bombs. He won't move before dark. The men will check out the empty buildings. We'll go there at dusk. If we don't find him, we'll wait outside the embassy."

*　*　*

Atcho had sat in the mezzanine above Klaus and Etzel, shocked at the part of the conversation he had understood until the brothers switched to the language they had used in the tunnels. *Three nuclear bombs in the hands of those thugs?* The prospect was unthinkable. He had to get back into West Berlin and alert authorities.

Nighttime was still hours away. He had eaten nothing since the day before, and he felt lightheaded. As he peered at the brothers conversing below, he spotted the bag of food that Klaus had tossed there. When the two men left the building, he retrieved it. The food was passable. He settled in to wait for nightfall.

Several hours later, he crept downstairs. In a side office, he found a window on the back of the building. He pried it open and slid through into darkness. The brothers had not returned. Nevertheless, he kept a watchful eye while he gained his bearings.

He figured he must be near the Wall—the Mövenpick had been close to it, and the trek through the tunnels had gone at a snail's pace. He sat for several minutes, listening to the sounds of the night. A few crickets clamored intermittently, but otherwise, all was quiet. In front of him, the horizon was dark, but looking about, he saw a glow in the sky to his right. *Not many city lights in East Berlin. West Berlin must be in the opposite direction.*

As he considered a route, he saw glimmering of a different type to the east. The first sliver of a full moon rose over the edges of the rooftops.

The air was cold, and he was not dressed for it. The silver orb would soon illuminate his position. He had to move. He hugged the shadows as he skirted abandoned buildings and made his way to the street.

Glancing toward the ascending moon, he took a deep breath and scurried across to the welcoming darkness on the other side. There, he stopped again to listen. He was in an alley. In the distance he heard the sound of light traffic.

A slapping sound in the bricks next to his head startled him—*a bullet*—and then the loud report of a rifle followed by shouts and the scurry of running feet. He moved over a few feet and dodged into deeper shadows. He held fast there, assessing where the attack had come from.

A dark silhouette moved past him, a man, his shape outlined by moonlight. Atcho crouched. The man continued down the alley. Atcho remained still. Another man moved past, and then a third. *Klaus' network.*

Atcho froze. He had seen the brothers in action and guessed members of their group might have similar capabilities. With at least three on his tail, he had to assume the worst, and they had already shot at him.

The third man halted. Atcho held his breath. The man turned toward him and seemed to stare into the dark recess. Atcho could not see his face to know for sure. The man stepped toward him. Atcho lunged.

Hearing movement, the man swung his weapon around, but too late to use it effectively. He fired a burst. The bullets missed. The staccato of submachine gunfire broke the stillness.

Atcho and his adversary connected. The other man was stronger, and possibly more physically capable. Atcho planted a foot behind the man's leg and barreled his left shoulder into his clavicle. As the man fell backward, Atcho locked his own right arm around his adversary's neck. When the two hit the ground, Atcho felt the snap of the man's spinal column. The fight was over.

He heard a yell from the direction the other two men had gone, and then running footsteps. Looking up, he saw them.

Light reflected off the MP5 next to his dead opponent. Atcho grabbed it and fired off a burst. One of the men shrieked and went down. The other darted into shadows. Then Atcho heard a voice he recognized.

"Etzel?"

Klaus. He called to his brother in their native tongue. As before, Atcho understood not one word, but he knew the context. He glanced down at Etzel's dark corpse. *Things just got personal.*

Out on the moonlit street, the wounded man writhed in pain. Klaus yelled at him to shut up and called for Etzel again.

Atcho backed further into the shadows against the building and slid in the direction he had come. He watched for other men. Seeing none, he rounded the corner, crouched against the wall and scurried along its length. Just as he reached the far end, he heard an anguished cry. *Klaus found Etzel.*

"I'll kill you," Klaus screamed. "Do you hear me, Atcho? I will find you, and I will kill you. Nowhere is safe for you." He continued wailing into the night.

Atcho heard more cries, and men running toward Klaus. He shrank into a dark place and checked the MP5. The magazine was empty. He slid the weapon under a bush and stayed in darkness until the last man was well past him. Then he dodged from shadow to shadow, heading for the darkest areas he could find. His breath came in staggered heaves. Sweat streamed from every pore. He slowed to a walk, but kept heading east, away from where they would continue to look for him, away from the bright glow of the West Berlin sky.

* * *

After Sofia had finished her meeting with Wolfgang Sacher, Jeff dropped her near the US Embassy, situated adjacent to the Wall. She walked the remaining distance. Inside, she found Nina. They once again swapped clothes.

"Is this plan going to work?" Nina asked. Gone was the blithe attitude of a young East Berliner seeking a cigarette. Instead, she was a dead-serious professional contemplating a dangerous mission. She was about the same height and build as Sofia, but she had blonde hair cut in short curls framing a light-skinned face with hazel eyes.

Sofia sighed. She worried about Atcho, where he might be, and what torture he might be suffering. She also fretted over how to get her relatives out of East Berlin. She had planned to collect them from their house, bring them with her to the hall where Wolfgang would read the press release, and then have her undercover team encircle them along with Wolfgang's family. Then, they would walk together into West Berlin with the crowds.

She saw now that she had underestimated the resistance of hard-liners. They knew who she was. They suspected her mission. They intended to thwart her because that could frustrate bringing the Wall down.

Any approach she made to her relatives could endanger their lives. She would have to find another way to rescue them, but she had no more resources at her disposal.

"If I didn't think the plan would work," she replied to Nina, "I'd call it off. I've got to get back to the west side. Make sure that the rest of the team knows to plan for contingencies as intently as the mission. If the Wall doesn't come down, we want everyone out alive and safe."

Nina nodded soberly. A staff car took Sofia back to the Mövenpick on the west side. There, she found Detective Berger looking for her. He was visibly angry. "Tell me about this Tony Collins. The reporter." He uttered the word with disdain.

"What's he done?" Sofia asked, startled.

"He identified your husband as a kidnap victim before we made a statement. He had the news published to the world before we had our press briefing. How did he know those things? Did you tell him?"

"I haven't seen him. After I left you, I went to the embassy. You can check."

"I did already. You were logged through Checkpoint Charlie at nine seventeen. Two minutes later, Collins logged through. He stayed only twenty-one minutes, and then came back to the west side. What did you talk about?"

"I didn't see him," she repeated, annoyed. She recalled that Jeff had described a man in the café who looked like Collins. "Do you think that if we were going to talk about something, we'd go into the East to do it?" Her eyes smoldered. "Why are you wasting time chasing Collins instead of finding my husband? Maybe when you find Collins, you should take lessons from him."

The detective was clearly chagrined. "My worry is that he might make things more difficult."

"You announced that Atcho had been kidnapped, so where's the harm?"

Berger hesitated. "There isn't any, really. That's what we normally do. Get as many people alert to finding him as possible."

"Then I don't see how Collins hurt anything. Where is he now?"

Berger looked sheepish. "He checked out of his hotel a little while ago and took a flight to Terceira."

"Where?"

"It's an island in the Azores. He must have had another incident to cover."

Sofia thought that over. Leaving a story he pursued was unlike Collins, but maybe he had another priority. "Do you have any leads?"

Berger shook his head. "Only the van we found the other night. The Stasi would never sanction an operation like the one this morning. Those two guys must have had inside help. That's the only way they could have avoided security. We still don't know how they left the building."

"Have you checked the cellars? Seems like people are always finding new tunnel entrances the Nazis left behind."

"My men are checking, but so far nothing."

"What do you need from me now?"

Berger sighed in frustration. "The sketches we took from your descriptions don't resemble any known Stasi officers. You said the kidnappers were brothers, but they're new to us. That's worrisome. They might be independent players. The trouble is, why haven't they asked for ransom? What could be their motive?"

The questions were obviously rhetorical. Berger stared at Sofia, seemingly hopeful that she might produce answers. She could tell him nothing. "Do you have anything for me now?" she asked.

Berger shook his head. "You're free to go."

* * *

Sofia tried to rest that afternoon, but her thoughts returned to Atcho. She recognized that she was emotionally tied to her mission, a prescription for disaster. Her plan to extricate her relatives with Wolfgang's family had become impossible. It was unsanctioned anyway.

With all the factors weighing in, good judgment indicated that she should withdraw from the mission. Let other professionals proceed.

On the other hand, unless the Wall came down on its own, if she did not stay with it, Wolfgang might balk. The chance to end the East German government, with its cruel Stasi and its machinery of oppression, might evaporate. Her dream of seeing her family living freely could be extinguished for several more decades.

She dozed fitfully and woke up while night still darkened the city. A rare sense of helplessness seized her. A shower didn't help, and neither did watching TV. Her mind churned over how to untie the Gordian knot that engulfed her. As dawn crept across the sky, she curled up on the sofa in the living room, exhausted, and finally slept.

14

While Sofia had met with Wolfgang, Collins had carried on a long discussion with Jakes. "I can't be in the Azores long," Collins said. "Get a local to meet me at the airport—someone who can get me around and translate. I need to visit the family of that fisherman, Gonçalo Alvarenga."

"What do you expect to find?" Jakes asked. "I haven't approved the trip yet."

"I don't know. There's too much coincidence. A native fisherman is lost at sea in the same vicinity that a US helicopter carrying Yermolov goes down. No bodies turn up. Then someone tries to kidnap Atcho in Berlin. Who has a beef with him here? The Stasi is implicated. The Soviets control that sector. My gut tells me either holdovers of Yermolov's organization are after Atcho, or it's Yermolov himself."

Jakes was silent a moment. "That's a leap. Why would they do it?"

"I don't know, but someone came after him twice in barely over a day. The second time, whoever it was came to his room in a highly secured location. Someone wanted him badly. I can't think of another explanation that accounts for that."

"So, again, what do you expect to find?"

Collins sighed. "Look, if Yermolov survived, he had to get from that string of islands to Europe. Someone had to have seen him." Another thought struck him. "There's something else."

"What?"

"Give me a minute to collect my thoughts." He reached into the dim recesses of his memory. "You recall that during the coup attempt, Yermolov acquired a briefcase-sized nuclear bomb?"

"Yes, and US intelligence couldn't track down its origin."

"They couldn't, but I did."

"You what?

"I tracked down the origin. Well, at least partway. I spoke with the bomb builder. I interviewed him."

"You what? And you didn't report it?" Jakes' voice revealed rare exasperation.

"The main stories surrounding the conspiracy had already been published," Collins replied. "When I learned his identity, he was a source."

"Still..."

"Hear me out. After the coup story broke, I spent months tracking down and getting to know the members of the Rasputin group in Paris. Do you remember that I took a long vacation at the beginning of this year?"

Jakes grunted his response.

"I tried to find out where the bomb came from," Collins continued, "and where they got the nuclear material. It turns out the bomb maker was one of their members, a retired nuclear engineer. The group is harmless. The engineer is a guy who saw his parents executed in the Ukraine as a boy. He escaped to France and lived quietly."

"They're a harmless group that financed and assisted a nearly successful coup against the Soviets." Jakes' tone revealed his anger. "They gave the ringleader a nuclear bomb. What were you thinking?"

Collins' ire rose. "They thought they were striking a blow against the power that destroyed their countries, killed their families, and drove them from their homes. They lived quiet lives, and none of them were ever involved in crime."

"Until they gave Yermolov a nuclear bomb. So, where did the fissionable material come from?"

"They wouldn't say," Collins said, chastened. "There's one more piece I should tell you. The engineer is a distant cousin of Yermolov's. They even resemble each other."

Jakes groaned. "Good lord. Can this get any more convoluted?"

"Reality is that way." Collins heard Jakes exhale as another urgent thought struck him. "I have to chase this down, Jakes. Think about the implications. If our instincts are right, Yermolov is alive, he could be in Berlin, and his cousin the bomb maker could be just a stone's throw away in France."

"You think Yermolov's after another bomb?"

"Maybe. He got one before. Atcho stopped him."

Jakes thought that over. "OK, but why would he go after Atcho now?"

"I don't know. Revenge maybe, or to get him out of the way. Maybe just because he's in Berlin. Think of what's going on there now." He reminded Jakes that public pressure to bring down the Wall was huge, that a backlash from hard-liners was bound to happen, and Yermolov would gravitate to them. "They'd welcome him. I don't think the reason why he's after Atcho matters. I told you what I saw Sofia doing in East Berlin. She's up to something. Maybe Yermolov caught wind of it. Don't forget that she was the person who disabled his bomb last year."

Agitation crept into Jakes' voice. "All right. See what you can find out in the Azores. Keep me informed. *Fully* informed."

* * *

Collins watched the ground rise to meet the descending airliner through the perpetual haze that hung over the Azores archipelago. The flight terminated at Lajes Field on Terceira, the largest of the chain of "magical islands." This was where the huge Antonov An-225 Mriya had landed and delivered Borya Yermolov into the hands of the US military nearly a year ago.

Collins observed the air traffic, taking note of the directions of approaches and departures. Then his guide found him. Fifteen minutes later, they entered Vila Nova, a scenic village along the coast where the Alvarenga family lived.

The interview with Gonçalo Alvarenga's widow had been arranged.

Thank you, Jakes. Collins anticipated that it would be a sad affair. He was right. The widow clearly still grieved. She was matronly, and the house was neat, but a quick look around revealed that it needed work. She explained through the guide that her eighteen-year-old son had taken on her husband's responsibilities, but with school and continuing the family's fishing occupation, he had little time to keep up with repairs.

Not comprehending how Gonçalo could have been lost at sea, she provided no new information. "He was so experienced, so careful and deliberate. He knew how to spot storms and move out of their way. But," she shrugged, "such is life. And death."

The son, João, a polite young man, sat close by. He said little beyond greetings until Collins prepared to leave. Then he asked, in good English, if the newsman would come see his boat. "I want to speak with you alone."

Surprised and not knowing what to expect, Collins left the guide behind. João led him downhill through the picturesque rough-hewn streets, the bright and pastel colors of the houses set against waves crashing on rocks and a deep blue ocean.

The young fisherman startled him. "Why are you interested in this story?"

"I'm a reporter. I follow stories."

"My mother told you I'm a student. A good one. I will go to university."

"That's wonderful," Collins replied sincerely. "I wish you all the best."

"The point is, I stay informed. I know who you are. I read your stories. I know you wouldn't be here if there were not a bigger story."

The reporter peered at João. While he wasn't a household name, Collins had an international following. He was surprised to learn that it included a student on this small island in the North Atlantic Ocean. "What do you want to tell me?"

João lowered his head. "I don't want to upset my mother." He looked around for other listeners. "You'll see when I show you my boat." He turned to face Collins. "My father was murdered."

The young man's lips quivered as he fought to control his emotions. He looked away. "His boat was found on the east side of the island, south of the airport. That's miles from here. There was no reason for him to be over there, and he would never have been that far off course. I tried to tell authorities, but they only patronized me."

Collins studied João's face. "Let's see your boat."

The dinghy was beautiful. Painted bright yellow with green trimming, it was tended to with pride. "My father always took care of his things," João said. "He was a careful man. A good man."

"I'm sure he was," Collins said softly. "What did you want to show me?"

João went forward of the cabin and brought back a long pole with a crook. "Look at this. I saved it. I bought another one to use for fishing." Just below the curve were several dark patches caked into dents and scrapes on the pole. "That's blood."

While sympathetic, Collins remained professionally skeptical. "You're a fisherman. Don't you see a lot of blood?"

"We use fishing nets," João retorted. "We don't see a lot of blood, and never enough to cake like that, and not on a pole that always goes into the water. But there's more." He went into the wheelhouse and returned carrying a bundle. "This is one of my father's blankets. It also has blood on it. Look at the stain."

He sat down and spread the blanket over his legs. The stain fit as though blood had soaked along his left leg. "Then, there's this."

He stood and lifted two more objects he had brought from the cabin. "This is a military uniform." He pointed out two holes in the trousers surrounded by dark stains, and two pieces of insignia on the jacket. "It belonged to a Soviet Army officer. I found it in the cabin."

15

Borya Yermolov paced in his apartment. He had placed a call to Cousin Veniamin, but the engineer had been out. While Yermolov awaited his cousin's return call, he mulled over his conversation with Klaus earlier in the day. *Those two were valuable to me. Ranulf's incompetence blew a hole in that situation. And we're running out of time.*

Pressures that bore on Yermolov were new to him. For most of his career, organizations had supported him. He had controlled resources. During nearly three decades of his double life as the spy Paul Clary, he had had subordinates to do his bidding in both the US Air Force and the Soviet KGB. Even during the coup attempt, he had commanded military, intelligence, and logistics assets, placed at his disposal by disgruntled Soviet officials opposed to Gorbachev's policies.

Now, he had only his wits, knowledge, and force of personality to induce his wishes to be converted to action. His position was tenuous, and possible only because of the upheavals taking place in Eastern Europe. The odds of success were infinitesimal. His face broke into a roguish grin. He liked a challenge.

His mind reached back to his capture. He had no idea how he had escaped the sinking helicopter or what had happened to the crew or other passengers. His first clear memory was of the fisherman staring down at him, at his Soviet uniform, and his bloody leg with a hole through the trousers. His action against Gonçalo had been instinctive, to survive.

The storm had been beneficent. It had tossed for hours, rocking the boat unmercifully. He had found a dry crawl space in the bow with a thin mattress and blankets. Taking off his soaked Soviet uniform, he had tossed it into a corner of the cabin.

For three days, he had rested, becoming aware that in the distance, airplanes ascended and descended at regular intervals. *An airport.*

Early on the fourth day, he had set the boat adrift. Then he had set out limping toward the distant air traffic. His leg was stiff and ached dully, but he had averted infection, and profuse bleeding was no longer an issue. Nevertheless, he had stayed close to the coast and avoided roads.

For the next few days, he had approached isolated farmhouses, invading those whose inhabitants were absent. In some he had eaten; in others, he had taken money or pieces of clothing or cleaned himself up. From each, he had taken what he needed in amounts small enough to attribute to the owners' lapses of memory. Otherwise, he had taken care to leave the homes as he had found them.

After several days, he had had sufficient cash and looked presentable enough to mix in public. He had learned that he was on Terceira. He had also heard about a fisherman who went missing after a recent storm, and whose boat had been found listing in the waves to the southeast of Lajes. No foul play was mentioned.

In the guise of a retired US Air Force general, Yermolov had ingratiated himself to pilots and crew in the private aviation part of the airfield. He had plied them with drinks and swapped war stories.

Ten days after the helicopter crash, he had hopped a flight in a small plane to a remote airport outside of Lisbon. On arrival, he had feigned weakness attributable to his injured leg, followed an immigration official to an infirmary, rendered him unconscious, and escaped into Portugal. He had placed a call to his cousin, Veniamin. Within another day, he had arrived at Veniamin's house in a village north of Paris.

* * *

While waiting for Veniamin's call, Yermolov thought through a dilemma. Fortunately, his contacts in the black market were strong. His source still had access to weapons-grade plutonium and the other materials Veniamin needed to build the bombs. Yermolov arranged payment and delivery through sympathizers in Moscow. However, his cousin had become increasingly difficult. When Yermolov first brought up building a new bomb, Veniamin balked.

"I regretted doing it the first time. I can't do it again."

"I know you love your family," Yermolov replied with a menacing undertone. "I'll get the materials to you. You build what I need and bring it to me in East Berlin. This is not a request."

Taken aback by the implied threat, Veniamin understood for the first time the full nature of his distant cousin. He threw out a question, and immediately regretted it. "Did you know that a news reporter came to see me at the beginning of this year? Tony Collins. He traced the bomb to me and wanted to know where I got the plutonium."

Startled, Yermolov hid his annoyance that he had not learned this before now. "I know Collins. He interviewed me as General Clary a few years ago. What did you tell him?"

"Only that we were distant cousins. He would have guessed anyway. We resemble each other."

Yermolov was skeptical that Collins could have pieced that tidbit together, but he was not immediately worried. Collins would believe him to be either dead or incarcerated by the Marines. He pressed Veniamin on the issue of the new bomb, once again issuing a veiled threat. "I want only the best for your family."

That conversation seemed to have resolved Yermolov's problems with Veniamin, at least for the present. Handling him should not be difficult. *Keep the vision of lots of money in front of him—and keep him afraid.*

Baumann's underling, Ranulf, also presented an obstacle. The fool's failed mission to abduct Atcho had forced Yermolov into a more visible role.

Ranulf had balked when told that a second bomb was needed. That had been in Baumann's office. "Who is this guy?" he had demanded, glaring at the Stasi director. Then he had turned to face Yermolov directly. "Do you think it's easy to get two million dollars together? In East Germany? And do it so that no one knows? Can you even get the materials on that short notice?"

Baumann's pointed reprimand had brought Ranulf to heel. Yermolov's face had distorted with anger. "The materials are not the issue," he had retorted. "They will be delivered to Veniamin. You don't need to know how I do that. Let's leave it that my network is stronger than yours. You just need to deliver the money to pay Veniamin."

Ranulf had sat back with reluctance bordering on hostility as Yermolov and the director had continued talking. Then suddenly his eyes had narrowed, and he had leaned forward with interest. At the conclusion, he had seemed eager to proceed.

Yermolov had watched Ranulf closely, studying his changed expressions. *With that much money, he might imagine himself in a chalet in the Swiss Alps.*

Further complicating Yermolov's situation was how to make all the pieces come together. He thought he understood the motivations of each person in his plan, starting with the Stasi director. Having planted the seed of ambition, he thought the man now aspired to East Germany's highest leadership position.

Klaus and Etzel were more difficult to assess, but Yermolov believed he understood them as well. Their motivations sprang from religious and regional resentment against Russian rule. Yermolov had overheard the brothers conversing. They were both fluent in at least one Chechen dialect.

That region of the Soviet Union, Chechnya, had long writhed under the Communist yoke. It harbored a desire to be free of its godless masters. The tensions there against Russia stretched back into pre-Soviet history for centuries. During that time much of the population had converted to Sunni Islamism to resist Russian rule.

Throughout those centuries, Chechen history and culture had been inextricably linked to Persia, now modern-day Iran. When students in Tehran had occupied the US Embassy by force in 1979 and held it for 444 days, that action had sparked a movement beyond Iran's national borders, and specifically into the heart of Chechnya.

Yermolov had overheard the brothers speak of *jihad* and refer to each other by different names. Etzel called Klaus "Sahab," and apparently Etzel was known as "Alvi." Their last name was Kadyrov. They could be counted on to strike at the US and the Soviet Union as long as they could hit a target of their own choosing.

The problem with the brothers was that they operated independently and had a network of their own. *How else could they have gotten into and out of the hotel in West Berlin and spirited Atcho to the east side?* And now they held Atcho—or said they did. *Controlling them relies on meeting their ambitions, which cannot conflict with mine.*

Then there's Atcho. Yermolov realized he had made a mistake in ordering his abduction: killing Atcho outright could have been made to look like a random mugging gone bad. That would have solved the issue. *The brothers could have done it easily.* He heaved a sigh. *Play the cards you've got. When it's an empty hand, bluff.*

The phone rang. Mindful of intelligence listening posts, Yermolov kept the call short, delivering a brutal message cloaked in a pleasant tone.

"You'll be a rich man, Cousin," Yermolov laughed. "I know you love your family. I need three of those items. The price is right. The materials will arrive tomorrow. Deliver them personally in three days. Am I clear?"

When Veniamin started to protest, Yermolov allowed an edge into his voice. "It's difficult, but I have confidence in you. You'll get it done because of what it means to your family. Call again tomorrow to report progress." Having no doubt that Veniamin grasped the implied threat, he hung up.

His next phone call was to the Stasi director. "There's been a new development. I need to see you and Ranulf at your office in one hour." He waited only long enough to hear an affirmative response and hung up.

Command is never granted. It is taken.

16

Yermolov strode into Baumann's office exactly one hour later. As he had expected, Baumann had alerted security to let him through. The rogue general took a position against the wall behind the desk. "Where is Ranulf?"

The director had been writing at his desk. He looked up, startled at Yermolov's brusque demeanor.

Baumann stood, a look of consternation crossing his face. "What's happened?" His voice wavered. He was not accustomed to such take-charge confidence in his presence, and he was not yet sure of Yermolov's capabilities. He suddenly felt his age.

"Wait until Ranulf gets here. Is he on the way?"

At that moment, Ranulf entered.

"You're late," Yermolov snapped. The other two men were taken aback. The effrontery was obvious and deliberate. "Listen to me, gentlemen." Yermolov spoke harshly. "We've played around long enough with this plan to save East Germany. It's time to act." He turned to the director. "Who assigned those men who first went after Atcho?"

Still struggling to conceal his shock at Yermolov's brazen entry, the director gestured toward Ranulf. "He did. Naturally—"

"Exactly. And whose men got the job done?" Neither Ranulf nor the director could hide their unease. Yermolov answered his own question. "Mine. I brought them here. They got Atcho. I have a whole platoon just like them ready to come on my order. Let's hope things don't come to that."

His hard eyes fastened on Baumann. "Do you want to save this country? Or are you hoping for the best when your trial takes place in The Hague?" The director's eyes glittered. "Let me tell you," Yermolov continued, "if we don't act, East Germany is finished, within days."

The director opened his mouth to speak, his expression ominous.

"Don't," Yermolov growled. "We don't have time for histrionics. Your government is already irrelevant. The Stasi is the only remaining force capable of reversing course. As of this moment, I command the Stasi. It—you—report to me." He cast a piercing glance at Ranulf. "You are at my personal disposal. Do you understand?"

Both men stared in shock. "I'll be plain. Time is critical. If you do what I say, you will prosper." He straightened to full height. "If you don't, you won't live out the day."

They understood the direct threat. Yermolov indicated a sofa and chair in front of the desk. "Please, have a seat."

Baumann reached for his phone.

"Don't," Yermolov warned. "You'll be dead before anyone comes through that door."

Baumann hesitated. Yermolov strode to his desk and ripped open the middle drawer. "You're old," he said, jerking a pistol from the drawer. "Ranulf can't help you."

The two men stared at him. "I mean you no harm," he said, "but I demand your cooperation."

While Ranulf and the director sat down, Yermolov circled purposefully behind the desk and took the director's chair. "You'll get your office back," he told Baumann. "For now, the Stasi will act at my direction to govern East Germany. When our plan is executed, you'll become the Party general secretary, select your own Stasi director, and help me make my move on the Soviet Union. Do you understand?"

Baumann's face had turned a ghostly white. He nodded.

"Good. Then you will now develop a plan to arrest the ministers, directors, and of course the general secretary. Make sure the army senior commanders and staff are under control at the outset. When the bomb goes off, you'll round them up. Some might be allowed to keep their positions. We'll see. Do you understand?" He did not wait for a reply. "This action will reinvigorate your officers. We need people who will not hesitate to shoot into crowds."

Color had returned to the director's face. "What happens if we have another mass exodus through Czechoslovakia? Honecker tried to stop it. He failed."

Yermolov knew Baumann referred to the crowds that had traveled through Czechoslovakia to Hungary earlier in the year and then on to West Germany. Hungary had intended to facilitate East German tourist travel to West Germany. As word had spread, people had left their homes and belongings and flocked to Hungary. From there, they had crossed the border into West Germany by the tens of thousands, never to return.

Then General Secretary Erich Honecker had responded by closing East Germany's Czech borders. The population had protested. Small demonstrations across the country had escalated into large ones, culminating in the huge protest in Leipzig that had been broadcast to the world and precipitated the current crisis.

"Honecker was no longer prepared to shoot people in masses," Yermolov said. "I am. We'll make sure the border with Czechoslovakia stays closed. The first person who resists will serve as a bloody example to everyone else."

Baumann fought down his reaction to the menace in Yermolov's voice. "What about my KGB liaison? He could be a problem? Let's face it—the KGB still controls actions here. Gorbachev—"

"Forget Gorbachev. The Kremlin won't know how to react. The people on this side of the Wall will stay in their houses. We'll order a curfew and shoot anyone violating it or moving toward the Wall. We might throw a few people into the street and shoot them to make the point. Make sure they're people without useful skills." He smirked. "I like that idea.

"When the second bomb goes off in Chechnya, that will be the end for Gorbachev. Use discretion with your KGB liaison. If need be, shoot him."

Baumann raised an eyebrow. "Why Chechnya?"

"Because the Chechens hate the Soviets. They would gladly blow up something belonging to Moscow. They'll hope that will end Soviet rule." He laughed. "It won't. But the threat of the breakup of the Soviet Union will end Gorbachev and his silly policies. As soon as he's gone, we'll send troops to quell any revolt in Chechnya."

Despite his years of practiced cruelty, Baumann was startled at Yermolov's willingness to betray. He asked his next question cautiously. "Why will Soviet leadership turn to you?"

Yermolov smiled. "Because I'll be in Moscow then. I'll make the arrest and take charge of the politburo, by force if necessary. My team is there now. You're familiar with how close we came last year?" *He still doesn't know I'm bluffing.*

The director nodded. He said nothing.

"It'll be a bloody day," Yermolov said reflectively. "Do you have any questions?"

Ranulf had sat quietly, unnerved by the sheer audacity of what he heard. It was too big-picture for him to evaluate, but one thing he noted: Baumann accepted Yermolov as his direct superior, maybe even warming to the notion. "Sir." He directed his question to Yermolov. "What do you need from me?"

In his practiced manner, Yermolov reverted to the amiable personality of Lieutenant General Paul Clary, US Air Force. "It's good that you asked. You have a very important part to play. First of all, I need another bomb. Three, total."

Ranulf sucked in his breath. "Three bombs? Do have any idea of the cost?"

"Yes." Yermolov smiled agreeably. "And I have an idea that you wouldn't mind living out your existence in Switzerland or one of the tax havens in the Caribbean. With such a large sum, no one would miss an extra million or so."

Ranulf pulled back. "Please, sir. I never thought such a thing. I live to serve the East German state and the Communist Party."

"I'm sure that's true. I need three million dollars here in two days. I've studied your record enough to know that you're the man to get it done. If you need to use extreme persuasion..." His voice took on dark overtones. "If you're not up to the task, I'll get someone else. I'm sure you've already started the process. And"—he feigned a friendlier tone— "if you want to take out a larger amount to reward yourself and your helpers and share in this office"—he cast a glance at the director—"I doubt you'll find an objection." He paused again in thought. "As we settle into this new world order, I'll need someone to be my eyes and ears in other parts of the world. Will you be up to that?"

Ranulf could not believe his good fortune. "Yes, sir. Anything that serves the Party. I'll get the money here. Anything else?"

"Yes. Call your hit squads off of Klaus and Etzel."

Ranulf squirmed.

Yermolov glared at him. "I need the brothers to move about freely without getting shot." He paused to reflect. "Who knows—when you go traveling, those squads might prove useful." His voice turned deadly again. "Take care of that. Do it now." He looked at his watch. "I want a report tomorrow morning by ten o'clock that you have corrected the situation." He swung around to Baumann. "We'll meet again here then for updates."

Baumann acquiesced with a nod. Ranulf hurried from the office.

17

A gray overcast dawn broke over Berlin. Atcho stirred. He had walked for miles through the night, always staying in the darkest areas, with West Berlin at his back and ducking into hidden spaces when other people or a vehicle approached.

Around midnight, he had found shelter in an old shed at the back of an abandoned garden. Hungry and approaching exhaustion, he rested there. With winter cold setting in and just his sweaty jacket to provide warmth, he slept only intermittently.

He woke with a start, his mind numb, his body responding to survival instinct. He had to move before someone spotted him and reported a stranger in the neighborhood. The embassy was his objective, but without the ability to speak German, not knowing how many men Klaus had, or how omnipresent the Stasi and its informants were, he was in no position to stop strangers and ask for help. The best he could do was find the Wall and use it as a guide.

Scanning around before he made a move, he left his hideaway. The cold permeated down into his bones. He ducked his chin into his jacket and walked against the wind toward the sounds of a waking city.

Soon he turned onto a street with heavier traffic and pedestrians along the sidewalk. He watched for clusters of people walking by and gravitated into the center until they naturally dispersed. Then he waited for the next group in which he could hide in plain sight. He looked scruffy after his two-day ordeal, but, in a city of unhappy people, he did not stand out.

He had entered a main thoroughfare when he saw something unexpected: an olive-drab–colored sedan. It was noteworthy only in that it was larger than most of the few cars on the road, and it was American made. *A Flag Tour sedan.*

Sofia had told him about the elite intelligence teams whose attention concentrated on East Berlin. She explained that per an agreement signed in 1947, each of the Alliance members governing Germany could send small groups into each other's sectors. "Their formal job is to assert our continued rights of travel and circulation in the other sectors. In reality, we all use our groups to collect intelligence. And we all follow each other's cars in our own sectors. It's a game, but it can be deadly."

Sofia had said that each of the American sedans would carry a US decal and a US military license plate. Because they were designed to blend in, those items were difficult to spot.

A loose plan formed in Atcho's mind, but it depended on being certain that the vehicle was one of the US Flag Tour cars. He moved to the edge of the sidewalk. Although traffic was sparse, detecting a tailing vehicle was difficult from street level. He would have only seconds to act.

The car moved closer. Atcho's breath came in short, staggered gasps. He glanced around to see where policemen or other security personnel might be.

Two stood directly across the street. Another was off to his right and a fourth was close to his left rear. He slowed his pace and let a gaggle of pedestrians move ahead of him.

Edging closer to the street, he gauged the car's speed and the distance between the point where it would pass and the closest policeman.

Then he spotted the flag decal. When the car was only ten feet to his left front, he darted in front of it and threw up his hands.

"I'm an American!" he yelled. "I'm an American. I was kidnapped."

The car screeched to a halt. The men inside looked stricken. They stared at him, and then turned attention to their surroundings.

Startled pedestrians halted in shock. They fell away as policemen blew shrill whistles. Atcho heard running footsteps behind him. He raced to the passenger's side of the vehicle and pounded on the window. "I'm an American," he repeated, panting. "I was kidnapped. Let me in."

A major in the front passenger's seat reacted. He retrieved a photograph from his jacket and glanced at it. "It's him," he said tersely. "This is the guy in the BOLO." He rolled down the window. "Get in. Fast." He whirled around in his seat and unlocked the back door.

Atcho swung the door open and dove in. Before it had closed, the driver mashed the gas pedal. The tires squealed as the car took off. Angry faces of police officers and East German soldiers flew by the window.

"Take the next right," the major ordered his driver. "Get on our fast route and shake any followers. I need speed, but I do want to get home to Mama. Understand?" He glanced through the back window. "There's two behind us closing fast. How far are we from Checkpoint Charlie?"

"Two miles."

"Step on it, but don't kill anybody." He wiped his forehead. "Cripes! Of all the times for East Berliners to decide to take a walk." He looked out his side window at groups of pedestrians, all seeming to go in the same direction. "These crowds have been building and building." He glanced back again. "OK," he told the driver, "take it a bit easier. Those guys are falling back, I reckon because of the crowds. You might still need to take a couple of back streets before heading to the gate."

He turned around and extended his hand to Atcho. "Hi, sir. I'm Major Joe Horton. We were told about you." He wore a huge grin and laid his Texas accent on thick. "You sit back and relax. We're taking you home."

Atcho nodded his gratitude. He leaned against the rear headrest and exhaled.

18

Sofia awoke suddenly. The sun was already high in the sky. She felt physically rested but emotionally drained. Her first thought was about Atcho and what he must be enduring. She felt guilty for sleeping in the suite while Atcho was God only knew where.

She got up and showered and was still dressing when she heard a sharp knock on the door. A man's voice called her name.

"Sofia, are you there?" The voice was gruff and deep—and most welcome. She threw her robe on, rushed to the door, and opened it to reveal a big man, balding and several years older than Atcho.

"Burly!" She flung her arms around his neck and fought to contain the emotions of seeing a cherished friend.

He held her as she fought back tears. "Things will be OK," he reassured her. "Let's get inside where we can talk." He nodded to the state department security man posted outside and closed the door.

"I'm in shock," Sofia said. "How—What are you doing here?"

Burly sat down on the sofa and leaned back. "Your husband called the night before last. That must have been several hours before he was taken. He told me you were asleep on the couch and said he needed me here, pronto. I came as fast as I could. I talked to some of my old buddies at the station before I came to the hotel and they filled me in."

Sofia stared at him; he referred to the Berlin CIA station, Shelby's office. Burly had retired from the CIA and was one of Atcho's oldest and closest friends. They had trained together in Cuba for the Bay of Pigs invasion. He had helped Atcho in two operations since then.

"I'm confused. What were you supposed to do?"

"I don't know. We didn't talk long. By the time I got on a plane, the news was out about his kidnapping. Our old buddy Collins did that." Sofia scowled and started to speak, but Burly stopped her. "Collins is a good guy. He was a huge help last year, and he's always kept his word about not revealing information that would jeopardize national security. He does his job."

Sofia nodded. "I know. It's just that he can be such a bother."

"He beat the police and intelligence agencies on putting pieces together, and he got word out so that international attention focused here. That will help in finding Atcho and might even help to bring the Wall down."

"I hope so."

"Start from the beginning. Walk me through everything that's happened."

For the next few hours, Sofia told Burly all she could remember about the situation, starting with the first phone call and ending with her trip into East Berlin and her meeting with Wolfgang Sacher.

Burly listened, asking few questions. When Sofia finished, he took his time to respond. "Two things pop out." He spoke slowly, still formulating his thoughts. "One, the people trying to stop you know who you are. They can trace your family connections. Your relatives might already be in danger. Wolfgang and his family too."

"That's possible," Sofia replied. "But my records were purged long ago to hide my family contacts in the East. That was done so that I could meet with Wolfgang in other places over the years."

"OK, I'll buy that. The other thing is that Atcho wanted me here for a reason. I'd guess he wants another team to get your family out. That way you won't compromise your mission. If you fail in that, all else could be lost."

Sofia rose from the sofa and walked over to gaze out the window across the city. "That sounds like Atcho," she said softly. "What do we do now?"

Burly stood. He crossed the room and placed an arm around her shoulder. "You concentrate on what you're doing. Let me worry about getting Atcho back." Sofia turned and nodded into his chest.

"Is Shelby going to let you stay on the mission?"

Sofia shrugged. "For the moment. The last time we spoke about it was before Atcho was kidnapped. That might be the last straw. I met with Wolfgang yesterday. I still have to report to Shelby on that."

"How did the meeting go?"

"No hitches. Wolfgang is scared, but he'll do what he has to." She gulped. "Burly, if you have any influence with Shelby, don't let him pull me out. Atcho's tough. He'll get away one way or another. But if he doesn't, and if the Wall stays put because I wasn't there, and my relatives keep living under that monstrous regime..." Her voice caught. She wiped her eyes. "I don't think I could live with myself." She sniffed. "One thing. Shelby doesn't know about the plan to rescue my relatives."

Burly's head snapped around. His eyebrows arched. "You're playing with fire, Sofia." He squeezed her shoulders. "Shelby could scrub the whole thing if he finds out. Or if you go through with it without telling him and he finds out, that could end your career."

"I don't care about my career." She spun around, and her tears began to flow freely. "I care about my husband," she said, her voice cracking. "I care about my family. I care about the people who've suffered in the East all these years."

The phone rang. Sofia took a deep breath, collecting herself, and answered it.

"Turn on the TV." She recognized Brown's voice. "Do it now. I'll hold."

Sofia did, and the screen opened to a street scene in West Berlin. The camera panned to a journalist. "I'm standing outside Checkpoint Charlie," the young woman reported. "We are told that Eduardo Xiquez, the American businessman, has just passed through in a daring rescue. We reported yesterday that he had been kidnapped from the Mövenpick Hotel in a brazen early morning attack. No information of how he escaped is being divulged. The news now is that he's safe. We'll provide details as we get them."

Sofia stared, hardly believing what she heard. Her eyes brimmed, and her throat constricted. She dropped the receiver.

"Atcho's safe," she rasped. That was all she could manage.

Burly picked up the phone. "Sorry," he said into the receiver. "Sofia is still watching the TV. What's the latest?"

"Who are you?"

Burly chuckled. "I'm a friend of Atcho's and Sofia's. They call me Burly."

Brown was silent a moment. "I know who you are. My team told me you arrived this morning. I'm glad you're here. I just got off the phone with brigade headquarters. The state department and the Army will debrief Atcho and release him as soon as possible."

Burly grimaced. "How soon is that?"

Brown grunted. "You know how these things go."

"All right. I'll tell her," Burly replied, sighing. He hung up and spun around.

Sofia faced him, eyes wide. "You'll tell me what? When's Atcho coming here?"

He told her what Brown had said.

"I'm going there. Now." Her eyes burned with fury. "I've been scared out of my wits, and they can't keep me from Atcho." She headed toward the bedroom to change clothes.

Burly watched her. "Take it easy," he said softly.

Sofia whirled on him. "You too? I didn't know if I'd ever see Atcho alive again. No one's going to keep me away from him."

"I'm your friend, Sofia. Think. Get out of your emotions. You could jeopardize your mission—and that includes your family. The stakes are huge." He paused. "Atcho is safe now."

Sofia took a deep breath, walked to the sofa, and sat down. "I'm sorry." Her voice took on a collected quality. "You're right." She dropped her elbows onto her knees and rested her head in her hands.

"Hey, are you okay?" Burly crossed the room and sat next to her.

"I'm fine. I'm glad Atcho's safe." She leaned against him. "You're a great friend. Take me to him when it makes sense. I'll be fine."

19

Klaus walked into Stasi headquarters like a man on a mission. The guards at the front desk blocked his entry.

"Call Director Baumann," he snapped. "He'll see me."

The guards backed away. While one kept a wary eye, the other placed the call. Three minutes later, Klaus burst into the director's office—and stopped short. Yermolov and Baumann glared at him. Behind him, the door closed. He heard the steel slider of a pistol near his ear. He froze. Ranulf moved around to face him.

"Where is Atcho?" Yermolov snapped. He stepped aside. Behind him, the street scene of the journalist at Checkpoint Charlie played on a television. "Never mind. Atcho is back in West Berlin. Tell me why I shouldn't shoot you right here, right now."

Klaus stared at the screen, then shifted his eyes to Yermolov. An expression of resignation crossed his face.

Yermolov notice it. The Chechen usually exuded confidence laced with an odd humor that sometimes lapsed into insolence. Now, there was only fury behind his eyes, mixed with hatred. His gaze was riveted on the television scene.

Yermolov looked beyond Klaus to the door. "Where's Etzel?" He watched Klaus closely out of the corner of his eye.

"I'll do what you want," Klaus said, almost in a daze. "Atcho escaped."

"That's obvious," Yermolov retorted, gesturing toward the television. "You're no more competent than Ranulf's men. Why would I trust you again?"

Klaus' face contorted. His low voice rumbled with savagery. "Because I'm your best asset. I'll plant both bombs—the one here at the embassy and wherever you want the second target. You can have the third one too. I'll make sure Atcho never interferes again. I won't rest until he's dead."

Yermolov looked past Klaus to the door once more, and then studied him closely. "Where is Etzel?" he asked again, emphasizing each word.

Klaus' eyes smoldered, like a man accepting a fatal sentence. Yermolov repeated his question a third time, although he anticipated the response. "Where is your brother?"

"Dead." Klaus' voice was hollow. "Atcho killed him. It's personal now. I want him dead."

As the exchange took place, Ranulf kept the pistol pointed at Klaus, his eyes on Yermolov as he waited for direction. Baumann remained silent, standing to one side as if he were merely an observer.

Yermolov continued to scrutinize Klaus. *I have a dog on a leash.* He signaled to Ranulf to lower the weapon. "Before you came in, we were reviewing actions. We have work to do. Let's sit down."

They sat in the group of chairs in front of the desk. Klaus joined them. Yermolov opened the discussion. "Ranulf, when will the money be ready?"

"Tomorrow afternoon. It was expensive. I had to pay a lot of bribes." He shifted his attention to Baumann. "I pulled in enough to make us all comfortable."

"Good," Yermolov interjected. He addressed Baumann. "How are plans to arrest the ministers, etcetera?"

"The Stasi section leads are alerted. The arrests will be carried out on order."

"Detain the general secretary first, and anyone who could issue counterorders. Impress on your officers that this is our only chance to prevent the end of East Germany and their careers. Remind them of what the trials in The Hague could mean."

He turned to Ranulf again. "Two things. When the arrests happen, include the people you bribed. We can't have them doing the same thing to us. They can be examples to anyone who tries to stop us. Also, have your hit squads shadow the arrest patrols. Take out anyone who could provide early warning or who makes noise that could draw attention or get in our way. Do you have enough men for that?"

Ranulf felt a wash of pride. To be included in such high-level planning and execution was beyond any ambition he had ever entertained. To be entrusted with such a crucial part... He put on his most serious expression. "We can augment what we need from the regular Stasi." He glanced at the director for confirmation. Baumann nodded.

"All right," Yermolov said. "Get the money to me this afternoon. My cousin will deliver the bombs this evening." He directed his next comments to Baumann. "Make sure nothing happens to him. We might use him again."

He turned his attention to Klaus. "How will you get the bomb into the embassy?"

Klaus scoffed. "That building was never meant to be an embassy. It was a Prussian officers' club, and then a school for artists. It's old. All the security was added in the last couple of years. It's not even a standalone building. I can go through the ceiling or a wall or come through the basement. The US hires locals to work there. Some of them don't like Americans. Getting in and out will be no problem. If you get the bomb to me tonight, I can have it placed by the day after tomorrow." He gave a short, cynical laugh. "It's a nuke. It doesn't matter where I put it. Just that it's not discovered before it explodes. And since it's right next to the Wall, it'll blow out a big part of West Berlin too." He sneered, malice darkening his eyes. "Make sure you're more than a mile away and deep inside a cellar when it goes off."

Yermolov took that in and then turned his attention back to Baumann. "Once Klaus is out of the embassy, can you get him to Moscow quickly?"

"Depending on the time. We have daily diplomatic flights to Moscow. He can fly on one of those. I'll arrange it."

"Set it up, and Klaus, before any of this goes down, be sure you have a flight to Chechnya. Your second target is there. You pick the place. We need noise and heavy destruction. The people need to see lots of blood and the bodies of women and babies. The Soviet government will implode." He nudged Klaus. "Do you understand, Klaus? The second bomb will detonate in Chechnya."

Klaus nodded, expressionless. "I understand. Sacrifices must be made."

Yermolov studied him. He saw a man with dead eyes and only revenge on his mind. "And Klaus..." Yermolov paused to make sure he had Klaus' full attention. "When you've accomplished both things, I'll get the third bomb to you."

Klaus growled his response. "I'll put it under Atcho's bed in Washington."

The room fell deathly quiet, all eyes on Klaus. Yermolov broke the silence. "That works." He glanced around the group of faces. "This is the sequence. Klaus plants the bomb at the US Embassy. Then he travels to Chechnya and places one there. We detonate the bomb here remotely. Director Baumann takes charge of the government. He arrests the opposition, institutes martial law. Execute anyone, as you see fit. Request Soviet assistance. I'll travel to Moscow and join my team there. A day after the first explosion, Klaus, you detonate the bomb in Chechnya. I'll move in with my team to arrest Gorbachev and anyone else who resists. Frankly, I don't expect much opposition. I'm known, and everyone is tired of Gorbachev's foolishness. Then, Baumann, you'll get the assistance you require."

"What do you think the US response will be?"

Yermolov chuckled. "Confusion. This war hero president is no Ronald Reagan. He's a globalist and will first think of how to protect his new world order—his country's people and national interests be damned. He won't know how many other bombs we have or where we'll put them. My guess? He'll put a perimeter around the damaged area in West Berlin, well away from radioactive contamination. He'll proclaim, 'Read my lips. The perpetrators will be brought to justice,' and he'll have the FBI and the CIA investigate. He'll get Congress to form committees to 'get to the bottom of this.' Then, he'll move fleets of ships around the world."

Yermolov's tone turned to one of disgust. "He'll send humanitarian assistance to demonstrate resolve that the 'free world will not be deterred by aggression.' And ten years from now, the Wall will still stand, East Germany will still be sovereign, and the Soviet Union will continue as it has." He looked across at Klaus. "Who knows? The US might not exist as we know it today."

Yermolov took questions and adjourned the meeting. They began to disperse. Then Yermolov had a sudden thought. "Atcho killed your brother?"

Klaus nodded. Yermolov turned to Baumann. "Demand that the US deliver Atcho to Soviet authorities on murder charges. They'll never do it, but we can harass them with it. Keep repeating it. That's another distraction to keep them busy until we execute."

20

"You killed a man in East Berlin." Jerry Fenns looked grim. He stood at the end of a long table in a conference room of the state department's US Mission – Berlin, in the same building as the US Army's Berlin Brigade headquarters. Housed at Clayallee in the upscale Zehlendorf section of West Berlin, it also operated the consulate. "The East Germans are demanding your return to stand trial."

"Self-defense," Atcho rumbled.

"Don't get belligerent," Fenns retorted. "Lucky for you we had you in the West by the time the death was reported."

An army colonel at the end of the table stood and leaned forward on his fists. He was an imposing figure. "We're not giving anyone back to anybody," he said firmly.

Fenns started to protest, but the colonel cut him off. "Let's make this clear. The Army is in charge in Berlin. If we were anywhere else, you could tell me where to stick it. But our rules rule here, and we're not giving Atcho back. *Capiche*?"

The room was quiet, its occupants shifting their gazes among each other. Brown and Detective Berger sat across the table in the sparsely furnished conference room. Neither had said a word.

The colonel broke the silence. "Who was the dead guy?"

"He was one of the two brothers who kidnapped me," Atcho replied. "I escaped. They both shot at me. I got to this one before he got to me."

"How did you kill him?"

"I broke his neck."

The colonel grunted. The others in the room remained silent. Atcho turned to Brown and Berger. "Tell the East Germans to produce the dead man's identity. They can't. The brothers worked under the radar. They spoke in a language I don't recognize. Based on where they locked me up— a vacant building in some war ruins—I'd guess they're on the wrong side of East German law." He glared at Fenns. "Are you going to listen to what I told you about those bombs?"

Fenns ignored his comment, glancing instead at Detective Berger. "What will you do? Do you want to take him into custody?"

"That's not going to happen." The colonel took a step to position himself between Fenns and Atcho, who rose to his feet.

"Fenns, are you ignoring me?" Atcho glared at the consular officer. "I told you about three bombs. Three nukes. They're coming to Berlin."

"What's this about bombs?" the colonel demanded.

"I heard you," Fenns replied to Atcho. "We get three to four bomb threats a week. Everyone wants to blow up the world for peace." He smirked. "Did you *see* the bombs?"

Atcho shook his head.

"So, some guy can whip up three nuclear bombs," Fenns continued, "and carry them through East Germany into Berlin. Tell you what: we'll get our Geiger counters out, and if we find anything, we'll let you know. Now, can we get back to the subject?" He faced Berger.

"Hold up," the colonel interrupted again. "I want to know about the bombs."

"It's nothing," Fenns replied. "What do you want to do?" he asked Berger.

The colonel was now visibly angry. "Mr. Fenns," he bellowed. His eyes bulged. "Atcho is being detained by no one. I'm sure I speak for the general, but if we need to, I can call him." He grabbed the receiver of a phone on the table in front of him and waved it at Fenns. "Do I need to make that call?"

Fenns whirled on him his eyes bulging. "Do you really want to push that? Let me remind you that your brigade CG reports to a two-star chief-of-mission here, who works for a senior state department officer. That puts the state department in charge."

The colonel thrust the phone toward Fenns. "You call your two-star, sir, and I'll stand right here and wait to find out what he has to say."

Fenns hesitated.

The colonel replaced the phone receiver on its base. "Now, either you get on the subject I want to talk about, or I'll have you escorted out by force."

Fenns took a breath, visibly chastened. "We get bomb threats all the time. So far, they've turned into nothing."

"So, we should wait until one goes off before we believe a warning?" the colonel growled, his expression scathing. "Dismiss them if you want to. The Army will decide for itself." He swung around to Atcho. "Tell me about the bombs."

Atcho told him in detail about the conversation he had overheard between Klaus and Etzel. "They were excited. They were supposed to plant one at our embassy. They didn't specify the second target when I overhead them. The third one is for anywhere the brothers want as long as it's outside of Soviet interests."

The colonel studied him. "You think they can pull that off?"

"I don't know where they're getting the bombs, but these guys are capable. They overcame our security at the hotel. They move between East and West Berlin with ease, and they set up a headquarters in the war ruins. I wouldn't underestimate them."

The colonel nodded. "Detective Berger, what do you think?"

"I don't know," Berger replied. He redirected his attention to Atcho. "It was strange how the demand came through from East Berlin. Almost like an afterthought." He paused in reflection. "We've checked out the tunnel in the hotel. It was right where you said it was. I have men going through it now. It seems coincidental that you were staying in the hotel where it comes out on this end."

Brown had been listening without speaking, but now he stood. "You're saying that Atcho had something to do with his own abduction?" he said incredulously.

Berger grimaced. "Sorry. That wasn't my intent." His Germanic intona-
tion accentuated his words. "I am...," he paused, searching for the correct
word, "uneasy about the coincidence that the hotel Atcho was staying in is
the one where the tunnel came out. I don't believe in coincidences. So, how
did that happen?"

Atcho was disheveled, tired from lack of sleep, and starved. Fenns had
brought him some sandwiches, but they had only taken the edge off his
hunger. He stared, dazed, at Berger. "How am I supposed to know?"

Berger shook his head. "I don't expect you to. These are crazy times." He
stretched. "I'm betting that we're going to find more open tunnels into
buildings along the Wall. Those tunnels were used by people in the East
attempting to escape to the West. The East Germans closed the ones they
found with concrete and rebar. Either they didn't get them all, or some have
been re-opened. Now, we'll have to seal them to keep the bad guys out.
But," he cast a steady gaze at Atcho, "East Berlin is pressing hard for your
return. We've had calls channeled through our foreign ministry three times
already."

"Doesn't matter," the colonel retorted. "He's an American citizen. He
was kidnapped, and we've got him. End of story."

A knock on the door interrupted them. A big man with a balding head
walked in. On seeing him, Atcho's countenance brightened. "Burly!" he
exclaimed. He leapt to his feet and bounded across the room. Sofia
emerged from behind Burly.

Atcho diverted to embrace her. "I'm fine," he said softly. He held her a
moment longer, and then turned to greet his big friend. "Thank God you're
here."

"Reinforcements are on the way," Burly said in a low voice. He
enveloped Atcho in a bear hug. "I'll tell you about it later."

The other men watched, stone-faced. Finally, the colonel asked, "Who
are you?"

Burly looked over at him, then released Atcho and strode across to him.
"Sorry. I'm an old friend of Atcho's and Sofia's. I came to help." He
presented his CIA ID.

Fenns leaned in and examined it. "You're retired."

"I know who he is," Brown interjected. "I suggest you check on his current security clearances and orders. You'll find he's authorized to be active in this matter."

"I am," Burly confirmed. "I'm here to cut through red tape and make sure assets are directed where they're needed. I'm up to speed on the broad brush, but as soon as you've checked my clearance, I'd like you to fill me in on the details."

"What's your mission?" Fenns demanded.

Burly arched his eyebrows. The corners of his mouth turned up slightly.

"Got it," Brown muttered. "Classified, need-to-know."

* * *

"We checked out of the Mövenpick and moved to Army headquarters," Sofia told Atcho. "With two attacks on you, you need to be in a more secure place." They were alone with Burly in a soundproofed room in the Berlin Brigade headquarters.

'I'm confused on one point," Atcho said, changing the subject. "Fenns said that the brigade's commanding general reports to a major general who works for a state department officer. How does that work?"

Sofia blew out a breath. "It's complicated. Fenns is right about the command structure, but he's wrong if he thinks either general would give up an American citizen, he doesn't know them."

"But why does the Army report through the state department."

"I'm not sure I understand all the ins and outs. The arrangement came about because of the shared authority of the of the four powers governing Berlin. Regardless, that two-star is not going to override the one-star in a matter like this. Fenns has to know that. He just let his mouth run. The Army still runs Berlin."

Atcho contemplated a moment and turned to Burly. "Who else is coming?"

"Rafael and Ivan. They'll arrive tomorrow."

"You got them," Atcho breathed, "on short notice. I wasn't sure you could."

Rafael Arteaga and Ivan Chekov were two of Atcho's closest friends. Both men had worked with Atcho in previous operations.

Burly's voice brought Atcho back to the present. "I don't know what it is about you, Atcho." He grinned. "You're such an ornery cuss, but when you get in trouble, the free world comes running. All I had to do was ask, and your comrades dropped everything. I stopped off at the White House to speak with the national security advisor. He's fully read in on what happened here in Berlin and called the CIA director to get the clearances set up. I've got a free hand with direct access to him, if needed."

"Great to have friends in high places," Atcho muttered. "What's the plan?"

"Hey, I'm just the case officer. This is yours and Sofia's show. Tell me what needs to be done, and I'll coordinate as much support as I can scrounge up." He faced Sofia. "Does your team have what it needs to complete your mission?"

Sofia nodded. "It's just…" Her voice trailed off.

"She's worried about her relatives," Atcho interjected.

"She explained that," Burly replied. "She'll be stretched thin to get them safely to Wolfgang's press briefing and secure both families while moving across the border. What was your idea, Atcho? Why did you call me here, and why did you want me to bring Ivan and Rafael?"

"Sofia needs to concentrate on Wolfgang and his family. That mission must succeed. We need another team to get Sofia's relatives out."

Burly nodded. "That's what I thought. What can I do?"

"Throw your weight around, get us the equipment we need to communicate, and be here coordinating when everything goes down."

"OK. I can do that."

"The rest of us will operate in the field. We'll need radios and firearms, and a way to get into East Berlin."

"That equipment should be easy but getting everyone into East Berlin will take some work. What else?"

Atcho told him about the bombs.

Burly whistled. "I need to stop hanging around you," he mocked. "You're going to get me killed."

Atcho ignored the comment. "Sofia can't miss Wolfgang's briefing, and his family has to be there. Rafael and Ivan can get her family to safety. Is anyone else coming to help them?"

Burly nodded. "Yep. Rafael will bring along some of your Brigade 2506 compadres." He referred to the army of CIA-trained Cuban refugees who had stormed Cuba at the Bay of Pigs. Many of them had suffered imprisonment on the same Isle of Pines towers where Atcho had been incarcerated. After their release, some had fought Castro's forces in Angola. Two years ago, under Rafael's leadership, several had protected Atcho's family while he hunted down Yermolov in Havana.

"Ivan is coming too?" Atcho asked.

"Yes." Ivan was a defected KGB officer with a penchant for Louis L'Amour novels. He had always wanted to bring his family to live in the United States. The price of his willing participation in a Siberian mission with Atcho had been safe passage for his family to emigrate to the US.

"Let me get this straight," Burly continued. He went over details of the situation and the plan as he understood them, asking many questions. "Sofia, how will you get past the security checkpoint at the door to Wolfgang's news conference?"

"I have press badges for that. When Wolfgang sees me, he'll take the first opportunity to read the news release. Then, he'll take a few questions and make his departure."

They discussed other aspects of the plan. "Execution is going to be very much on the fly," Burly commented. He glanced at Atcho. "So, Rafael and his guys will get Sofia's relatives?"

Atcho nodded. "It's the same plan that Sofia had, except rescuing her relatives will be carried out by a dedicated team. It's a little trickier because none of the operators has met Sofia's relatives. We'll be asking for a huge amount of trust."

"My family will be expecting someone," Sofia interjected. "It'll work." She was silent a moment. "It has to work, even if we can't get Wolfgang and his family out."

Startled, both men studied Sofia's face, a mask of unwavering purpose. She saw their consternation. "They've suffered under this regime their whole lives. We're getting them out," she said with finality.

Atcho and Burly scrutinized her face again. She held their gazes. "I'll get my part done," she said steadily. "You do yours."

"All right," Atcho said after an interval. "The third thing we have to do is find and neutralize those bombs. We don't have much time."

"Do you have any idea where they came from?"

Atcho shook his head. "No. I'd suggest you get the listening surveillance people to intensify their effort in East Berlin. Klaus didn't say anything about how they were getting the bombs. We'll have to track him down and either follow him to the source or take them from him after delivery." He glanced from Burly to Sofia. "That's my job."

Sofia stared at him. She felt the muscles tense along her legs and up her back as she contemplated the implications of what Atcho had just said. She would lead a crucial mission to try to secure the freedom of millions of people while others brought her family to safety. As that occurred, her husband would once again go alone to hunt down and stop the source of potential mass carnage.

She said nothing. She suddenly felt extremely tired, but now was not the time to allow fatigue or emotional stress to inhibit her mind. She walked over to gaze at a map of the city hanging on the wall. "I was thinking," she mused. "Atcho, you said you were held in wartime ruins not far from the Wall."

"It can't be far from the Mövenpick, but on the other side. We twisted and turned in those tunnels for an eternity, but straight-line distance can't be more than a mile."

"Is that where you're thinking of starting your search?"

"Yes, but Klaus will guess that I can find my way back there. He's long gone."

Burly stared at him. "Any idea where else to look?"

"No."

21

While Atcho and Sofia conferred with Burly at brigade headquarters, Tony Collins called from the Azores to Jakes in DC prior to boarding a plane for his return trip to Berlin. "I hate to say we were right, but that seems to be the case. This is going to fall under national security considerations."

"Tell me as much as you can."

"I stayed another day after interviewing the family. The son took me to talk with several people who claimed to have seen a man with a hurt leg. They said he was an American, but he fit Yermolov's description."

"Did they say how he hurt his leg? As I recall, Atcho shot Yermolov in the thigh."

"No one seemed to know. The man didn't offer an explanation. That's not unusual. Strangers don't normally ask why someone limps."

"Did the authorities follow up?"

"A little. They didn't believe João. There's not much of a murder rate here. They don't have top-notch homicide investigators, and no one wanted to upset the widow. They attributed the blood to fishing, and since the limping man was believed to be an American, they thought João had found the Soviet jacket somewhere and rationalized the story. They pointed out that no recent Soviet accidents had occurred. Just American. They thought he couldn't accept that his dad had made a fatal mistake."

"But you believe him." The editor's voice betrayed skepticism.

"Jakes, Yermolov spied as Paul Clary—an American—for nearly thirty years. If he decides to play American again, no one meeting him for the first time will think he's anything else. He was presumed dead. No one was looking for him."

Jakes sounded unconvinced. "The Marines sent out a rescue/recovery team. No bodies were found."

"Yeah, but a storm blew in and delayed the search. In fact, that storm is what the police say caused Gonçalo's death.

"Also, a boat that leaves from Vila Nova and goes out just a few miles northeast would be under the approach pattern for Lajes. Gonçalo could have seen the crash. A helicopter departing the airfield for a ship over the horizon would be below commercial routes. That's the area where Gonçalo was and where the helicopter went down.

"He seems to have been a very nice man. If Yermolov survived and Gonçalo rescued him..." He paused to let the thought sink in. "The other factors add up. Yermolov could have hitched a ride on a private aircraft to Lisbon. From there he's a hop, skip and jump from Berlin. If the guy has proven anything, it's that he's resourceful. Napoleon escaped from Elba, and he didn't have airplanes."

"OK, one last question. Why would Yermolov kill his rescuer?"

Collins scoffed. "You know the answer. Yermolov killed Gonçalo because he was the only person who could say that a man survived the crash."

"I had to ask. All right. I'm not sure I'm totally on board, but I'll give you the benefit of the doubt. What do we do with this information? Is it something we can print?"

"Not yet. It's explosive, but we don't have to worry about anyone scooping us. Our competition never knew about Yermolov, aka Clary. Get it to the Pentagon. I'll let Sofia know as soon as I get back to Berlin."

After his conversation with Jakes, Collins settled into his seat aboard the plane. His mind was restless. *Could Yermolov have survived that crash?*

* * *

With an overnight layover in Lisbon, Collins arrived in Berlin the next morning. As soon as he cleared customs, he headed to the Mövenpick. There, he learned that Atcho and Sofia had checked out. Although relieved to hear that Atcho had escaped, he felt pressed to get word to him about Yermolov.

He went to the Berlin offices of the *Washington Herald* and watched in fascination the news clips of Atcho's rescue. He surmised that Atcho must have moved to a safe place under the Army's protection. At midmorning, he arrived at Berlin Brigade's headquarters, and after a few inquiries and phone calls to Jakes in DC, and to the Pentagon to confirm his credentials, he was directed to a guest apartment. A pair of sentries frisked him, and then one called up to the room.

Atcho answered the phone. Upon learning who sought admittance, he told the guard, "We don't have time for interviews," and hung up.

"Call him back," Collins insisted. "Tell him that Borya Yermolov escaped."

The young soldier complied reluctantly. After a short conversation, he told Collins, "He wasn't happy about your arrival, but he said to escort you in."

When they knocked on the apartment door, Atcho answered. "You've meddled enough," he said by way of greeting. "We don't need you broadcasting to the world before we can figure out what's going on. This had better be good."

"You need to hear this," Collins retorted. "There are things you need to know about besides Yermolov's probable escape."

Atcho glowered but led him into the living room. Sofia and Burly were there, seated. Sofia appraised him guardedly. Burly stood and greeted him. "Great to see you, man. It's been a long time."

Collins returned the greeting coolly. "The last time we met, you weren't so congenial."

Burly laughed. He remembered the encounter a year earlier at Camp David, during which Collins had been treated less than courteously. "All in a day's work," he replied. "Professional distance. But you did a superb job."

"Can we get down to business?" Atcho cut in. "Collins says that Yermolov escaped."

Astonished, Sofia and Burly asked in unison. "Has that been confirmed?"

Collins shook his head. "The helicopter that took him away crashed in the Atlantic. No reported survivors. The Pentagon thought he was dead." He related his investigation in the Azores, including that João thought Gonçalo had been murdered. He told them about the bloody uniform with the entry and exit holes in the left leg.

Atcho groaned. "That's where I shot him." His jaw had drawn taut. "Any idea where he's gone?"

"Maybe." Collins took off his glasses and rubbed his eyes. The burden of weighty matters showed on his face. He felt on edge. "Our DC office informed the Pentagon, but no one has had time to run it to ground." He wiped his glasses. "He could be here in Berlin. He might be behind the two attacks on you."

Atcho, Sofia, and Burly exchanged startled glances. Burly was the first to speak. "Are we off the record?" His tone left no room for nonsense.

"Of course," Collins replied testily. "Until you tell me otherwise. Do you want to hear the rest?"

The three remained seated. When no one's expression changed, Collins turned to leave. "Suit yourselves." He headed toward the door.

Atcho stood. "Wait. Let's hear it. Please sit down."

Collins still felt on edge. "I haven't asked questions or requested an interview," he snapped. "I came to give information. It gets worse. If you don't want to hear it, I'll take it to Army intelligence across the parking lot." He paused. "I have a family too. I want to see my kids grow up." He rubbed his eyes again, obviously fatigued.

Burly beckoned. "We'll listen. Have a seat."

"As I said, Yermolov might be in Berlin," Collins began, not relishing the news he had to pass along. "He's either seeking or already has a nuclear bomb."

Now he had their full attention. Sofia put her hand over her mouth. She started to speak, and then stopped herself.

The group asked Collins a few terse questions about what else he had learned in the Azores. He informed them of his visit earlier in the year with the Rasputin followers, including Veniamin.

Twenty minutes after he arrived, Burly walked him to the door. "Thanks for coming. You know we can't reciprocate, at least not now. We'll have to escalate this to the White House immediately. You could lose your scoop."

Collins nodded grimly. "I know." He paused when they reached the front porch. "I know I screwed up by not reporting Veniamin." He shrugged. "I thought Yermolov was in prison…" His voice trailed away, his shoulders drooped. Then he straightened his back and locked eyes with Burly. "Get that bastard. Before something bad happens."

"We'll give it our best shot. And when there's a story to tell, you'll be the first to hear it." He clapped Collins on the shoulder. "You'll probably know it before us anyway."

* * *

"What do you think?" Burly asked after Collins had gone.

"Wolfgang's announcement is in thirty-six hours," Sofia blurted. "The time for talking is over. It's time to put plans in motion."

"I agree," Atcho interjected. "We'd better brief the commanding general and Shelby. We need to know what other resources we can get."

"I'll set it up," Burly said. "This new information needs to get to the White House. Now." He went to the phone.

Atcho stroked his chin. "That must be how the East Germans know so much about you and me," he said to Sofia. "That had to be Yermolov on the phone with Klaus the other night. Collins could have saved us a lot of trouble if he had told us about Veniamin last year."

"We can't dwell on that," Sofia cut in. "I'll get the intel listening guys to see if they can pinpoint the cousin's location. The Paris office can run down the Rasputin group there. That should give us a good start. We might get lucky and intercept Veniamin before he makes delivery."

Atcho stood quietly with arms crossed. "Tell them to use their best guys on the intercept. We want the bombs *and* Yermolov. I promise you, he has bigger plans."

While Atcho spoke, Burly returned from the phone.

"What does he want?" Sofia asked.

"That's not hard to figure," Atcho replied. "He's always been after major roles in the Soviet Union. If he blows a hole in the Wall with a nuke and blasts another critical Soviet target, Gorbachev is done. Yermolov sees himself as top dog in Moscow."

"I agree," Burly said. "Sorry to interrupt. The general wants a full briefing this afternoon with all parties present. Sofia, you need to get your team over here from the east side. He understands the urgency but won't go off half-cocked.

"Atcho, to complete what you were saying, if Yermolov succeeds, the only good part for us is that the Soviets will be so busy stitching their empire together, they won't have time to mess with the US for years. They'll have to use military force. Poland is about to seize its independence. Chechnya is always a problem. The Baltic states are agitating to follow Poland, and the neighboring Eastern Bloc countries won't be far behind. Czechoslovakia is moving in that direction. The farther east you go on the Soviet border, the less control they have.

"Then they're smack in the middle of Islamic countries, who don't like the Soviets anyway. Hell, Moscow already pulled its troops out of Afghanistan ten months ago." He shook his head. "This can turn ugly real fast."

Sofia listened, her worry deepening. "Look," she said, "so far, there's no evidence that Yermolov knows about my mission, but if he's calculating like we are, he'll anticipate a move to open the Wall in less than a week. That means the bombs must arrive soon. They might already be here. We've got to move. I've got to go get my team.

"Burly, while you're running this up the chain, check on signal intel." She stopped, her face grave as a thought struck her. "You know the Soviets have to be informed."

Burly nodded grimly. "I'm sure our higher levels are thinking of that, but I'll check to make sure."

"The president should talk to Gorbachev quickly. If word gets out, Yermolov could accelerate. When is the rest of Atcho's team arriving?"

The phone rang. Atcho answered, spoke briefly, and hung up. "Collins wants another minute of your time," he told Burly, "and my guys just arrived."

22

A guard knocked on the door. Burly opened it and showed Collins and five other men into the apartment. The newcomers were in excellent physical shape and walked with a quiet calm that turned into exuberance when they saw Atcho, Sofia, and Burly.

Atcho recognized his old Bay of Pigs comrade, Rafael. Behind him was Ivan.

Sofia greeted them quickly. "I'm sorry," she told them. "I have to go retrieve my team. Atcho will explain." They hugged her, and she darted out the door.

Rafael clasped Atcho in a bear hug. "There's trouble whenever you and Sofia and Burly show up at the same time." He spoke in a jocular tone with a Cuban accent.

"I'm glad you came, *hermano.*" Atcho stepped back so that Burly could greet Rafael. Then he turned his attention to the next man in the group, one who bore a passing resemblance to the comedian Bob Newhart, but with a serious countenance and a muscular physique. "Ivan!" Atcho's enthusiasm was unbridled. "You came! Sorry the circumstances couldn't be better."

"No worries," Ivan said. "That's why I'm here. I didn't even have to be coerced." The former KGB officer spoke with an easy midwestern American accent, one for which he had trained prior to being assigned in the United States on a Soviet intelligence mission. He greeted Burly while Rafael introduced Atcho to the three remaining individuals.

The men had laid-back smiles and projected good natures, albeit with an unstated warning that said, "Cross us at your peril."

"These men didn't stop fighting Castro at the Bay of Pigs," Rafael said. "They were also part of Brigade 2506 supporting the CIA in the Congo. They rescued those missionary children in 1963. If not for them, those kids would be dead."

Atcho stood back to scrutinize them, his demeanor demonstrating increased respect. Rafael broke in again. "That's why I chose them. They've done this before."

One of the men stepped forward. "I am Juan," he said. He indicated the other two. "This is Fernando and Pepe." He faced Atcho. "We're honored to work with you."

"Don't get all gushy," Rafael interjected, laughing.

Atcho looked critically over the men. He liked what he saw, but still had reservations. "That Congo operation was more than twenty-five years ago."

The three stared back in sudden silence. Rafael stepped close to Atcho. "When you called me to go to Siberia last year, you didn't ask my age. You called. I came." He spoke firmly. "These are my brothers. They fought alongside of me many times. They would have come just because I asked, but when I told them it was you who called, they were eager. I trust them with my life. You can trust them with yours."

Atcho looked into the weathered faces of each man and held out his hand. "Thanks for coming. Do you know why you're here?"

"Just a general outline," Juan replied.

"Burly couldn't tell us much," Rafael chimed in.

"Well, things just became a lot more urgent," Atcho said. While he filled them in, he looked across the room to where Collins talked quietly with Burly. After a few moments, Collins made eye contact with Atcho and left.

"What did Collins want?" Atcho asked Burly a few minutes later.

"He thinks he might be able to help," Burly replied, "like he did last year with that Rasputin story. The one planted in *Pravda*."

"He wants to plant another story?"

"This time he'll do it on television. Time is short. We have to be sure Yermolov hears it. Collins' editor is contracting with a Berlin videographer to join him. He also thinks he can do some more ferreting. He's going to France to find Veniamin."

Atcho felt uneasy. "You're okay with that? We don't know where the bombs are."

Burly shrugged. "Can't hurt. Everything Collins knows about this situation he found out on his own. He doesn't need our permission to do the digging or to run with the story. If his report is dropped on the public at a critical juncture, it could give us an advantage and get Yermolov's supporters to turn on him."

"Maybe, but this is Germany, not Russia. Yermolov couldn't have much of an organization behind him now."

"Sure. That's what we thought last year, but it turned out that he had a good chunk of the Soviet military and intelligence services behind him, and a huge part of the bureaucracy. He even had a couple of politburo members and the head of the KGB. He's been out on his own for nearly a year. The last thing we should do is underestimate him."

"You're right," Atcho acquiesced. "Collins gets full credit for smoking Yermolov out last year. Maybe he can do it again."

23

That afternoon, the entire team moved to a secure conference room at brigade headquarters, prepared for a discussion with Commanding General Marsh. Sofia arrived with two men and two women trailing behind her. "This is my team," she said quickly. After introductions, she told Atcho, "The commanding general is on his way. I briefed him before I came in. With a possible nuclear bomb in the mix now, he wants to be informed up to the minute. His intelligence and operations officers are coming, too. You already met the intel guy yesterday morning at your debriefing."

Before Atcho could respond, an orderly stepped in and called out, "A-tten-tion!" The room fell silent. "The commanding general," the orderly announced.

Atcho swung around for a better view. Two generals walked into the room. Atcho shot Sofia a questioning glance.

"General Marsh is in command now," she whispered, pointing him out. "General Shachnow will take over in a few days. They both want to be in the loop."

Atcho knew both men by reputation. Marsh's career already spanned twenty-nine years, and he showed no signs of slowing down. He was a quiet man who did not speak of his accomplishments, but they were many, including two tours in Vietnam. As an infantry officer, he had also trained for airborne operations and was a distinguished helicopter pilot. Before assuming command of the Berlin Brigade, he had been the assistant division commander of the storied 101st Airborne Division. His awards and medals included those of the highest levels. Atcho had little doubt that his further career would be equally sterling.

Prior to coming to Berlin, Atcho had studied the incoming commanding general, Shachnow, out of curiosity. The man was a legend. Born in Lithuania, he had spent three years in a German occupation prison during the war. After his release when the war ended, he had enlisted in the US Army and had risen rapidly. Upon reaching the rank of sergeant first class, he had attended Officers' Candidate School and became a commissioned officer. His assignments had included command of Special Forces units.

And here he is at this historic moment, Atcho thought. *How incredible for him to witness Berlin's liberation after decades of Nazi and Communist occupation.*

"Where's the two-star?" he whispered to Sofia.

"On his way stateside, to brief his state department boss, the Army chief-of-staff, and the chairman of the joint chiefs. The situation here is gaining a lot of visibility. He'll back whatever the commanding general here on the ground decides."

Two colonels stood by the sides of Marsh and Shachnow. Atcho recognized one of them, the intelligence officer, from yesterday's debriefing. The colonel guided the generals to meet Atcho.

"I know about you," Marsh said, "your whole story." He spoke in low, clipped terms. "I came to tell you and Sofia personally that you have the full support of my command and my highers." He introduced General Shachnow and the other colonel. "Colonel Melger is my ops chief. He'll coordinate whatever you need."

As they were about to begin, the door opened, and Sean Shelby came in. He made eye contact with Sofia and moved to the front table with the generals.

After they had taken their seats, General Marsh turned to Burly. "I understand you have the president's ear?"

"I did have, concerning the mission to rescue Atcho. When I first spoke with the CIA director, Atcho had been abducted, but by the time I got here, he had escaped."

The general contemplated that. "What's your role now?"

Burly shrugged. "You know the nature of Sofia's mission?"

"I know the outline. I know that she and her team will be disavowed if things go wrong. And I know things just got a lot hotter with Yermolov and his bombs. The president is keenly aware of both situations and wants frequent updates." He steepled his hands under his chin. "I can confirm that Yermolov was on the helicopter that went down in the Azores. We do not have confirmation of his continued existence."

Silence settled in. Burly broke it. "Atcho will tackle going after Yermolov and the bombs. He'll be in radio contact with me. Sofia will continue with rescuing Wolfgang and his family. I'll coordinate between those two missions, and the third one."

Marsh's eyes narrowed. "I'm not familiar with a third mission."

"I'm not either," Shelby interrupted, his voice steely. His expression did not change. He shifted his attention to Ivan, Rafael, and the Brigade 2506 veterans. "Is that why they're here? Do they have clearances?"

Sofia stood. "I'm responsible." She directed her comment to Shelby. "I didn't brief you. I apologize. They're here because Atcho sent for them, to get my relatives out."

The general shot her a piercing glance. "I hadn't heard about that." He turned to Shelby. "Had you?"

"Negative."

Marsh shifted his eyes back to Sofia. "Fill us in."

Sofia did, including who the men were and how they were connected to Atcho. "My husband called Burly a few hours before he was taken," she concluded. "No one knew then about the bombs, or that Yermolov might have escaped. Atcho knew I couldn't ask for Army, CIA, or state department support to get my family out. He sent for his own team."

The general listened thoughtfully. He conferred in hushed whispers with Shachnow, Shelby, Melger, and the brigade intelligence officer. When they were finished, he addressed Sofia.

"I'll tell you frankly, I don't like operational surprises." He shifted his attention to Burly. "We don't have time for formalities. Are you vouching for these men? Including the Russian? I hear he's former KGB."

Burly stood. "Yes sir, I am." He gave a rapid rundown on each person.

When he had finished, Atcho stood up next to him. He indicated Juan, Pepe, and Fernando. "Sir, I met these three men a few hours ago, but I fought alongside Rafael and Ivan. I'd trust my life to either of them. Rafael tells me these men are good. On his word, I'll trust my life to them too."

The general sat quietly, and then turned his attention to Sofia. "Are you okay with that? Your mission is critical. You can't afford to be distracted. Your husband will hunt down Yermolov and three suitcase nukes." He paused, contemplating the gravity of what he had just said. "He'll do that simultaneous with your mission, and it hinges on Wolfgang Sacher seeing you personally. That's a lot of pressure. Can you handle it?"

Sofia gestured toward her own team members. "They've proven themselves on other ops. I trust them. I can handle it." Then she cast her eyes at her husband. "Atcho can handle his part. If he trusts these men, I do too."

All eyes were trained on Marsh and Sofia. Burly eased the tension by retaking his seat. Sofia followed suit. After a few moments, Atcho also sat down.

Marsh looked across at Shelby. "What do you think?"

The station chief took his time to answer. "I don't like that I wasn't clued in on the third mission earlier," he began.

Sofia held her breath.

Shelby fiddled with a pen while he collected his thoughts. "Sofia." His direct address startled her. "Do you understand that your primary mission is Wolfgang, his family, and his intended announcement? The stakes are high." He tapped his pen while he leaned back in thought. "Substituting someone for you would spook Wolfgang, that's for sure.

"I don't want to stand in the way of the Wall coming down, but I can't have you going rogue to do something else mid-mission." He frowned. "You've been known to go off on your own."

Sofia's cheeks flamed. "I understand, sir. I have one mission. I won't interfere in the others or fail to complete mine."

Shelby turned his attention to Marsh. "Can you get them all into East

Berlin and provide the logistical support? And get them back out if things go wrong?"

"I can," Marsh said. "But I won't take them in unless you approve the missions." He looked through his notes. "To clarify, I'll support only those missions you approve."

Shelby fiddled with his pen again. "I'm inclined to go with the first two," he began. "That third one…" He started to shake his head.

Rafael sprang to his feet. "Sir, may I speak?" Marsh consented with a nod. "These men and I," he indicated Juan, Fernando, and Pepe, "we all have military backgrounds. Every operation we've been in was organized by the CIA. Ivan was KGB, but he's proven himself and he's also worked with the CIA."

He turned his attention to Shelby. "Sofia's mission was planned with her in mind before she was even consulted. I've worked with her. She is one of the most effective officers in the CIA. You know that. She'll give the mission her all. But how could you ask her to do this and not think about her loved ones living a short distance away? And her husband out chasing nukes? Yermolov is a sideshow.

"If you want to give her the clearest mind possible, then support this third mission. She's already factored in the dangers to Atcho, but when she knows that her family is being rescued, then the only mission for her to concentrate on is her own."

He searched Shelby's immutable face. "Sir, I have only one thing left to say. Meaning no disrespect," he gestured again toward Ivan, Juan, and the others, "we will complete the mission with your help or without it. We will rescue Sofia's family." He stopped talking and looked at the floor. When he looked up again, he grinned impudently, and his voice returned to its normal jocular tone. "But we sure could use your help."

Shelby felt a half smile slip onto his face. He surveyed Rafael's group and saw five sets of determined eyes returning his scrutiny. Sofia looked straight ahead, professional. Atcho and Burly watched without expression.

Shelby heaved a sigh. "I'll approve…" he said. Seeing immediate reaction among the group, he held up a palm. "…with caveats." He focused on Atcho. "The idea of you going out alone to do this thing is not realistic. You don't know where Yermolov is, and neither do we. But we have a lot of resources. The president is personally interested.

"You know this Yermolov better than anyone. We'll support you with all the assets we can. That includes listening intel and human assets on the ground. If we see him first, we'll nab him. If you hear something, you tell us. That goes for his cousin and the Chechen too. Is that understood?"

"I don't have a death wish."

Shelby half smiled again, looked across at Marsh, and heaved a sigh. "General, you have your answer. All three missions are a go."

Marsh leaned back in his chair. He took a deep breath and addressed the group. "Let's be clear. The mission to get Yermolov and the nukes is primary. It requires irregular entry into East Berlin. We'll add our assets to the CIA's. If we see those SOBs first, we'll haul them in, dead or alive.

"If things go wrong and we can't rescue you, all three missions will be disavowed. Do each of you understand what that means?"

"We know the lay of the land," Atcho said.

Marsh sat quietly, his fingers drumming on the table. "What do you need from me?" he asked Burly.

"Get our teams into East Berlin, and provide us with secure radios. Give me a secure room with radio and personnel support where I can coordinate mission execution."

Marsh leaned forward. "All right. We can do that. You can use this room." He turned to Colonel Melger. "Get him set up."

He shifted his attention back to the full group. "Now, let me tell you what we know. The White House Situation Room is active and following the situation. I told them an attack could be imminent. We don't have time for studies, commissions, specialists, etcetera. We're going with what we have in this room to deal with the problem. That's a go with POTUS."

Another layer of gravity seemed to descend on the participants. "The embassy is taking quiet action to safeguard our personnel," Marsh continued. "The Soviets have been notified. I imagine they're doing the same thing.

"The KGB was already aware of Yermolov's presence in Berlin. For reasons I don't understand, Gorbachev seemed to have been left out of the loop until the president informed him.

"Nestor Murin, the KGB chief, has a personal relationship with Johann Baumann, the Stasi director. That should have made Yermolov more visible, but it didn't. Both countries are in political turmoil, so it's anyone's guess what's going on. My view: there's an internal struggle for control of the KGB. Anyway, Gorbachev promised KGB cooperation on the ground here, but so far, we haven't seen it."

The general looked down at his notes. "Veniamin Krivkov, the bomb maker, is on the move. With the information Collins gave, our people in France tracked down his house. He left a day ago. If he's coming this way, he won't drive up the corridor—too many checkpoints. We'll monitor that route, but I'll bet he comes through East Germany, under protection. Only one organization can pull that off."

"The Stasi." The intelligence officer's eyes narrowed as he spoke. "In which case, it's cooperating with Yermolov. The East German government's lost control of it. It's operating on its own."

The general stood abruptly. "That makes sense. Baumann is the last hard-liner left in place. It stands to reason that he might bolt and try to take his organization with him. He could be harboring Yermolov. I'll alert Washington about that possibility."

Marsh looked around at the concerned faces. "Colonel Melger will coordinate with the CIA and provide top priority support for the missions." He turned to Atcho. "I have more questions about your piece of this. Let's discuss in my office. Now. We'll do everything we can to prevent use of the bombs." His eyes narrowed. "The president was happy to hear that you're safe and on the case."

He glanced around the room. "Thirty hours is not much time. That leaves no room for error." Then, leaning toward Atcho, he pointed a finger. "You're going to find that son-of-a-bitch Yermolov. Don't walk away until you've confirmed he has no pulse."

24

As soon as Tony Collins had left Burly at Atcho's guest quarters, he had taken a flight to Paris and rented a car. That was yesterday. He had dispensed with caution when he decided on this trip to France. Feeling guilty about not having reported his contact with Veniamin Krivkov last winter, he hoped that intercepting the bomb maker might help defeat Yermolov.

He spent that evening at a tavern in the village north of Paris where he had interviewed Veniamin all those months ago. There, he found members of the Rasputin group he had befriended. Through subtle questioning, he learned that Veniamin had gone to a weekend home several miles farther north.

Collins drove out the next morning and located a barn that Veniamin had converted into a weekend getaway. He arrived just as Veniamin pulled out of the gravel driveway. Collins followed, hoping to catch him. After a few miles of back roads, Veniamin turned onto a highway headed northeast.

Collins groaned. *He's headed to Berlin.*

He glanced at his fuel gauge and his dismay deepened: his gas tank was low. He followed as long as he dared, noting that Veniamin drove at a languid pace.

They crossed into West Germany and entered the Autobahn, famous for unlimited speed limits, where Mercedes and Porsches whizzed by at more than a hundred miles per hour.

Veniamin continued to poke along.

Collins pulled even and glanced at him. Veniamin drove as if in a trance, his eyes fixed on the road ahead, seemingly oblivious to anything around him. His jaw was set, his shoulders slumped. To Collins, he looked like a man on his way to meet Fate.

Collins' stomach knotted. His fuel would run out soon. He watched in dismay as Veniamin continued down the Autobahn while Collins was forced to exit and fill up.

A few minutes later, his fuel replenished, Collins pulled back into traffic and raced along the highway, watching for Veniamin's car. Ten hours later, he entered a lot and parked near the border crossing into East Germany. He had not seen Veniamin along the way. *He must have stopped somewhere.*

Collins peered at the cars lined up on the side of the border closest to him. The crossing took its name from the nearest village in West Germany, Helmstedt. The East German side was named for the corresponding closest village, Marienborn. Together they comprised Checkpoint Alpha, aka the Helmstedt–Marienborn checkpoint. It was the largest and busiest of the border crossings between the two halves of divided Germany, situated on the line separating the British and Soviet occupation zones.

Another hour turned into two more, and still Collins saw no sight of Veniamin. He was about to give up and head back to Paris when he saw Veniamin's car limp into the area. It seemed to slow further, as if Veniamin were taking stock of his surroundings. Then it entered the flow of traffic and headed toward the crossing point.

Collins cranked up his engine, jammed the car into gear, and maneuvered to follow. The lines of cars converged and slowed to a crawl.

Veniamin was several cars ahead of Collins. Closing the gap was impossible.

Ahead, a British soldier stood beside each lane, clearing travelers to proceed into East Germany. Collins watched Veniamin drive up to one of them. Moments later, Veniamin had passed the British checkpoint and driven into East Germany.

Collins hurried after him as quickly as traffic, prudence, and the East German machine gun–armed border guards allowed. By the time he caught up with Veniamin, the engineer had parked at a customs inspection station.

Collins watched Veniamin climb out of the vehicle as if in a daze and walk to the back of his car under the vigilant eye of two border guards and a uniformed passport control officer. A man in plain clothes strode up behind them. From the way the others reacted to this official's presence, the reporter could tell that the man exercised authority.

Collins gulped. *Stasi!*

He watched Veniamin, trembling visibly, lean down and open the trunk.

25

When Veniamin had driven into Helmstedt, he had looked about worriedly, taking in the mass of cars and trucks converging on the border crossing ahead. It terrified him. The prospect of entering East Germany struck fear to his core, more so now given his deadly cargo.

Running off either side of the complex as far as Veniamin could see were two parallel razor-sharp fences with wide killing fields between them, and concrete watchtowers, guards with machine guns, minefields, hungry dogs, and motion-activated shotguns. Those fortifications were well lit at night and ran over eight hundred miles, from the Baltic Sea to the Czech border. They assured that the citizenry did not escape.

After nearly fourteen hours of driving, Veniamin was almost sick with exhaustion. His stomach churned. He had barely paid attention to the scenic countryside on his five-hundred-mile drive from his town north of Paris. For the duration of the trip, Yermolov's words uttered four days ago had replayed ceaselessly in his mind. *I know you love your family. The materials will arrive tomorrow. Deliver the completed items personally in three days. Am I clear?*

You were all too clear, Cousin. He had no doubt about Yermolov's willingness and ability to carry out the implied threat. To Veniamin's chagrin, the delivery had indeed been ready. In the trunk of his car now were three small matching suitcases.

Yermolov had been right about Veniamin's family. Veniamin doted on a son and a daughter. Each had blessed him with three grandchildren, who now ranged in age from infancy to twelve years. He loved weekends when both families came to his house.

He cursed the day he had learned of the existence of his distant cousin. He knew little of Yermolov's background. They had almost nothing in common except that they both had descended from Grigori Rasputin, the Siberian mystic. The legendary political vagabond, known for an insatiable sexual appetite, had left behind an unknown number of bastards, including two sons who had sired the cousins.

Yermolov had been born in the United States. He had spent his adult life there as a deep cover spy for the KGB, in the US Air Force. Veniamin, on the other hand, had escaped from Ukraine and had grown to maturity in France.

Yermolov had found Veniamin through a group of Russian refugees in Paris. They belonged to an obscure sect of the Russian Orthodox Church that revered Rasputin. Oddly, despite their disparate backgrounds, both cousins had become nuclear engineers—the only other element common between them.

Yermolov had offered one million dollars for each nuke to tantalize Veniamin. Despite the sum, only the real threat to Veniamin's family had motivated him to comply. Now, he found himself in the grip of unspeakable horror: *Yermolov will set off three nuclear bombs that I made.* He pictured cities in flames with radioactive fallout raining down from darkened skies on the skeletal remains of innocent humans. *How will I live with that?*

He had aided Yermolov in the last conspiracy out of his desire to help strike a blow against the Soviet Union—against the Kremlin—the power that had destroyed his childhood home and murdered his parents. Yermolov had put him in direct contact with a black-market arms dealer who had provided required amounts of plutonium and other materials. Veniamin had never known the source or arrangements: he had not asked.

He had brought the technical skill to design and build the bomb.

Yermolov had assured him that he intended to use it as a last resort, to blackmail the Soviet regime into capitulation.

Veniamin recalled his secret feelings at the time. *I wanted* him *to bomb the Kremlin.* Now the thought caused him shame. To his relief, the conspiracy seemed to have died, because he had heard nothing more about it. The Soviet government had continued about its business with no outward show of disruption.

This time, though, Yermolov intended to detonate the bombs: he had made that clear.

Veniamin recalled the moment that Yermolov had called from Lisbon, requesting funds to travel to France. Veniamin had felt suddenly nauseated. Two days later, Yermolov had arrived at the train station in his village. His cousin had looked thinner than when they had seen each other a few weeks earlier. He now walked with a limp. No explanation had been offered, and Veniamin had not inquired about the injured leg.

Yermolov's behavior had changed too. Whereas he had exuded confidence while organizing the conspiracy last year, now he seemed furtive, urgent, desperate—even more lethal.

* * *

Veniamin had blocked many of his childhood memories, but the most horrific of them intruded uninvited. He recalled near-starvation during the famine engineered in Ukraine by Joseph Stalin. He relived visions of a fine red mist spraying out from his parents' heads as troops executed them with shots to their skulls.

He remembered running, running, running. Bullets split the air. His lungs heaved. He reached a fast-flowing river, jumped in, and floated in the current.

Nine years old then, his survival instinct was already well developed. The executioners did not pursue him, he guessed, because shadows stretched long in the approaching dusk. Spotting him would be difficult, and a skeletal boy would die anyway.

His memory of the following days was murky. He recalled crawling from the river in darkness, long, aimless treks at night, skirting farms with barking dogs, and sleeping during the day. Always came the terror of being discovered.

One early morning, a local policeman spotted him, half-dead, huddled in a woodshed. The officer left him in a displaced persons camp, one of hundreds spread across postwar Europe.

Thousands of refugees populated each camp. They had first sought sanctuary from the Nazis and then from Stalin's Communists as the tides of war turned. Being a disarmed population, they had no means of defending themselves against either tormentor.

For months, Veniamin lived in the misery-ridden camps, transferring from one to another for reasons he was too young to comprehend. At some point, a kindly woman smuggled him out of his last camp. She took him to a warm place and fed him hot soup. He slept on a real mattress that night, under thick blankets.

The next morning, another woman ferried him south to yet another set of strangers. This sequence repeated numerous times, always furtively. He traveled many hours over bumpy roads, stuffed into dark spaces in battered vehicles spewing suffocating fumes.

After several weeks, Veniamin found himself in an orphanage in France. This was to be his home until either he was adopted, or he reached adulthood.

Years later, Veniamin searched for the kind lady who had smuggled him from the first camp. He had learned with horror that the entire refugee population had been herded a thousand miles northeast to the forced labor gulags of Siberia.

Catholic nuns ran the orphanage. Although strict, they were kind. They labored to provide each child with an excellent education. However, no one adopted Veniamin.

He studied diligently, blocking out his dark memories, and he graduated at the top of his class. As a result, he went straight into university on scholarships. His professors recognized his keen mind and promoted his academic career.

The North Atlantic Treaty Organization formed in 1948 to provide a nuclear shield against the Soviet threat to the United States and its European allies. By 1960, when Veniamin completed his doctorate, countries that had been allies during World War II had split into competing factions. He had no recollection of the treaty's start, but he remembered vividly the day after his graduation. An officer of the French nuclear defense forces visited him. "President de Gaulle believes that France should have its own nuclear arms," the officer told him. "You're one of the brightest nuclear engineers to graduate recently. We want you in the program, to help design France's weaponry."

* * *

Two days before reaching Helmstedt–Marienborn, Veniamin had left the house he had inhabited since joining the French nuclear program, thirty years earlier. He spent the day at his countryside barn-home.

A man had visited Veniamin that day. He had come unannounced, but Veniamin had expected him. He was the black-market arms merchant delivering Yermolov's plutonium. He had delivered the deadly packet along with other materials Veniamin would need, and he left without ceremony.

Having built the bomb last year and an identical one for the new plan, Veniamin had needed only a few hours to construct the remaining two. He had worked late into the night.

The next morning, as he had prepared to leave, he stepped into his shop to retrieve the suitcases. Before he left, his eyes had rested on his sawdust-sprinkled table saw, a power sander and other tools, and finally his half-dozen wood projects—a rocking horse, a child's playhouse, a bookcase. He inhaled the comforting scent of cut wood. Then he turned off the light and carried the suitcases to his car.

He had spent the day driving the Autobahn to the Helmstedt–Marienborn border crossing. On the best of days, traversing to the eastern side of the checkpoint with its bureaucrats and authoritarian police inspectors was an ordeal. Running the gauntlet with three nuclear bombs in the trunk of his car terrified Veniamin. He felt lightheaded.

The complex comprised the gateway to the ribbon of highway known as the "corridor" that traversed East Germany to Berlin. Established under the Four-Power Treaty, it allowed ground passage for French, British, and US troops and materiel needed to administer their respective sectors.

Civilian traffic also used the corridor, the most tightly controlled highway in the world, to travel to and from Berlin. They drove it under rigid surveillance of both East German police and Soviet soldiers.

For Veniamin, the corridor represented another petrifying obstacle. He had voiced his concern to Yermolov.

"Keep to your right as you enter the Marienborn side," his cousin had replied. "An escort will meet you there. Give me the license number of your car."

"Can't I make delivery to your escort?"

Yermolov's response was direct, his tone menacing. "No. I need you here."

26

Veniamin took a deep breath and maneuvered his car into one of the two lanes of traffic flowing under the aluminum canopy at the border crossing. Night had fallen.

The lanes moved slowly but steadily as British soldiers checked the credentials of drivers ahead of him. Finally, a British soldier stood outside his window. Veniamin's heart beat furiously. He presented his passport.

"Sir, have you driven the corridor before?" the sentry asked. Veniamin told him he had not.

"Then listen carefully to this briefing. We're required to give it to all Westerners traveling the corridor. You must stay on the Autobahn all the way to Checkpoint Bravo in Berlin. Do not exit anywhere, and don't speed. If you do either of those things, you are likely to encounter members of either the East German police or the Soviet Army. If that happens, your treatment will be unpleasant.

"As a civilian, you don't have the protections afforded to Allied military members. If you're stopped, don't agree to anything. Insist on seeing a government representative and make no statements. Do you understand everything I've said?"

Almost overcome with anxiety, Veniamin could only nod. The soldier waved him through.

Ahead of him, other cars moved forward, their short briefings with border guards completed. Veniamin pressed his accelerator. As he approached the other end of Helmstedt, the line of cars in front of him spread into several lanes.

Veniamin's heart pounded. Sweat poured down his face. East German guards equipped with automatic rifles scowled at him, their weapons pointed in the direction of traffic.

As Yermolov had instructed, Veniamin tried to get to the right. He was one lane over, so he signaled and started to maneuver. The horn of the car behind him blared. Guards swiveled their eyes his way. One pointed at Veniamin. His every nerve froze.

Before leaving his village, he had asked about transiting the crossing. "You enter another world," his friend had said. "A strange, dark one. After getting through the Helmstedt side of the checkpoint, you cross a white line. You're in East Germany. A seventy-five-foot watchtower is right there—and three guards with AK-47s pointed at you.

"You come to a concrete platform under bright lights with more armed guards and enormous thirty-five-ton red and white cement blocks. Don't crash them. Those roadblocks catapult across the lanes in three seconds. They will squash you like a bug.

"You get to the border control a half mile farther on. It has many lanes with even more lights. They'll take your passport and put it on a conveyor belt, and you're a nobody, nameless and homeless. No defenses. No rights.

"Finally, you make it through. You think you can breathe easy, but two miles farther on there's another checkpoint, complete with lights and those thirty-five-ton blocks and more guards with AK-47s. It's like they're giving you a final warning.

"Then you drive two or three hours and arrive at the checkpoint in Drewitz. You go through there to get into Berlin. It's like the ones you went through at Helmstedt–Marienborn, and you do it all over again.

"Only a fool would volunteer to live in a Communist country."

With his friend's vivid descriptions whirling in his head, Veniamin stared at the soldier signaling him to stay in his lane. He maneuvered back.

The cars crawled along for what seemed an interminable time. Veniamin passed the first set of bright lights and arrived at the second. It was as his friend had described, and so was his feeling of helplessness.

A border guard signaled him into an inspection station. When he parked, an immigration control officer took his passport. "Open the trunk," he ordered.

Legs shaking, Veniamin got out and went to the rear of the car. Taking a breath to steady his nerves, he put the key into the slot on the trunk.

Another officer arrived and hovered over his shoulder. He wore plain clothes. Veniamin guessed he was Stasi. When the lid to the trunk flipped open, the officer stepped forward and stared at the three suitcases. "Open that one," he ordered, pointing at the middle suitcase.

Veniamin felt his stomach turn. His temples pounded. He steadied his hands and reached down to unclasp the latches. First one, then the other. Clothes covered the metal plate above the bomb.

A feeling of surreality engulfed Veniamin. The officer reached into the luggage. He groped around. An indecipherable look crossed his face. He pulled back the clothes and stared at the metal plate. Whirling, he fixed his eyes on Veniamin.

"Take him," he barked. Immediately, the immigration control officer signaled to two guards, who came running. They grabbed Veniamin's arms.

The Stasi officer lifted the case out of the trunk and turned to the immigration control officer. "Impound the car and bring the other two bags." He turned to the guards holding Veniamin. "Take him to the interrogation room below."

Veniamin's mind went numb. He staggered between the guards. Other travelers watched, and then averted their eyes.

The guards dragged him into the building. The Stasi officer led the way down some stairs into a tunnel. They entered a room. Two chairs faced each other across a table. Otherwise, the room was bare.

The Stasi officer set the suitcase on the table. The immigration control officer placed the remaining two next to it.

Veniamin slumped into one of the chairs. The Stasi officer stood over him, hands on hips, glaring.

Veniamin's mind reeled. He breathed in short, quick gasps. His heart felt like it would pound out of his chest. He dropped his head onto the table. *What will happen to my family?*

27

Veniamin lifted his head from the table. It felt heavy. He had dozed. He wondered how long. The windowless room was painted a dreary yellow. Aside from his own chair and one across the table, there were no other furnishings. He was alone. The three suitcases had been moved, set in a neat row against the wall near the door.

His nerves felt paralyzed. The last time he had felt such fear was when he had raced away while bullets whizzed by, pursued by men who had just executed his parents. That seemed to have happened centuries ago. This time, he saw no escape.

The authorities would want to know who the customer was for the bombs. All he could tell them was they were for his cousin, a former Soviet general, but he was not even sure that Borya Yermolov was his real name.

The door opened, and the Stasi official stepped through, alone. Veniamin braced for the worst. The officer crossed to the chair on the opposite side of the table and sat down. For a time, he studied Veniamin soundlessly. Then he jerked a thumb at the suitcases against the wall. "We both know what those are, so let's not play games." He spoke in English. "I know you understand me. Don't pretend you don't. I want to know now: will the bombs work?"

Veniamin sucked in his breath. "They work." His voice sounded distant to him, like it belonged to someone else.

"How do you arm them?"

"There's a remote-control device in each suitcase. Before the bombs are placed, the frequencies between each unit and its corresponding remote are set. Then they are detonated from a safe distance."

"Do they have a fail-safe against tampering?" The man's accent sounded different than most Germans when speaking English. His tone was more guttural, with hard-sounding *h*'s and *r*'s, more like a Russian accent. He regarded Veniamin thoughtfully.

Veniamin nodded. "The switches aren't activated, but the operator could set the internal mechanisms to prevent tampering."

"Show me how to set the fail-safe and the remotes."

His face a mask of fear, all Veniamin could say was, "Here? Now?"

In response, the Stasi man retrieved one of the suitcases, laid it on the desk, and opened it.

Veniamin's eyes widened. "I—I can show you," he stuttered, "but you wouldn't want to set that now. If you did, you couldn't open it back up without exploding it."

"What about the remote-control frequencies?"

"They have to come from a list of frequencies that you know for sure are not being used. Otherwise, someone else might set it off inadvertently at the wrong time. I don't have that list. My cousin was to give it to me in Berlin."

The officer's eyes narrowed. "Your cousin?" He regarded the device warily. "Who is your cousin?"

Veniamin watched him nervously. "Borya Yermolov," he blurted. He stood and leaned across the table. "Please don't rummage around in there." Sweat ran down the sides of his face.

"I know your cousin," the man said. "My name is Klaus. He sent me to get you. Before we go, I want to know if the bombs work. Show me how to set the fail-safe, how the frequencies are entered, and how to test to the system." He rotated the open suitcase to face Veniamin. "Show me."

Veniamin stared into it and swallowed. With shaking hands, he pointed out to Klaus the etched outline on the metal sheet in the bottom half of the suitcase. "This shows the orientation of the bomb, so you know where things are."

He lifted the metal sheet. Inside, a cylindrical tube was secured from the lower left corner of the case to the top right. Veniamin gazed at it, thinking fleetingly how innocent it looked.

He indicated the tube. "Everything happens inside here to cause the explosion. At the bottom end is a triggering device. It starts the reaction in the plutonium at the top end..." He started into an explanation, but Klaus waved him off.

"Just show me how to set it up."

Veniamin trembled as he pulled the remote control from a side pocket. Then, he pointed to a timer and a console for entering data. "If you want, you have the option of using a timer instead of the remote control."

He showed Klaus the switch to set the anti-tampering safeguard and how to enter the frequencies in both the remote and the receiver on the bomb. "You can test the individual components by pressing a button on each one. If the diode lights up green, it's working. Notice that the battery has one too.

"To test the whole system, push this button." He pointed to one that was larger than the others. "When that one is green, your bomb is active. Then you push the fail-safe switch, set the metal sheet back in place, and close the lid."

Klaus studied the components. "How much damage will the bomb do?"

Veniamin heard a new note of anxiety in Klaus' tone. "It'll take out a square mile," he replied. "Total destruction, and of course, there's much wider fallout."

Klaus saw that Veniamin had set the fail-safe switch, and that the overall system diode shone green. "Is it active now?" he asked, alarmed. His face had gone deathly pale.

"What? Oh, how silly of me." Veniamin moved the fail-safe switch to off and pushed the various component buttons until all the diodes were dark. "Don't worry. Until the timer is set, or the frequencies are entered into the remote, there's no way to detonate the device."

He glanced back up to see Klaus' fearful eyes. "If you arm it and close the lid without turning off the fail-safe, you've got a problem." He laughed lightly, feeling gratified at Klaus' discomfiture. "In that case, unless you intend a suicide bombing, you'd best drop it in a deep ocean. A very deep ocean."

Klaus scowled. "Let's go."

28

Yermolov grabbed the phone as soon as Baumann handed it to him. He recognized Klaus' voice.

"I've got Veniamin. And his suitcases." Klaus stayed on the line only long enough to relay that they were returning to Berlin.

After hanging up, Yermolov leaned back in the chair behind Baumann's desk. The Stasi director sat on the other side, looking diminished. He glanced at Yermolov but said nothing.

"Klaus has Veniamin," Yermolov said, his eyes half-closed, "and the bombs." He felt a sensation that was rare for him: exultation. *Plans are coming together.* He momentarily envisioned a future with himself sitting in the office of the General Secretary of the Soviet Communist Party at the Kremlin, in Moscow. *I came so close last year.*

Those plans had been thorough, laid out well in advance, closely guarded, and precisely coordinated. *They would have succeeded but for Atcho.*

He felt no antipathy toward his nemesis—he was incapable of such emotion—he just held a deep understanding that Atcho was a constant threat to his survival. *Where is he now?*

Yermolov pulled himself out of what he recognized as a slide into muddled thinking. *Stay focused.* The current plan had been pulled together out of thin air, starting with no support. Only the physical threat he represented to Baumann, and the promise of installing him as dictator over East Germany, held it together. Even that might have been insufficient but for the imminent danger to East Berlin's existence. *Otherwise, he would already have had me put in chains and delivered to the KGB.*

His entry into Russia would be orchestrated to deliver the same shock that Berlin would feel, although in Moscow, it would be on a greater scale: he would make his triumphal entry amid apocalyptic chaos from the twin explosions. *I'll be there when Chechnya blows up.*

He foresaw two potential, immediate, and key allies on arrival. One was the chairman of the KGB, Nestor Murin. The portly official had been his case officer when Yermolov had spied in Cuba as a US Air Force lieutenant at the beginning of his career. In last year's conspiracy, Murin's support had been crucial in organizing military, intelligence, and politburo support.

He arched his eyebrows at a sudden discomfiting realization. *Murin might want to be general secretary himself.*

His second potential ally was the Supreme Commander of Soviet Forces, Generalissimus Kutuzov. Last year, Kutuzov had been the Regional Army Commanding General in the vast Siberia Oblast, the Soviet Union's largest military command. He had succeeded in coalescing the major military commanders behind Yermolov.

Somehow, neither Murin's nor Kutuzov's roles had been detected. *Either that, or Gorbachev is keeping his enemies closer. He can't fight the whole military and intelligence structure.*

In any event, following the conspiracy's defeat, Gorbachev had kept Murin in place and promoted Kutuzov to the Soviet military's most senior command. *If I can get Kutuzov's and Murin's support again, we'll continue last year's plan as if it had never been disrupted.*

"It's almost time to implement," he snapped at Baumann. He walked to the window. "Make sure your subordinates are prepared to execute. Report back when the arrest and hit squads targets are identified and they're ready to go. When we give the order, they must act forcefully and without hesitation."

The Stasi director nodded distantly.

"Notify Ranulf to get over here with the money," Yermolov continued. "Klaus and Veniamin will arrive in a few hours. I want two of your best nuclear engineers on hand to check out the bomb mechanisms and make sure they work." He gazed across Berlin's rooftops. "The world meets its destiny within forty-eight hours."

Thunderstruck, Baumann stared at Yermolov. Despite the rapid pace of events, he clearly had not fathomed that the time of reckoning was upon them.

Sensing his reticence, Yermolov glanced at the director. *He's weak, but I have no replacement.* "Director Baumann, please take your rightful seat behind the desk. I no longer need it. By the day after tomorrow, you'll occupy the desk in the general secretary's office." He moved to a small table on which several bottles of beer had been set out. "Let's drink to that."

29

Early the next morning, Atcho observed Rafael and Ivan with the other three men of their team clustered in front of a large-scale wall map of Berlin. They had pinpointed Sofia's relatives' residence and now discussed alternative routes. The atmosphere was tense. In little more than half a day, Wolfgang would read his announcement. Predicting the aftermath was impossible.

Burly sat at a desk at the end of the room talking on the telephone, his voice low. Atcho could not hear him.

Abruptly, the door opened. Sofia stepped in. Spotting Atcho, she hurried across the room. "Veniamin is in East Germany. He crossed the border a short while ago."

Atcho fixed disconcerted eyes on her. "How do you know?" Before Sofia could respond, he called across to the others. "You all need to hear this."

Rafael and his group ceased discussion and gathered around. Burly lifted a finger to indicate he had heard and would wind down his conversation.

Sofia took a deep breath. "I just came from the intel section. Remember the general said Veniamin had left his house? That was three days ago. Just before then, our listening surveillance intercepted a call from East Berlin to a number in Paris.

"The caller demanded that three items be delivered by today. The man on the Paris end of the line was nervous about traveling in East Germany. He was told that someone would escort him. He gave his license number.

"That car crossed the border in the last hour. We ran the number with Paris authorities. It belongs to Veniamin Krivkov. The timing is right. It's him."

When she finished, the room was quiet. Rafael spoke up. "Great work, but how did the intel people find that specific car? Thousands come through that checkpoint."

Sofia waved him off. "I can't go into specifics. The Brits were alerted to watch for the make and model of car and the license number. We have eyes on the East German side of the border too." She shrugged.

"Why didn't the Brits stop him?" Rafael persisted. "They could have ended the threat right there."

Sofia sighed. "They were supposed to, if they saw him. I don't know why they didn't. I can speculate that the word didn't get out soon enough, or the guy on the ground wasn't informed until too late. There are many reasons why he could have gotten through." She shrugged. "I don't have any good answers."

"The threat is real now and headed our way," Atcho broke in. "Sofia, is there any way to speed things up with Wolfgang's announcement?"

Sofia shook her head. "We have to go with the flow. The crowds in Alexanderplatz get bigger every night. They're openly hostile to East German officials, including Wolfgang, but if he tries to speed things up, he's likely to blow it. We're relying on surprise to keep the East German government from preparing counteractions, and we're counting on the crowds to provide major screening to get him out of East Berlin.

"The latest word is that the official announcement is scheduled for tomorrow, the tenth. That means tonight is the night for Wolfgang."

"Why not wait to see if the announcement will happen?" Ivan asked.

"That would seem logical, but the date of the announcement is still not published. If the East German government decides not to go through with the policy change, it will likely use military force to crush the crowds. It could be a bloodbath."

The room descended into silence. At length, Rafael broke in. "We've got another concern." He indicated Ivan and the rest of his team. "Atcho, you said the target of the bomb is our embassy, and that the impact area is a mile wide." Atcho nodded. Rafael faced Sofia. "Your family's home is within the blast area."

Sofia's eyes narrowed, but she remained stoic. "Go on."

"What do we do if the announcement doesn't happen, if Wolfgang gets cold feet, or if someone countermands his order to the guards? It could be a massacre."

Sofia regarded him without expression. "What do you recommend?"

Rafael drew a breath, reluctant to speak. He turned to his companions. Ivan and the others nodded their support. Rafael turned back to Sofia. "You want them out, no matter what?"

Sofia nodded.

"Okay, but there are some extreme risks that can't be avoided."

"Give me the worst."

"All right. Our recommendation is to take them directly to the embassy."

Sofia's reaction was immediate. "That's where the bomb will be planted!"

"True, but security at the embassy is beefed up. They don't know us. They could think we're bad guys and open fire. But, if we go to where the crowds are, the danger could be greater. What are there, six people to move?"

"Yes. My uncle and aunt, their daughter and her husband, and two children."

"Exactly," Rafael cut in. "Your uncle and aunt are elderly, and one of the kids is a little girl, a toddler. The embassy is much closer than the nearest border crossing. Keeping six people including two old-timers on canes and a toddler together in a fast-moving crowd that could turn into a mob will be tough. If things go bad..." He shook his head and left the sentence unfinished.

"There's another issue," Burly cut in. "The embassy is prohibited from assisting political escapees in East Berlin."

"We thought of that," Rafael rejoined, "but as soon as Wolfgang's announcement is made, all the rules go out the window. We'll plan on having the family close to the embassy around the time we expect the announcement. When the crowd starts getting excited, we'll make our move. Keep in mind that the embassy has a bunker belowground. Staff should move there as soon as Wolfgang starts his speech." He diverted his eyes to Sofia. "It could end up being the safest place for them."

Sofia looked drawn. She assented with a nod.

"Burly," Rafael continued, "can you arrange recognition signals with security at the embassy? Let 'em know we're the good guys." He gestured toward his group. "We're all American citizens. They shouldn't keep us out, but we don't want a shooting argument on the subject."

Burly nodded. "As you said, all the rules will be out the window. I'll see what I can do. What happens if you get stopped by the local police or, God help us, the Stasi? Do any of you speak German?"

Rafael grinned and glanced at Ivan. "We've got a handle on that."

"I speak broken German," Ivan chimed in, "but..." He reached into his pocket. "As you know, Russian is my mother language, and," he held up an ID card, "this says I'm a colonel in the KGB. That holds a lot of authority here. No one will dare cross me."

Atcho had to smile. Ivan had used the ID on their last mission into Siberia. It was as good as genuine, having been produced at the Soviet Embassy in Paris.

"I kept it as a souvenir," Ivan said with an ironic smile. He shifted his view to his compatriots. "Given the company I keep, I should have expected to use it again."

"Is that still valid?" Burly asked.

"Not really. It was fake from the start, but the expiration date is still months away. No street cop or Stasi goon is going to question me."

"I believe that," Atcho admitted. "I've seen you in action." The atmosphere had lifted to one of jocularity, as often happened when mission details were pounded out and execution was still hours away.

"Have the Soviets been informed?"

Burly shrugged. "I don't know. General Marsh elevated our concerns. It's on Washington now. We have to keep doing what we're doing. Don't forget that officially the state department is miffed at West Berlin's mayor for having lunch with Wolfgang in East Berlin. Their meeting violated the treaty, but it's a great cover story for deniability and to reduce the probability of the bad guys guessing what we're doing."

The room turned somber again. "The bombs," Sofia cut in, her voice hoarse. "What about the bombs?" All eyes shifted to her. "Veniamin is on the way with them. If my family makes it into the embassy, and that bomb goes off... We're supposed to rely on the bomb shelter?"

The mood dropped further. Atcho shifted in his chair, then turned and addressed Burly. "I'll need my pistol and a radio. One more thing: I told General Marsh that I want that major with me—Joe Horton, the one who rescued me." He saw Burly scribble a note. "I told the general that I won't accept just anybody. It has to be him." He smiled slightly. "Horton and I bonded. I know what pressure he'll stand up to." Then he turned to Sofia. "Don't worry, darling. I'll take care of the bombs."

Burly took note of the tension. "All right, folks," he said. "We're almost set. Go take care of your last preparations. We'll get together here in," he looked at his watch, "five hours to go over everything one last time. After that, we execute."

30

Burly hurried through the door into the secured room at Berlin Brigade that now functioned as the team's operations center. "I need your attention." he announced.

Every member of the group ceased activity and fixed their eyes on him. They had been joined by Major Joe Horton, the Flag Tour officer. Horton seemed perplexed as he was read into the situation. He spoke infrequently and appeared detached to the point that Atcho wondered if selecting him had been an error.

But he had checked the man's record. Horton had deployed for several tours in Vietnam, worked with the CIA, and advised the Montagnards with Special Forces.

Atcho knew little about the Montagnards, only that they were tribesmen deep in the mountains of Vietnam who fiercely opposed the Viet Cong and the North Vietnamese regime. They had been reliable allies of the US. *If Horton operated with them, he's no slouch.* Atcho refocused his attention.

"I just spoke by phone with Collins," Burly said. His narrowed eyes and pursed lips revealed the gravity of what he was about to say. "He's on his way back from Checkpoint Alpha. The news just got worse: the Stasi has Veniamin and his bombs."

Atcho felt the blood drain from his face. He maintained his composure and looked at Sofia. Whatever emotion she was experiencing, she too held it in check.

"Ordinarily, we might think this is a good thing," Burly went on. "But if, as we suspect, the Stasi is cooperating with Yermolov, then no government controls the bombs. Not even the Soviets."

Burly related that Collins had followed Veniamin into the checkpoint at Marienborn. When he saw Veniamin dragged away, he had reversed course and called.

"Why didn't Collins stop and let us, or the police know while he was following Veniamin?" Ivan asked. "He followed, the man through two countries."

"He isn't read in on what we know. He suspected what Yermolov was up to, but he had no confirmation until he saw Veniamin led away with the suitcases."

"We knew this morning that Veniamin crossed the border," Ivan intoned. "If Collins saw him with the bombs, why did he take so long to telling us?"

The room fell silent. Burly looked annoyed. "Give the guy a break. He knows he screwed up and he's trying to set things right. Because of him, we know who the players are, and now we know where Veniamin and the bombs are. Collins was in East Germany already and had to go back through that border cluster to call us. And incidentally, he'll have to go through it again and drive up the corridor to get here in time to do us any good. That's the fastest way for him to get back here now. If he comes back via the route he went, that could take a couple of days instead of several hours—we might not have a couple of days or hours, and we need him to do one more thing.

"Keep in mind that he didn't have to do any of that. He put his life and freedom at risk."

Silence. Horton was the first to speak. Before Burly's briefing, he had sat staring at the ceiling, seemingly bored, for much of the team discussion. He scraped his chair toward the table and leaned forward.

"Sir, I'm just a dumb grunt, and I'm late to this party." He looked around the room as if he might be talking out of turn. As he spoke, he seemed to intensify his Texas twang. "If you don't mind, I'd just like to reiterate—can I use that word? I sometimes use big words when I really don't know what they mean." He laughed at his own joke, and then caught himself, his face turning serious again. He cleared his throat.

Next to him, Atcho felt his own tension dissipate a bit. He remembered sitting in the back of the sedan on the east side of the Wall. There, Horton had taken immediate command. With a combination of humor and uncompromising determination, he and his driver had escorted Atcho safely back to the west side.

Atcho knew that Horton lived where the rubber met the road. He was the guy fighters wanted next to them in the foxhole. He had been an enlisted man, had risen through the ranks to sergeant first class, and then had attended Officers' Candidate School to gain his commission.

Atcho thought his antics must drive his bosses to paroxysms of frustration. But he also knew they would choose to take him into battle every time.

Horton drew a deep breath and continued. "As I understand, and I know you'll tell me if I'm wrong—y'all think this Wall is coming down in a few days, is that right?" He looked around for a response and went on without waiting for one. "And this little lady—" He gestured toward Sofia, then blushed. "Oops—no offense, ma'am. Sometimes my old-school manners get me in trouble." He laughed again in his disarming way. Sofia's eyebrows arched, but she could not help smiling. She felt her tension ease.

"Don't worry. I know some of what you've done," Horton continued, still addressing Sofia. "I sure don't want to get in a fracas with you. Did I use that word right?" He put a finger under his chin as though recapturing a thought. "As I was saying, this little lady—oops, tripped again." He waved a hand at her. "She's gonna make sure the Wall comes down by getting an East German official to make an announcement. And he's going to do that before he's supposed to, to make sure it gets done." He paused as if a thought had intruded. His eyes bored into Sofia's. "This guy's name is Wolfgang? And he's an East German politburo member, right?"

She nodded.

He grunted. "That's what I thought. Oh, well. Ripley's has lots of stuff that's hard to believe too. I don't know what a 'politburo' does anyway." He chuckled, enjoying the humor. As he spoke, he gestured wildly with his arms, his tone indicating he thought the plan ludicrous. He spoke directly to Sofia again. "Meanwhile, Miss Sofia already has a team in the East who'll swing by, get Wolfgang's family, and bring them to the site of the announcement. Did I get that right? How many people? Three?"

"That's right. Wolfgang's wife Leni and two teenagers—a boy and a girl."

Horton stared at her, open-mouthed. "Are you sh— I mean, are you kidding me?" He paused. "You're going to escape from East Berlin with teenagers?" He looked at the ceiling. "Ah, Lord. Do you know what kind of trouble teenagers can be? I got two of 'em.

"Anyway, after this politburo guy does his thing, Miss Sofia and her team will pick him up. Then they'll all walk together with the crowds? Out of East Berlin? Do you really think you can pull that off?" His tone became deliberate. He did not smile. "Ma'am?"

Next to him, Atcho stirred uneasily. Sofia looked dumbfounded. She began a retort. "Major Horton, if you don't want..."

"Now don't get your britches in a twist," he interrupted with his most charming smile. "I'm just trying to make sure I understand things."

"What's your point?" Burly broke in.

"Just checking to make sure I got a handle on everything," Horton said genially. "You want some of our Flag Tour teams to be part of this. I want to know what I'd be getting us into. Can I go on?"

Burly nodded impatiently.

"So, while Miss Sofia..." He winked at her. "While she's doing all of that..." He laid the Texan accent on thick now and pointed at Ivan. "This here Russian is going to play like a KGB agent, and these old guys from the *lost* Bay of Pigs..." The five men glared at him. He glanced at them. "No offense, fellas. I just wanna be accurate."

He addressed the full group again. "These guys are going to round up two old people on canes, a young couple, and two kids, including a toddler." As he spoke, his eyes swept the ceiling as if searching for sanity. "Then they're going to wander through the crowds in East Berlin to the US Embassy, which isn't allowed to help them, and where, by the way, we think a nuclear bomb will be planted."

He faced Juan directly and indicated Rafael. "Are you really going to take your team in to do that? Do you trust him to get you in and back out?" He pointed at Ivan. "Are you going to put your lives in this guy's hands? He might just want to turn you all over to the Russkies."

Ivan eyed Horton with an implacable expression. Juan locked his eyes on Horton, but otherwise showed no emotion. He turned slowly to Fernando and Pepe, who returned his gaze soundlessly. Then he shifted his view to Rafael, and then Ivan. Finally, he rested his eyes back on Horton. "We'll take our chances."

Horton studied him momentarily. "OK." He turned to Atcho. "And then there's you." He chuckled as he said it. "You get yourself kidnapped by a guy you thought you'd killed once and put in prison once, and I had to put my mission at risk to save your scrawny ass from wandering the streets—on the wrong side of the Wall? Isn't that about the size of it?"

A narrow grin crossed Atcho's lips. "You have a unique way of viewing things, Major Horton." He shrugged. "You summarized my entire existence in one sentence, but you are essentially correct."

Horton studied him. "I want to make sure I got a sharp picture." He paused a moment longer. "Now, you're going after this General Yermolov—I haven't got clear in my head yet if he's American or Russian—but he's bad. And you're going after him and three nuclear bombs, which, we just learned, are in Stasi hands. Oh, yeah—and we don't know who controls the Stasi."

He shook his head as if in total disbelief. "If you don't succeed," he waved his hand dismissively at the others, "it doesn't matter what they do, because it's all going up in a mushroom cloud anyway. That's the plan?"

Atcho held his steady gaze. "You have a good grasp of the situation."

Horton put his hands on the table in front of Atcho and stooped so that their eyeballs were even. "And you want to use my teams to help in all of this?"

Atcho met Horton's eyes. He leaned forward. "I'll get Yermolov and the bombs, Major," he said, his voice low and matter-of-fact. "With you, or without you."

Horton stared a moment longer. "OK." He abruptly sat down, stretched his legs, twiddled his thumbs, and stared up at the ceiling.

The room remained quiet. At last, Burly cleared his throat. "Major Horton, are you done? Do you have any more questions?"

Horton looked up as if startled. All eyes were on him. "Oh—sorry, sir." He scrambled back up to his feet. "Like I told you before, I'm just a dumb grunt. Sometimes I forget decorum." He winked. "See, there's one of them big words again. I hope I used it right." He looked around at the impassive faces and laughed. "I'm in."

Burly wiped the back of his neck. Atcho breathed a sigh of relief. Sofia remained unmoving.

"You S-O-B," Rafael called across the room. He grinned. Even Ivan subdued an involuntary smile, while Juan, Fernando, and Pepe nudged each other and chuckled.

"Major Horton." Atcho's commanding voice broke through the murmur. Immediately, the room fell silent again. "Do you mind telling me what your decision is based on?"

Horton stared at him. He tilted his head to the left and then to the right as if tabulating possible reactions to his response. Then he met Atcho's gaze once more. "Hell, sir." He appeared about to reveal a deep, dark secret. "I got a family too. I had to make sure you all would stick to your guns before I committed myself and my teammates. Besides," the corners of his eyes creased with the beginnings of a grin, "we already know we can't turn you loose by yourself in East Berlin. People get killed that way."

He laughed. Then his tone changed to one of deadly seriousness. "The way I got things figured, we're gonna need five of our Flag Tour cars to support those missions. That means ten members of our intel teams all at once."

"Why so many?" Burly asked.

Horton counted off on his fingers as he replied. "One to get Sofia joined up with her team in the East. Two more to get Rafael and his team over there. One to get Atcho and me in there. And one decoy. Don't forget, each car already has two people."

"Why the decoy?"

"Every time one of our cars goes through, the Stasi are on them like flies on buttermilk. One thing we got going for us is that the crowds are so thick these days. Nobody can hardly follow nobody. Does that make sense? You get my meaning, though.

"I'd suggest we send one car through carrying only the normal crew. That one will draw the chase cars. Then we send three more in fairly quick order. We'd need to stagger them, so they don't go through all at once. We don't usually send that many teams out in such a short time, so they won't be expecting them.

"Our guys will still have to assume they're being followed and take evasive action. The people in the back seats will have to duck down. It'll be cramped, but it should work. The border guards don't hardly know how to act these days, so I don't expect them to stop us. Atcho and I will bring up the rear."

While he talked, the phone rang. Burly answered it. "It's General Marsh," he said after a moment. "He wants an update."

"Tell him I'll come brief him now," Sofia said, preparing to leave.

"I'll let him know," Burly said. He looked around the room into the eyes of each team member. "Folks," he said. "It's time."

Horton had remained standing. "One thing before we head out," he said. "I know you know this, Miss Sofia." He caught her eye, and he did not smile. He looked around at the others. "This ain't a cakewalk. Four years ago, Major Arthur Nicholson, a great soldier doing my job, got shot and killed by the Soviets. It's serious business."

31

Early that evening, Wolfgang Sacher looked about the great auditorium and fought to maintain composure. On his way to his daily press briefings in the early evenings, he had seen the crowds in the streets grow. Each day they became more restless, more openly hostile to East German officials—to him. For the past three days, he had been jeered when he reassured people that their government would soon deliver a brighter future.

Each time he had made those optimistic comments, he had recited the East German Social Unity Party line, which he knew to be a lie. Even with the recent loosening of policy, the calcified Communist system could never deliver the quality of life enjoyed by Western countries. But Wolfgang knew that an irrevocable change was near. In a few hours, he would strike a blow that could culminate in the death of the tyrannical government. Delivering that blow, however, was fraught with risk.

He looked past the gaggle of Western press to the main entrance of the hall. Sofia's appearance there would signal that his family was under her protection. Then, he could proceed with his announcement.

As he shifted attention to other parts of the room, his view rested again on the Western press, and particularly on Tom Brokaw, the sonorous newsman of legendary fame. He scoffed. *How difficult to try to be both digni-fied and eager to ask the ultimate question at the same time. These reporters try to be different in exactly the same way, but they rarely know what is really happening.*

He scanned the door again and caught himself. *Still several hours to go. You can't appear overly interested in what's happening at the door.* His nerves felt stretched, taut. He must keep a normal appearance. He had to be congenial while bloviating about the dubious achievements of the East German socialist state.

He glanced one more time around the auditorium, steeling himself against his urge to look at the entrance. During a moment when no one paid him much attention, he reached into his jacket pocket and removed an envelope. He inserted it among the papers on his desk. Then he tapped the microphone. "We are ready to begin today's press conference. I'll make a few general remarks, and then take your questions." The crowd quieted. He leaned back in his chair and launched into his routine defense of the Communist system. "No one is unemployed, hungry, or homeless in East Germany..."

* * *

Ranulf entered Baumann's office carrying two duffle bags. His eyes widened when he saw the desk with three identical suitcases setting on it. A nervous little man he did not know sat in a chair in front of the desk. The man bore an uncanny resemblance to Yermolov, but was older, thinner, and bent, with no hint of arrogance. *Veniamin Krivkov.*

Klaus occupied a chair near him. Director Baumann sat across the desk.

Yermolov stared out the window. He turned only long enough to see Ranulf enter. "We're all gathered. Director Baumann, will the nuclear engineers be joining us?"

Baumann shifted in his seat. "They'll be here momentarily. Is there anything you need from them aside from checking the systems?"

Yermolov shook his head. He turned to Veniamin. "I trust you completely, Cousin," he said with slight sarcasm, "but everyone makes mistakes." He watched Ranulf cross the room and place the duffle bags on the desk. "Is that the money?"

Ranulf nodded. "Three million dollars in one bag, and two million in the other, all in old, untraceable bills. I used every bit of pressure I could and paid a lot of bribes to get it. This could be our only chance. I got as much as I could." He shifted uneasily under Yermolov's intense scrutiny.

A knock on the door interrupted their conversation. Two men entered. One carried a small satchel. Baumann stood. "These are the engineers."

Yermolov reverted to the cordial personality of General Paul Clary. ""Please come in. I'm sorry I don't have time for formalities. We need your assessment of these devices." He indicated the three suitcases and introduced Veniamin. "This man designed and built them. We need to know if they will work."

Visibly nervous, the engineers approached the desk.

Veniamin looked equally unsettled. He opened the first case, and then the other two. Without fanfare, he went through the same explanations he had given Klaus. As he showed the engineers the various digital displays and data entry screens, their eyes grew wide with horror, but they made no comment. When he flipped the switch to arm the fail-safe system and run through the testing cycles, their fear was palpable.

They asked a few questions about the structure of the elements inside the rocket-shaped tube, and then watched as Veniamin, with painstaking care, disarmed the one he had used to illustrate. Then he walked through the process on the remaining two bombs. When finished, he closed all three suitcases. "You can test communications between any suitcase and its corresponding remote by pressing this button." He showed them. "When this diode lights up, that tells you they are communicating but will not set the bomb off. To do that, you must press this button." He pointed it out. "You press it to arm it, hold it five seconds, and then press it down farther to detonate. I designed it that way to prevent accidental detonation."

Fear grew to incredulous terror on the engineers' faces. They stood, speechless. The one who carried the satchel removed an instrument from it. He moved forward with obvious hesitancy. "Do you have a port where I can measure radioactivity?"

Reluctantly, Veniamin re-opened one of the suitcases. He lifted off the metal plate and exposed the port.

The engineer studied the tube and its attachments. He opened the port and held the instrument close to it. A clicking noise sounded.

"Well?" Yermolov inquired, still in the genial personality of Paul Clary.

The two engineers glanced at each other and then at Yermolov. They nodded. The senior engineer spoke up. "The radiation levels are correct. As Mr. Veniamin indicated, all three of these devices are viable nuclear bombs."

Klaus watched in fascination. Only after Veniamin had closed the suitcase did he speak up. "I've seen the procedure four times, and it's been identical each time. I'm confident I can arm them and get to a safe place to blow them." His eyes gleamed. "This will work. I've scouted the target. I can have the bomb placed within an hour."

The room fell quiet. Yermolov looked pleased. He resumed staring out the window. "I might be imagining it," he mused after a moment, "but the crowds seem larger than ever tonight. They're filling the street, they're denser, and they're headed toward Alexanderplatz." He turned away and addressed Baumann. "Are you hearing anything out of the ordinary?"

The Stasi director shook his head. "The crowds have grown every day. There are rumors of announcements, but no confirmations. Just people building up silly hopes."

Yermolov thought that over. "Are your men ready to move?"

Before responding, Baumann looked to Ranulf, who nodded. "They're assigned to their targets. They can act on a moment's notice."

"Excellent!" Yermolov seemed genuinely pleased. He turned back to the window.

One of the nuclear engineers interrupted his thoughts. "Sir, do you still need us?"

Yermolov smiled. "No, go ahead, and thank you." As soon as the door had closed behind them, his demeanor transformed back to that of the cold, calculating renegade Soviet general. He snapped at Baumann. "Don't let them out of the building. We can't allow them to tell anyone what they saw here. Retire them permanently."

He saw a look of shock cross Veniamin's face. "What did you think," he demanded, "that we were playing children's games last year? How about now? You brought me three bombs. Those engineers are a tiny fraction of the carnage everyone will witness."

He shifted his glare to Baumann, who picked up the phone and placed a call. The director spoke in low tones and hung up. "It's handled. They won't be a problem."

Yermolov continued to watch through the window. The crowds grew. Suddenly, he whirled, startling the gathered men. "Gentlemen," he barked, "it's time to implement.

"Ranulf, move your squads into position.

"Klaus, plant the first bomb. Do it now. Let me know when it's done.

"Veniamin, help him set the remote-control frequency.

"Director Baumann, make reservations for Klaus and me to Moscow on the next diplomatic flight."

All four men stared, shocked. Klaus' eyes gleamed. He opened one of the suitcases and laid it flat on the desk. Veniamin sat in a stupor.

Klaus grabbed him by the collar. "Let's go," he snarled. "I don't have much time." He jerked Veniamin to the desk. "Walk me through it. Make sure I do it right."

His violent action spurred the others. Ranulf stood and lumbered out the door. Baumann appeared in shock but turned to his telephone.

"Veniamin." Yermolov's voice carried such force that everyone stopped to see what he would do. "Arm that bomb but disable the timing device. Set the frequencies and the fail-safe. Give me the remote. I'll keep it with the others."

Klaus scrutinized him. "If you want bombs set in Chechnya or anywhere else," he said evenly, "you'll make sure I'm safe."

Yermolov spoke calmly. "You have nothing to worry about. Come back when you're done." *You're my dog on a leash.*

Thirty minutes later, Klaus left Baumann's office. He carried one suitcase.

* * *

Klaus chortled when the American Embassy came into view. He drove one of the Stasi Wartburgs. Crowds flowed past him, ebullient, celebratory. Pedestrians' bright eyes over big smiles and laughter created an air of expectancy. Their mood and demeanor were strange anomalies in East

Berlin. But when they saw Klaus' Stasi vehicle, their expressions turned grim and openly contemptuous.

Klaus smirked. *You fools have no clue what's coming your way.* He pictured the suitcase in the trunk of the car and grinned with satisfaction. *A lot of infidels will pay the price for their sins tonight. The Great Satan will feel the wrath of Allah.*

He parked across the sidewalk in front of the embassy. A line of Polizei kept watch on both sides of the street. He stood at the edge of the passing crowd, legs apart, arms crossed, his face a mask of agitated authority.

Behind him, the US Marine embassy guards noticed his arrival. A Stasi car stationed near their entrance was not unusual. Given the crowds, that one should be there now was not surprising.

They had been alerted that strange events would likely take place that evening, including that a family could be seeking asylum—and that they might have to beat a hasty retreat into the fortified bunker in the basement. The group of asylum seekers would include a set of grandparents, a married couple, and two small children. If the family avoided the Stasi and Polizei successfully, the Marines were to assist their entry. The family would be escorted by an armed patrol of five men, all US citizens.

Klaus stayed in position for fifteen minutes. Suddenly, he yelled into the crowd at an imagined infraction and started to run. He stopped, whirled around to the line of Polizei on his side of the street, and shouted, "I'll be back for the car." He watched for acknowledgment. A dour-faced policeman nodded. Klaus took off running again toward the edge of the crowd, as if in pursuit. As soon as he was out of sight of the embassy, he ducked away from the crowd and into shadows.

He emerged a few minutes later looking like any other East German. He joined in the laughter and revelry of the crowds heading toward Alexanderplatz.

32

An olive-drab sedan belonging to the US Flag Tour group of intelligence specialists crossed into East Berlin at Checkpoint Charlie. Immediately, two Stasi Wartburgs pulled in behind it. The sedan maneuvered through a growing throng of pedestrians, making for a particular street usually open for fast driving. The Stasi vehicles stayed close behind.

As soon as Checkpoint Charlie fell out of sight, the major in the passenger seat radioed in. "Clear," he said. "We looked for more Stasi vehicles when we came through. None seen."

"Thanks for the help," Burly radioed back.

A short interval later, three more olive-drab sedans drove through Checkpoint Charlie, staggered apart by a few minutes. The first took Sofia to rejoin her team. The second and third dropped Rafael's team at secluded spots in back alleys. Then they drove away for other missions.

Rafael's teammates split up and walked through an area called Kreuzberg. They converged on an enormous apartment building roughly a mile north of the embassy on the west side of East Berlin. On arrival, they checked in with Rafael by radio and dispersed along a line near the front. The building was set mere yards from the eastern side of the Wall. The men stayed in the gathering shadows until dusk

The house where then ten-year-old Sofia and her father had last seen her cousin no longer existed. The original barbed wire installed that awful day had been replaced by a brick wall.

That structure had been eventually swapped for inner and outer concrete walls with the wide, brightly lit kill zone between them, augmented with the requisite towers, machine guns, and horizontal tubular tops. Houses in the immediate vicinity had been bulldozed, including Sofia's relatives' former abode. The family now lived in a crowded apartment building fifty meters from where their home had been.

Rafael's plan called for Ivan to go into the apartment and guide the family out. With his broken German and KGB identity card, he had the greatest chance of succeeding. Because Sofia's uncle held no position of note and would not be watched closely, Ivan expected no resistance. The uncle was an old man who had done his best to survive and raise a family within the shadow of the Wall. Freedom had never been more than a short distance away.

Rafael checked each man at his position. The last was Juan, on the right flank, crouched in shadows.

"Here we are again," Rafael said quietly.

Juan was big and dark-skinned. "Here we are again," he agreed. He was a thoughtful man who spoke little. He heaved a sigh. "Maybe someday the world won't need men like us. I'd like to stay home and enjoy my grand-children."

Rafael chuckled. The last mission he and his teammates had been on together was the CIA operation in the Belgian Congo in 1963. Their objective had been to rescue missionary children held by rebels opposing a new government. The country had gained independence from Belgium. The rebels had believed the new regime to be a puppet.

Civil war had raged with many participants but little international attention. Fidel Castro had sent forces allied with the rebels. One hundred and twenty-five Bay of Pigs veterans, including the members of Rafael's team, had volunteered to oppose them.

"Do you still worry about that little girl you carried out of the Congo?"

Juan took his time to respond. "I do. She was so scared. She was only four. I had one arm around her, and she hung on to me for five miles. We rode in the back of a truck over rough roads. Bullets struck within inches of our heads. We heard the *k-chinks,* and she jerked every time. We took fire all the way, and the smell of gunpowder hung in the air. I fired full bore on a machine gun with my other arm for the whole ride. We finally reached the rally point and I set her down. One of the missionaries took her away. I never saw her again." His voice broke. "To this day, I worry about ... well, maybe she lost her hearing. I had nightmares about it."

Rafael peered at Juan's face. In the darkness he saw only his outline. He clapped Juan's shoulder. "Well, brother," he said softly, "we made it out. They did too."

Juan laughed quietly. "Yeah, we all made it out, and here we are again." He scanned in the direction of his teammates. "Lord help us getting through this one."

* * *

While Rafael spoke with Juan, Ivan scrutinized the apartment building, a gray monstrosity stretching along the street and into the sky. It was offset from an identical one behind it, and another behind that one, and then another. A forbidding black-and-white likeness of recently deposed General Secretary Erich Honecker stared down at passersby. *They haven't had time to put the new guy up.*

Dim amber lights glowed from some apartments. Ivan recalled a similar sense of oppression in Moscow, with its huge buildings and few visible people.

He had had no chance to reconnoiter the building. Sofia had provided him with engineering drawings, which he had studied until he knew by heart the routes to her uncle's apartment.

The plan had anticipated crowds moving toward Alexanderplatz, but there were few pedestrians at the moment. Without large numbers of people, he would be more likely to stand out. The building was set back from the street a good fifty yards, which meant a large expanse to cross.

He keyed his microphone. "On my way." Then he stepped out into the street. He crossed in shadows and entered the building.

From far down the hall, a lone man walked toward him. The man glanced up and made eye contact. He moved closer to the wall as if to give Ivan a wide berth.

Can't let him tell anyone about a strange man in the building. Ivan stopped in the middle of the dim, narrow hall with its peeling walls. He deliberately watched the man, who approached cautiously. Ivan pulled his KGB ID from his pocket.

The man passed.

Ivan turned to watch him go by. "Halt!" he commanded in German.

The man froze. He turned.

Ivan shoved the KGB credentials in the man's face.

He stiffened.

"Come with me. Now. Do you understand?"

Terrified, the man nodded vigorously.

"Show me to this apartment." He gave the unit number.

"I—I don't know those people."

"I didn't ask if you did," Ivan growled. "Show me to the apartment."

Three minutes later, Ivan and his hapless escort stood in front of the door. "Stay here," Ivan ordered. The man's shoulders drooped. Ivan knocked.

The door creaked open. Ivan pushed against it and shoved his escort inside. He peered around the dimly lit room. A bent old man stared at him. Next to him, a trembling old woman wrung her hands in silence. Across the room, a younger couple sat close to each other, their eyes fearful. Two children played on the floor, oblivious to the drama unfolding before them. All wore overcoats, as if prepared to go for a walk.

A door stood open to Ivan's left. "In there," he growled to his escort. "Don't cause trouble or you'll be visiting Stasi headquarters." The man's eyes grew wide. He stumbled into the next room.

Ivan closed the door and turned to face the family. None of them had yet spoken. He put an index finger to his lips, stepped into the center of the room, and motioned for them to gather around. "Listen, and don't speak," he said, indicating with his eyes the man in the other room. He saw their worried expressions. His voice softened. "It'll be all right. I took my family out of Russia last year."

An unmistakable sense of relief showed on the adult faces, followed by restrained hope. Ivan cautioned them again. "Do exactly as I say. What are you taking with you?"

The old man looked about the room at the tattered couch and the tiny area that served as a kitchen with a two-burner stove. "There's nothing worth taking."

"You're going to a better life," Ivan said gently. "Do you know where the American Embassy is?" The adults nodded in unison. "That's where we're going. Here's how."

Four minutes later, the old man and his wife shuffled out the front entrance on canes with their grandchildren. They turned south and proceeded at a slow pace.

Rafael saw them. Having been alerted by radio, he dispatched Fernando and Pepe to keep them in sight.

Five minutes later, Ivan exited with the younger couple and the terrified escort. "Go the opposite direction," Ivan told the man. "Keep walking for thirty minutes. Speak to no one. Stay away for two hours, unless..." His voice sharpened. He indicated the young couple. "...unless you'd like what's coming to them."

The man bowed twice. "Thank you. Thank you." He tried to shake Ivan's hand, but Ivan pulled it out of reach.

"Go. Before I change my mind."

The man hurried away.

Across the street, Rafael and Juan watched Ivan's group start off. They followed at a distance. Several minutes later, the two halves of the team merged and proceeded toward the embassy. As they progressed, the sparse pedestrian traffic thickened. Rafael pulled his team into a tighter moving perimeter around Sofia's relatives.

* * *

After being dropped off, Sofia and her group headed for Wolfgang's neighborhood, two miles east of Rafael's team. They formed a loose protective circle around the home. It was an old, two-story structure with the semblance of a yard closed in by a collapsing fence.

Sofia recalled visiting this house as a young girl with her father. Wolfgang had grown up in it and had been allowed to live there because of his "dedication to the Party."

At roughly the same time that Ivan entered the apartment building, Jeff eased up next to Sofia. Nightfall was only minutes away.

Sofia sensed Jeff's approach. She remained still in the shadows that obscured her.

"We've got company," he murmured. "Three on the north side. Fanning out."

"Have they seen us?"

"No. We got here first."

"Okay then. Spread the word. Weapons free. Take whatever action required to protect family members. After that, follow the plan. Do you understand?"

"Each member will engage the nearest target."

"Good. I'll enter the house in ten minutes and stay inside for five. Make sure that when I bring the family out, there's no longer a threat."

"Roger. Any word on whether the crowds will materialize in this area?"

Sofia looked around. The foot traffic was not thick, but for this time of evening, it had to be heavier than usual. People generally headed in the same direction, toward Alexanderplatz. "This far out, we might not see large numbers, but if we take out the bad guys, this crowd should serve our purposes. Make sure—"

"I know," Jeff interrupted. "Don't disturb the populace and hide the bodies out of sight. We've got this."

"Try to keep them breathing. We don't need an international incident, regardless of how things go."

"Roger."

Ten minutes later, Jeff called an all-clear. "They'll sleep a while, and no one will see them anytime soon."

"Keep 'em warm."

"No worries. Go do your thing. By the way, these guys are thugs. They had bad intentions."

"Understood. Get word to Burly. Other teams might be after other targets." Sofia took a deep breath. "Going in." A group of pedestrians walked by her hiding place. After they passed, she stepped out quietly, approaching the house thirty feet behind them.

Suddenly, a dark figure sprang from the shadows directly into her path, landing in a half crouch. She could make out only a silhouette of a man, but light reflected from something in his hand. A knife or a gun.

She jumped high in the air and brought her trailing leg around in a wide sweep. It connected with her assailant's chin, sending him sprawling. The weapon flew from his hand—after she felt a hot stab of pain in her right arm and heard a muffled explosion.

The man rolled. He scrambled for his weapon.

Sofia struck again, bringing her right leg down on the back of his neck. He lay still. She looked around. No one else was there.

Sofia keyed her radio. "I found another one," she informed Jeff between rapid breaths. "He's asleep. Get over here and make sure he stays that way."

"Roger."

"Listen, he did me some damage. I'll have to check it while inside." She felt warm blood running down her arm inside her sleeve. "I don't think it's serious, but I might have to put something on it to stop the bleeding."

"Let us know if you need help."

Sofia continued to the front door of Wolfgang's house. The pain in her shoulder increased in intensity, and stiffness spread into her arm. Her lungs heaved. She paused to let her breathing return to normal.

Her apprehension mounted as she knocked on the door. She had met Wolfgang's wife, Leni, once before, but had no basis on which to gauge her personality or temperament under pressure.

Leni opened the door. A matronly woman with a face creased with anxiety, she beckoned Sofia inside. "We're ready."

"Good. We have to move, but first, I need help. There were men outside watching the house."

Sofia suddenly felt lightheaded and fought down a wave of nausea. "Get someone in here," she called into her microphone. "I might not make it."

"Nina's on the way," Jeff replied.

Leni took in the sight of Sofia's wounded arm, now with blood seeping through her coat. Alarm spread over her face.

"We don't have much time," Sofia gasped. "One of my team members is coming to help. I need anything that can soak up blood. If you have another coat or a jacket, I could use it."

A light knock rapped on the front door. After a nod from Sofia, Leni answered it. Nina entered and rushed to Sofia's side. "I'll need a blanket and a coat," she told Leni.

The old lady bustled away. Nina helped Sofia into a dimly lit living room. A man, a woman, and two teenagers stared at them. *Wolfgang's family.* Their eyes shifted to Sofia's wound.

"Don't worry," Sofia said between strained gasps. "We leave in five minutes."

"We'll leave when we're ready," Nina said in a firm voice. She lifted Sofia's arm over her head. "Lie down. We've got to stop the bleeding and prevent shock." She helped Sofia to a sofa and removed a small first-aid kit from her coat.

Leni hurried into the living room carrying the items Nina had requested. "I'm sorry, this is all I have."

"We'll make it do," Nina said. She took off Sofia's jacket and examined her wound. It was clean, but the bullet had nicked an artery. "Help me," she told Leni. "Put the blanket over her." While Leni complied, Nina applied a tourniquet above the wound and bandaged it. "That should hold until we get where we're going." Then she pulled out a syringe. "Brace yourself," she said. "This is going to hurt, but then the pain will ease."

Ashen-faced, Sofia grabbed Nina's arm. "I've got to get inside that press briefing."

"We'll cross that bridge later. Right now, we've got to keep you alive."

Leni interrupted. "Those men..."

"Don't think about them," Nina said. "They won't bother us, but when they're discovered missing, others might come. We have to hurry." She looked at the anxious faces across the room. "Those men are killers," she said sternly. "Let's move." She waited long enough for the painkiller to take effect, and then radioed Jeff.

"Coming out. Sofia will need help."

* * *

Oily, the little man running Ranulf's hit squads, was puzzled. He had sent out the teams, all of them reliable as long as he was able to pay them at the end of their missions. He could hardly call them professional. They were thugs, but each one knew his own capabilities and limitations.

Chief among their limitations was that they, like anyone else attempting to escape over the Wall, risked being shot. That threat kept them within the regime's bounds. Aside from that sobering prospect, they were free to come and go as they chose. A few of their ilk had escaped to the West through Czechoslovakia and Hungary, but most of them avoided the risk of catching a bullet. Sufficient numbers of weak and harmless people on whom to prey lived in East Germany.

Oily's thugs were apolitical, no threat to the regime. Their primary advantage was that they would undertake messy operations that official East Berliners must steer clear of or risk the wrath of either the international community or their patron, the Soviet Union.

Oily coordinated their assignments. Although cunning, he had no interest in politics or the "big picture." On this evening, he and his ruffians were about to realize the biggest payoff they had ever known. His perception of tonight's activities was that the list of high-profile targets seemed inordinately long, which led to thoughts of a coup in progress. The idea that tonight might be the end of the Wall had never crossed his mind. It had been there all his life. He had observed the growing anti-government crowds as an oddity, expecting that any day the military would mount a crackdown.

All of his teams had checked in via radio except one. That one had been dispatched to a neighborhood two miles northwest of Alexanderplatz. The leader had reported the team in position, but he had then missed two scheduled radio checks.

Oily was not concerned. Wolfgang Sacher and his family lived in the house in question. Being the mouthpiece of the party, Wolfgang's face was familiar to East Germans. He was known to be congenial, but lately he was reviled because of his steadfastness to the Party line at a time when people had become hostile to it. That said, Wolfgang neither made nor enforced policy, and thus was regarded as harmless.

On Oily's list, Wolfgang had been marked merely as a person to watch,

not one to arrest or execute. Still, the fact that the squad had missed scheduled reports rankled him. He sent another man to check on the situation.

While Baumann worked at his desk, Yermolov stood by the window
studying the swelling crowds. He had estimated that he had at least
another day or two to prepare before events precipitated an opening in the
Wall. Now, he was not so sure.

From his vantage point seven floors up, he watched the throngs stream
by. Only days ago, they had spread loosely along the street, passing in quiet,
tentative groups, glancing warily at the officers posted along their routes.
Now, their numbers had enlarged such that the crowd was endless. It took
up the entire length and breadth of the street, and the people were boister-
ous, openly contemptuous of authority. Officers on other main avenues
through East Berlin reported similarly growing crowds.

Yermolov turned on the television. The screen showed the inside of the
hall where the Communist Party spokesman, Wolfgang Sacher, held daily
court.

He watched Wolfgang with contempt. Just a few days ago, the crowds
had listened in scornful silence as he told them of the great achievements
of the Communist state. Today, they booed him. Wolfgang took the derision
with good-natured smiles.

His briefings had become nightly affairs, lapped up by the Western
press. Sometimes he lectured, apparently for no other reason than that he
could. Other times, he took questions and used his responses as opportuni-
ties for further dull exposition.

Yermolov turned down the volume and his thoughts returned to what
Baumann had told him. As the last hard-liner from the Honecker regime,
Baumann had been isolated from many senior meetings. As such, highest
level information was increasingly withheld from him.

Nevertheless, the director had picked up a rumor that the government
was considering loosening travel restrictions. As Baumann understood the
proposal, the intent was to install a policy that let East Germans travel back
and forth more easily while putting a check on emigration. The politburo

hoped that by satisfying some of the people's demands, discontent would be curbed, protests would die away, and East Germany could get about its normal business.

Yermolov had scoffed at the notion. *Better to kill those ideas. Give the people a little, and they want a lot.* "Any idea when the government plans to announce the changes in travel policy?"

Baumann breathed deeply. "They're not certain they'll do it, but it could be as early as tomorrow, November tenth."

"Well, then," Yermolov replied tersely. "We'll be ready."

33

The fifth Flag Tour sedan rumbled through Checkpoint Charlie. The guardhouse was lit up against the darkness. From his seat in the back-passenger side, Atcho glanced out the window to his right. His eyes locked on the Checkpoint Charlie Museum. He had visited it in the days prior to the first attempt to kidnap him and had studied in amazement the dizzying array of souvenirs and photos of people and the devices they had used in desperate escapes from East Berlin.

One photo showed an East German soldier jumping over barbed wire stretched across a sidewalk. His rifle was still on his back as he vaulted, and pedestrians in the background watched in shock. He was the first escapee, having taken his desperate opportunity two days after the first barbed wire was laid down. His action had precipitated the order in East Germany to shoot to kill those attempting escape.

On display was a mini-Austin used in a getaway. A live person had been sewn inside the front passenger seat and was driven through the check-point, there to be released. The escape succeeded.

Another display was a sports car with the windshield removed. The driver had raced under the barrier arms in a daring rescue of his fiancée. That successful attempt had precipitated the large concrete barriers set at odd angles on the eastern side of the checkpoint to channel traffic.

Atcho could scarcely believe the numbers. Over five thousand people had risked death to escape to the West. One hundred and forty had paid the ultimate penalty, and that was just along the Wall in Berlin. Countless others had lost their lives in other places along the East–West border. He shook his head now, recalling his own desperate struggle and that of his beloved Cuba. *Maybe it ends for East Berlin tonight.*

The sedan pulled through the East German side of the crossing. "I've never seen so many people on the streets at night, and this is November," Horton said from the front. He tapped his watch. "November ninth, to be exact. See, I got this watch that tells me the date." He laughed again. As he did, he looked out the back window. "We didn't get away clean," he said. "We got company." He turned to his driver. "Chad, be careful weaving through all these people, but as soon as you see an empty side street, lose these guys."

He turned back to Atcho. "That's Stasi following us. They drive those underpowered Wartburgs. Outrunning them is usually easy, but these crowds will slow us down."

Atcho barely paid attention. He looked out at the large numbers of people, all seemingly bound for the same location. "All these people going to Alexanderplatz," he muttered. "We'll soon see if they're serious."

"If they're not serious, they're going to an awful lot of trouble," Horton rejoined. "Some have started heading to the Brandenburg Gate."

Chad suddenly turned onto a narrow street. It was heavily populated, but the center of it was largely empty. He accelerated a bit. They traveled a distance with the Stasi Wartburg hugging close behind. The farther they went on the street, the thinner the crowds became.

Watching out the window, Atcho was again struck again by the stark differences between West and East Berlin. While West Berlin's houses and apartment buildings were neat and orderly and generally exhibited prosperity, East Berlin's were crumbling structures, crowded together and dimly lit. They bespoke human suffering.

Suddenly, Chad mashed the accelerator. They had come to a section that was thinly populated. Ahead of them was a stretch of straight road.

Horton turned, grinning. "I know where Chad's headed. This road will curve about a mile up. We should be able to outrun that Wartburg's headlights. When we get around the curve, we'll take a quick right. They'll antic-ipate that and radio ahead. With any luck, we'll get to the first turnoff before their buddies, so they won't know if we took the turn or not. Once we make that right, there are a lot more turns we can make."

He became serious. "One thing we got to worry about is their big cargo trucks. They like to sit and watch for us, and if they see us, they try to ram us. They killed a couple of Frenchmen that way. You know, members of the French army doing the same thing we do."

Atcho shook his head. There was nothing to see out the windows at this point, no crowds, no buildings, just the dark of night. The road was poorly paved and maintained, so the ride was rough. The sedan bumped along, and the lights of the Wartburg became pinpoints left far behind.

Chad found the road he was looking for and turned so sharply that Atcho was thrown to the other side of the car. Horton seemed not to have noticed. "We're going to circle south and see if we can find the place where you were—incarcerated?" He chuckled. "Big words again.

"If you see anything that looks familiar, holler at me, sir. We did a map recon, and there ain't but a couple of places it could be. This side of the wall, within a mile of the Mövenpick? Still in ruins? Most of those places have at least been bulldozed."

"Got it, Major. Would you do me a favor and stop calling me sir?"

Horton chuckled. "I'll do my best, sir, if that's what ya really want. Old habits don't break easy."

The car rolled into a built-up area. It headed south until it came within sight of the Wall and the back end of the crowds headed toward Alexan-derplatz.

"I got a hunch I know the place where you were held," Horton called back. Minutes later, he directed Chad to turn down a narrow street. It looked like it dead-ended after a short distance, but then an alley took off to the right. "I think the East Berlin government forgot this area," Horton said. "It's not very big, and it's hidden by the buildup around it. But there's some ruins back here—a good-sized building that looks like it could have been the headquarters of some bureaucracy way back when."

The car pulled around another corner. There, through the windshield, Atcho saw the building. "That's it."

"Are you certain, sir? You know things can look different at night."

"It *is* night, Major Horton. That's it. And look—it's vacant."

Horton directed the driver to halt near the front doors. Atcho started to get out and Horton swiveled in his seat. He grinned at Atcho. "Strictly speaking, sir," he chuckled in his disarming way, "this ain't really legal, you bein' here. In East Berlin. I know it, the generals know it, and you ain't really here, ya know what I'm saying?" He laughed and tossed his head back. "Then again, I was never in Cambodia. The point is, General Marsh took me aside, and he told me, 'You make sure our noses stay clean.' He told me, 'Don't forget, Atcho's a wanted man inside East Berlin.'

"So, you stay put. I'll go in and check things out. Chad'll stay here with you." He shifted his attention to the driver. "You keep your eyes peeled, and you let me know ASAP if anything's happening."

Atcho sat back, annoyed but also amused. He could not help thinking about the lighthearted manner in which Horton approached his mission juxtaposed against the enormity of events that could transpire within a few hours. Or what failure could mean.

He watched Horton climb the four low stairs and try the main door. It opened, and after a quick look around, he entered.

Atcho stirred impatiently. Two minutes later, he got out of the vehicle and went inside the building.

Horton was just coming out of the room across the foyer where Atcho had been imprisoned. His eyes narrowed when he saw Atcho. For the first time, his tone was stern. "Sir, I told you—"

"Never mind what you told me," Atcho retorted. "You never went to Cambodia, and I never got out of the car."

Horton leaned slightly forward, eyes steely and unblinking. Then the corners of his eyelids creased, and he grinned. "Fair enough." He looked around. "Nobody's been in here since you escaped." He made the assertion without qualification. "We ain't gonna find nothin' here. They vamoosed." He crossed to the dust-covered desk in the foyer and picked up the phone. "Line's dead." He looked at Atcho expectantly. "So, what's next, Cap'n?"

Before Atcho could reply, Horton pointed through the door of the small room where Atcho had been held. Clearly visible was the table against the inside wall, the chair still sitting on top of it, and the cot wedged against the opposite wall below the broken window. "That's some contraption you built there. Did you really escape on that thing?" He opened his eyes wide and dropped his jaw in mock wonder. "Well, go-o-olly!"

Atcho laughed involuntarily. "Go with the plan, Major. You know the next stop."

Horton peered at him. "You sure that's what you want to do, sir?"

Atcho grunted. "How do you get away with so much BS?"

"It's a talent, sir," Horton responded, his face deadpan. "Don't knock it. It's the only one I got. Now tell me again. Are you sure that's what you're gonna do?"

Atcho fixed his gaze on him. "I don't see any other way."

Suddenly Horton stared toward the main entrance. He crossed to the door and stood listening. Atcho followed. From the narrow alley, they heard the rumble of a large truck coming their way.

"Let's go," Horton yelled, "unless you want to get mashed flatter'n a pancake." They ran to the car and dove in, slamming the doors behind them. Chad had already repositioned the sedan facing the direction they had come.

A large Soviet Army cargo truck burst from the alley and barreled straight toward them. The courtyard had little room to maneuver.

Chad gunned his engine. The sedan's tires spun, throwing up clouds of dust, and the car lurched toward the truck. The vehicles accelerated toward each other. At the last second, Chad jerked the wheel to the right and the car flew past the truck. Metal scraped metal with a shrieking sound amid a shower of sparks as the sedan's trunk nicked the rear of the other vehicle.

The truck braked hard, coming to a sliding halt just in front of the building's entrance. Its driver ground the gears into reverse and the truck began backing toward them, picking up speed as it came.

The car was at too sharp an angle to steer into the alley, so Chad stomped on the accelerator, sped past it, then mashed on the brakes and spun the car in the opposite direction.

The truck closed the distance. Chad slammed the accelerator again and cleared the alley's entrance by inches.

With a resounding crash, the back end of the truck plowed into a corner building. Its engine stalled.

When Chad reached the far end of the alley, he slowed enough to make a sharp left turn, and then roared down the empty street.

Horton, who had been crouched down in the front seat, raised his head. "Tell me again where you want to go, sir." His eyes and mouth crinkled into his unique grin.

"How did they know where we were?" Atcho asked. He had been flung sprawling across the back seat and pulled himself to a sitting position. Streams of perspiration ran from his forehead.

"The Stasi makes sure everyone in East Germany knows how to spot our cars and call in reports. All those informants keep them in the loop. Let's hope that truck's the only one that got the word before we got out of there." Horton turned to get his bearings, and then swung around again to face Atcho. "Are you still bound and determined to go to Stasi headquarters? As you just saw, they'll more than likely know when you arrive."

Atcho nodded without saying a word.

Horton rolled his eyes and stared at the ceiling. "All right, sir. It's your neck."

* * *

Oily heard back from the man he had sent to check on his team at Wolfgang Sacher's house. All four members had been drugged, bound, gagged, and hidden. One reported being attacked. The only conclusion Oily could reach was that, whatever Ranulf's intentions and those of his superiors, they had been found out. Someone had discovered them and had taken counteractions.

He placed an agitated call to Ranulf. No response. Oily dropped the receiver and radioed each team. "We've got interference."

* * *

Burly met Collins in the foyer of the Berlin Brigade headquarters building. "Thanks for coming. I'm glad you made it through the corridor safely."

Collins raised his eyebrows. "That was no picnic. I won't do it again. I got back to Berlin early this morning."

"We need you at Wolfgang Sacher's press briefing. It's already started."

"I'm on my way now. If it's like his other briefings, I won't miss much."

"You're taking a camera crew?"

"That's the plan, per your request. Jakes contracted one of the best local freelancers. Doing video reports is new to me. I spent the day practicing."

Burly's brow furrowed. "You'll do fine. Get to the hall quickly. When the briefing terminates, go straight to Checkpoint Charlie. Report everything you see as it happens. Make your first report as soon as you hear anything significant. One other thing." He reached over and placed a meaty paw on Collins' shoulder. "Make sure your cameraman has lots of strong batteries and a powerful broadcast capability."

Collins studied him. "Maybe I should just go straight to the checkpoint now."

"No. You'll want to be in the press briefing. Believe me." He reached into his pocket. "Take this." He handed Burly a two-way radio. "Don't change the frequency. It connects directly to me. Use extreme discretion, but I need to know what's going on at ground level in real time. It's a secure channel. Do you understand?"

Collins almost gaped but checked himself. He looked at the radio. It was easy to operate. He nodded without speaking.

"I need it back when this is all over. And you and I never had this conversation."

Collins exhaled slowly. "Got it."

Forty-five minutes later, having navigated Checkpoint Charlie and the streets choked with pedestrians headed toward the Brandenburg Gate and Alexanderplatz, Collins and his cameraman entered the auditorium. Wolfgang was already into his good-natured defense of all things socialist. As on prior nights, he said nothing of international import, yet the air was electric with expectancy.

Collins recalled that, sixteen months earlier, Bruce Springsteen had entertained a huge audience at a concert in East Berlin. He had sung "Badlands." East Germans had reveled in the notion that "The Boss" had written the lyrics for and about them. The rock star had delivered a short speech calling for the Wall to be torn down, and then sang "Chimes of Freedom."

The concert had been a sensation. Millions in East Germany who could not attend had watched it on blurry black-and-white television screens.

Analysts credited the concert with providing the spark that led to East German citizens' demands for liberty. However, Collins wondered if one detail had been overlooked: of three hundred thousand attendees, only half had paid for a ticket. The rest had pushed through the barriers, forcing their way into the open-air concert. *Did they learn a lesson that night? Will they apply it here soon?*

He kept an eye on Wolfgang. At one point, the spokesman looked toward the entrance, and, for a second, he appeared unnerved. The look vanished as quickly as it appeared. Collins would have dismissed the observation but for the unusual urgency of his conversation with Burly. *Something will happen tonight.* He saw Wolfgang glance again at the entrance.

Apparently not seeing what he looked for, Wolfgang shuffled through some documents. He found a single sheet of paper and leaned back to scan it.

He glanced at the entrance again. When he did, his face looked stricken. He brought his chair upright. Then he seemed to catch himself and returned to his casual position. He scanned the paper again.

Collins glanced at the door to see what had generated Wolfgang's furtive response. Sofia had just entered and appeared not to have noticed whatever had generated Wolfgang's reaction, but she also looked pale. Another woman was with her. They stood along the wall to one side of the press audience. Collins watched them a moment longer. Sofia's weak appearance concerned him.

At that moment, Wolfgang's voice sounded over the speaker system. "I have a press release from the politburo. I want to read it just as I have received it."

34

Yermolov paced. An awful feeling of the turning of the tide gripped him. He could not shake it. The crowds in the street below Baumann's office window continued to grow, heading toward Brandenburg Gate or Alexanderplatz.

Baumann sat at his desk, shuffling papers. Yermolov glowered at him in disgust. *He's trying to look busy.*

In the corner, the television remained tuned to Wolfgang Sacher's press briefing, the volume turned down. Yermolov had watched the briefing intermittently. He saw Wolfgang study a document. Moments later, the Party spokesman leaned into the microphone.

Yermolov turned up the volume. He caught the transmission in midsentence. "...I want to read it just as I have received it." Wolfgang waved the paper.

"We want... through a number of changes, including the travel law, to create the chance, the sovereign decision of the citizens to travel wherever they want. We are naturally concerned that the possibilities of this travel regulation—it's still not in effect. It's only a draft."

Yermolov's eyes narrowed. A knot formed in the middle of his forehead. Baumann moved closer.

Wolfgang looked at the paper and once again read aloud, mumbling through a statement that was almost unintelligible. Then, his voice rang clear.

"... we have decided today to implement a regulation that allows every citizen of the German Democratic Republic to leave our country through any of the border crossings."

Yermolov gripped the side of the desk. His knuckles turned white and his mouth pressed into a thin line. A vein pulsed above the bridge of his nose.

Just then, the office door opened. Klaus entered. "The bomb is in place..."

Yermolov waved him away and turned back to the television. Having expected a more enthusiastic response, Klaus stared at the back of Yermolov's head and then at the television.

Sounds of men and women shouting questions came over the speaker. Wolfgang scratched his head and scanned his document again. "You see, comrades, I was informed," he paused to put on his glasses, "that such an announcement had been distributed earlier today. You should have it already." He read from it again.

"Applications for travel abroad by private individuals can now be made without the previously existing requirements of demonstrating a need to travel or proving familial relationships."

He continued reading through a paragraph filled with bureaucratic jargon.

"When does the new policy go into effect?" a reporter yelled.

Wolfgang scanned his paper again. "That comes into effect, according to my information, immediately, without delay." He put the paper down on his desk and shuffled his documents.

In Baumann's office, Yermolov gasped. "This can't happen."

He heard a reporter's shouted question. "Does it apply to West Berlin? You only mentioned the rest of West Germany."

The press conference was suddenly quiet. Yermolov could feel the pall that must be hanging over the hall.

Wolfgang shrugged, picked up the paper and read from it again.

"Permanent exit can take place via all border crossings from East Germany to West Germany and West Berlin, respectively."

In Baumann's office, all was quiet. Then, from outside the window, they heard a thunderous celebration. The protesters had received the news. He went to look.

For as far as he could see down the dimly lit street, people cheered. They waved flashlights, jumped in the air, and hugged each other. The ones close to the Stasi headquarters turned and almost as a body "shot the finger." The message was clear. *We no longer fear you.*

The office door flew open and Ranulf rushed in, his eyes desperate. He had run up the stairs. Perspiration streamed over his heavy forehead and down his shirt. "Did you hear the news?" he huffed, breathless. "This building is almost empty. A lot of officers went out to manage the crowd, but there's not even a skeleton crew down there."

All eyes turned to Yermolov. He circled to the desk chair, sat down, and leaned his head on the tips of his forefingers. "This will accelerate our plan, not stop it."

He looked down, thinking out loud. "Veniamin, set the frequencies in the other remote controls and bombs. Director Baumann, you should—"

He looked up as he spoke and found three sets of eyes staring strangely at him. Realization dawned as he looked around the office. "Where's Veniamin?" His mind raced, trying to recall when he had last seen his cousin. He stood, furious. "Where is Veniamin?" He enunciated each word.

"He was here when that broadcast started," Baumann volunteered. "Maybe he went to the restroom." He turned to Ranulf. "Go check."

Ranulf returned less than a minute later. He shook his head.

Yermolov grimaced. "We continue with the plan. Director Baumann, arrest the general secretary. Ranulf, order your teams to execute. Klaus, can you set the frequencies and arm those bombs?" Klaus nodded. "Do it."

Klaus grinned, clearly enjoying the prospect. He moved the duffle bags containing the money to the floor on the far side of the desk. Then he made room to open wide the two remaining suitcases.

Ranulf took note.

Baumann scrutinized Yermolov's face. "What are you going to do?"

"As I said, we continue the plan. You're about to become the general secretary of the party. You will arrest or execute resistors. Deploy the army for crowd control. Order them to shoot anyone who resists. When Klaus finishes, we'll head for the airport."

Baumann gestured toward Klaus working on the bombs. "Why do that here?"

"We might not have a chance later," Yermolov said impatiently. "Do you have any more questions?"

"The diplomatic flight is not scheduled until tomorrow morning."

"Order them to be ready in an hour. National emergency." Yermolov peered at Baumann, sensing a reluctance that could be fatal. "Keep in mind to stay a mile away from the US Embassy. I have all three remotes. I'll detonate the first one when we're in the air. Make sure my directives are followed."

Baumann held Yermolov's steady gaze. *He's reminding me that he can detonate from anywhere. Those bombs are guns aimed at my head.* He broke from Yermolov's glare and hurried through the door. Ranulf followed.

* * *

Oily slammed the phone down. He had received no response to repeated calls to Ranulf. He picked up the radio to call his squads. The phone rang. Ranulf.

"What's going on?" Oily demanded. "Have you seen the crowds? They're saying the government announced open borders with the entire West. Effective immediately."

"That's right. The situation is chaotic."

"What happens now? Do we have jobs tomorrow?"

"I don't know. The Stasi headquarters is almost empty. Officers are running for cover." Ranulf liked talking with Oily. Not only did he exercise authority over him, but he could also feel intellectually superior.

"What happens now?"

"Meet me at my office as quickly as you can. I have an idea. Call off the teams. Tell them they'll get paid for tonight."

"I'll be there in an hour." Oily hung up and keyed the radio. "Abort, abort, abort."

* * *

Wolfgang's heart pounded. From outside the hall, he heard the roar of a million people cheering louder than at any sports event. He watched the throng of journalists and television newsmen. Some still yelled questions at him. Others jostled out the door. *They all want the same scoop.*

A politburo member nudged him and put his mouth close to Wolfgang's ear. "You let loose the hounds. God help us—if there is one." He pulled back and leaned in again. "Watch your back."

Wolfgang gulped involuntarily and scanned the crowd. He had lost sight of Sofia and momentarily felt the rise of panic. Then he spotted her to the left of the entrance, right where she should be. They made eye contact without acknowledgment and Wolfgang settled in to wait for the rush at the door to abate.

After a few minutes, he headed toward the gaggle of reporters still shoving their way out. Some tried to press more questions, but he waved them away. "Please, I'm very tired." A few continued to push, but most were intent on contacting their news organizations.

From the corner of his eye, Wolfgang saw Sofia take up a position near his left elbow. She looked to be in pain. Another woman stayed close to her side. He kept moving toward the exit. Finally, he emerged at the top of the stairs. The bright lights of television cameras shone in his eyes. He shielded them with his hand.

The vast square was packed with people squeezed together as far as he could see. When the ones at the front saw him, they shouted his name. Then a mighty roar surged through the crowd: "Sacher! Sacher! Sacher!"

Wolfgang waved and descended the stairs. His security detail chief met him there. "Sir, where are you going?"

Wolfgang returned the questioning gaze. He put a hand on the man's shoulder. "Go home," he said. "Take care of your family. Send your men home."

The security chief gave him a grim look. "Sir, I have orders. You must come with me."

Sofia nudged his elbow. "This way, Wolfgang."

He stared back and forth between Sofia and the security chief, noticing how pale Sofia had become. He suddenly felt lightheaded.

* * *

Through the fog of pain and weakness from her wound, Sofia saw that the enormity of what Wolfgang had just done bore down on him. He seemed to be fading as fast as she was. Her arm hung in an improvised sling, and the pain was still excruciating. She focused her attention on Wolfgang. "Stay with me."

The security man tried to step between them. He held a pistol to Wolfgang's waist. "You will come with me. Now."

Sofia tried to push against the man, but she was too weak. Nina appeared from the other side and shoved her pistol in the man's side.

"If he dies, you die," Nina whispered in his ear. "You won't win any medals for making a martyr out of Herr Sacher and causing a riot." She jabbed him. "Put your gun in Sacher's hand and back away, out of sight."

The man grimaced, then smirked. "Don't think I'm here alone. You won't live out the night." He handed the pistol to Wolfgang, who took it as though handling an open bowl of acid. Then the man backed into the crowd and disappeared.

Nina took the pistol. "Your family is around the corner of the building. Our team is with them. We have to go."

Wolfgang wiped a hand across his brow. He was frantic. "I forgot to order the border guards to stand down. Without instruction, they will stop people from going through the checkpoints." He shook his head, clearly dismayed. "The journalists were eager to get out and report. Issuing the instruction slipped my mind. The politburo could disavow the press release or order the guards to shoot the protesters."

Sofia inhaled against the pain. She looked around at the crowd, already moving toward the border crossings, then she put her good hand to the side of Wolfgang's head and brought it close to hers. "Listen to me." Her voice faded. She gritted her teeth. "The genie is out of the bottle," she rasped. "You can't put it back. There's no way the border guards can hold this crowd now. Your family is waiting. Put these on." She handed him a slouch hat and a scarf. "Cover your chin. You won't be as recognizable."

Wolfgang scrutinized Sofia up and down. Realizing how weak she was, he swung around to Nina. "What's wrong with her?"

"She was shot. She's lost blood and she's in a lot of pain. Help me move her through the crowd until we link up with our team."

Wolfgang snapped to. "Of course. What do you want me to do?"

"Get out in front and make a way for us. Tell people she's sick. Get us to the corner of the building where your family is."

Wolfgang jostled through the crowd, doing his best to keep his face hidden. Some people recognized him and tried to thank him. He accepted but kept pushing.

Ten minutes later, all three were within Jeff's security perimeter. Wolfgang rejoined his family. While Nina briefed Jeff on what had transpired, Sofia leaned against her, fighting to remain conscious.

Jeff pulled the team together. "I'm taking charge. We have other threats." He explained to them what had happened with Wolfgang's security chief. "Nina will give you a description of the man. Stay close together. Rotate helping Sofia. Make sure she has plenty of water. Keep your eyes peeled."

"I'm on my feet," Sofia interrupted.

"Right. No heroics today. We still have a ways to go. Time to move."

They headed toward Checkpoint Charlie.

35

Collins could scarcely believe his ears. *Did Wolfgang Sacher just open the borders?* The move had been hoped for, even expected, but no one had anticipated it being done in such an offhand manner, without pomp or the presence of the highest officials from East and West seeking time in front of a camera. But for this history-changing announcement, the press conference would have been another obscure affair, notable only for the size of the international press corps.

As soon as journalists started shouting questions at Wolfgang, Collins grabbed his cameraman by the shoulder and headed for the exit. Just inside and to the left, he caught a glimpse of Sofia standing behind several reporters, quiet and unobtrusive. He started to say something to her, but she gave him a look with an almost imperceptible shake of her head that warned him off. He passed her by.

Outside, word spread fast: small groups whooped as they heard the news, and those cries quickly spread to the full crowd thundering its will. Only a few minutes before, the square had been filled with the low hum of angry, mocking, demanding people. Now, the howls of joyful incredulity traveled at lightning pace and suddenly, as one, the multitude raised its voice in a pulsating cry of victory.

Collins looked around, assessing the best spot for his news hit. Other crews had already set up, some with platforms. He grabbed his cameraman by the shoulder again and they moved to a position in front of the hall by the bottom step.

"This is historic news," Collins began, an unmistakable edge of thrill in his voice. "East Germany just opened the Berlin Wall. I'm standing in front of the hall where the announcement was made just moments ago in a routine press briefing. As you can see, it's an announcement the people of Berlin and of Germany itself have hoped for, indeed demanded." He signaled the cameraman to pan over the crowd, which thundered its celebration. "Is this a permanent opening that will finally bring freedom to this country? We don't know yet, but this historic event is surely one sign that things are going in the direction that everyone here hopes for. I'll interview people on the street and report as events occur."

As he signed off, Collins felt the radio vibrate. He pulled it from his pocket and fumbled with it.

"Don't talk," Burly said. "Listen carefully. Your on-camera broadcast came through. Looking good. Wolfgang will come out shortly. He didn't order the border guards to stand down. We'll have to fix that. His family is waiting around the corner." He told Collins where to find them. "Go there. Don't speak to them. I need you to break trail ahead of them, all the way to Checkpoint Charlie. Do man-on-the-street interviews to get people to let you pass. Do whatever it takes but keep moving.

"Get our party to the front of the crowd. When you're there, stay to your right. Keep your lights and camera aimed at the border guards. One more thing: keep pressing the message that the East German government announced the right of its citizens to travel anywhere without interference. Effective immediately. Key the radio twice if understood."

Incredulous, Collins keyed the radio. Just then, he spotted Wolfgang slowly picking his way through the press to the bottom of the stairs. The crowd broke into a deafening chant. "Sacher! Sacher! Sacher!"

Collins gasped involuntarily—Sofia was at Wolfgang's elbow. His eyes widened as he realized what had just occurred. He recalled Sofia's strange rendezvous in the café near Checkpoint Charlie. *I thought that odd for a woman whose husband had just been kidnapped.* The pieces of the mental puzzle fell into place. "Oh, my Lord," he whispered ecstatically to no one. He whirled on his cameraman. "Let's go." They pushed their way toward the place Burly had directed.

* * *

Burly radioed Rafael. "How's your progress?"

"Slow. Crowds celebrating here. Assuming announcement made."

"Affirmative. How long to destination?"

"Twenty minutes at current pace."

"Double up. Have new mission for Ivan."

"Wilco. Out."

Rafael surveyed his small group. They had made steady progress despite being surrounded by a growing number of people hurrying in the same direction. At one point, the crowd burst into spontaneous cheers and stepped up its pace. They jostled the family as they passed. Rafael drew his team into a tight barrier around them.

The grandparents and the children were tiring. The father had carried the smallest child most of the way, but when he had struggled under the weight, his wife had taken over. Now, she labored to keep up.

Rafael offered to carry the toddler, but the huge cheering crowd frightened the girl. She wanted nothing to do with strangers. The father took over again.

The old couple trudged more and more slowly on their canes, each footstep more painful. Rafael pulled his group together. "We have to step up the pace."

"How much farther?" Juan asked.

"About five blocks. Here's what we're going to do." He gave terse instructions. When he had finished speaking, Juan loaded the grandfather over a shoulder. Fernando picked up the grandmother, who wrapped her arms around his neck. The older child climbed onto Pepe's back. Rafael took the screaming toddler and did his best to quiet her.

"Go out ahead," he told Ivan. "Scout the front of the embassy. Do whatever you have to do to get us in there."

After what seemed an interminable time, Rafael saw the embassy.

Streaming sweat, the group paused before it came into full view. Juan, Fernando, and Pepe set down their charges. Rafael returned the toddler to her father. Then they proceeded.

Rafael surveyed the area around the main entrance. US Marines had formed a defensive half circle in front of it. The crowd overflowed the street. Police and Stasi officers formed a line to keep people away from the entrance.

Ivan stood at the rear of a Stasi Wartburg. He conversed with an officer, their voices raised. Suddenly, he reached into his pocket and pulled out his identification card. He showed it to the Stasi officer and the man snapped to attention.

Ivan spotted Rafael and motioned the group forward. A policeman stepped ahead of them. Ivan called to him angrily and started his way. The policeman looked to the Stasi officer, his eyes questioning. The officer hesitated, and then nodded.

Ivan reached Rafael. "Keep walking," he said, his voice low. "This Stasi guy doesn't know what to do. He might not stay that way for long."

"What did you tell him?"

"That this family is to be allowed entry on philanthropic grounds by order of the Kremlin. I threatened to expose him for crimes against humanity and suggested he should join those headed across the border."

Rafael looked around. "He might have taken your advice. He's disappeared."

The group continued their slow way to the entrance. The Marines formed a line and showed them the way. When they were safely inside, Rafael called Burly on a secure telephone line. "We're in."

"Put Ivan on."

Ivan took the receiver. "Get to Checkpoint Charlie," Burly said. "Fast. Look for Sofia and Collins." He told Ivan where to look. "Call when you get there. If you arrive before them, keep an eye out. FYI, Sofia is wounded. It's bad."

Ivan inhaled sharply. Checkpoint Charlie was not far, but the hordes would slow progress. He looked out the entrance. The Stasi Wartburg was still parked there.

He strode to the Stasi officer nearest the vehicle. "Where's the driver of that car?" The officer shrugged and turned away.

Ivan whirled him around by the shoulder and jammed the KGB ID in his face. "You just became my driver," he snarled. "Get me to Checkpoint Charlie. Do it now."

Twenty minutes later, with sirens blaring, the Wartburg arrived at the east side of Checkpoint Charlie. People already pressed the border guards to let them through.

The sentries milled about, unsure what to do. They held their automatic rifles ready and continued to block the remaining few yards to freedom.

Ivan radioed Burly. "I'm here. No sign of the others. What now?"

"Wait."

* * *

Veniamin had seen no way out. From the time Klaus had confiscated his passport at Marienborn, he had felt like an animal led to slaughter, smelling blood. The feeling had intensified in Baumann's office when he came face-to-face with Cousin Yermolov.

It had grown yet again when he had shown the inner workings of the bombs to the two nuclear engineers who were then "permanently retired." And finally, he had felt abject terror when Yermolov admonished him about the "carnage everyone will see."

He had watched with fascination as Yermolov fixed his attention on Wolfgang Sacher's speech. Veniamin's knowledge of German was insufficient to follow what was said, but he recognized that something momentous was occurring.

Then Baumann had become engrossed, and Ranulf had moved closer. When Klaus entered to announce that he had placed the bomb, and Yermolov had waved him away, Veniamin thought he might have found his moment.

All attention except his had fixed on the television. The other men had clustered around it, their backs to Veniamin. He had moved closer to the door. They were oblivious to him. He had opened it and stepped through. They had still paid him no heed.

Leaving the door ajar, he had crept to the staircase. Slowly, he had descended. He reached the next level and had increased his speed.

He had hurried down another flight. A door had burst open and a man had rushed toward him. Frantic, Veniamin had looked for a direction to run, but there was none. He had lifted his hand reflexively toward the man, although he had no idea what to say. The man had hurried past without looking at him and climbed the stairs.

Veniamin had leaned against the wall and wiped sweat from his forehead. He had glanced up the stairwell. No sign of pursuit.

He had almost run down the remaining flights, amazed by how few people seemed to be in the building. To see the dreaded Stasi headquarters almost deserted had itself been unnerving.

He reached the last set of stairs. An orderly lounged at the reception desk watching the crowds go by. Veniamin heard a huge cheer erupt.

Now he ran past the orderly and out the door and raced the few remaining yards to the crowd. He slowed to match its pace, allowing it to engulf him. He had never been to Berlin and did not know where these people would go. As he walked, he cast furtive glances over his shoulder. The policemen lining the streets worried him, but they looked befuddled, seemingly uncertain of what to do.

As he struggled through the crowd, he found a few people who spoke broken French and English, and he came to understand the reason for the cheering. "Has the border opened yet?"

"We don't know," came the reply. "We're going to Checkpoint Charlie to find out."

Veniamin now faced a dilemma: he had never been given back his passport after it had been taken at the border. He had no way to prove his French citizenship. If the crossing points were open and he got through, he could make his way to the French Consulate and report a lost passport. If, on the other hand, the checkpoints remained closed, he would face difficulty beyond what he cared to imagine. *Especially if my cousin detonates...* He killed the thought.

After he had trudged some distance, he became less concerned that someone might recognize him. He moved closer to the edge of the crowd, where he was able to make faster progress by moving around slower people. He began to feel the effects of travel, lack of sleep, extreme stress, and walking for miles without food or water. For the last few days, he had been spurred by adrenaline. Now, he felt dangerously close to exhaustion.

Finally, he turned onto Friedrichstrasse. There in front of him stood the iconic US guard shack at Checkpoint Charlie.

The contrast in lights between East and West Berlin at the crossing was stark. They shone brighter by magnitudes on the western side. The effect was heightened by spotlights aimed into East Berlin. As Veniamin drew closer, he saw that they belonged to camera crews videotaping every detail. Behind them in West Berlin, huge numbers of people waited, calling their deafening welcome to long-lost families and friends.

As Veniamin drew closer, he saw the Wall and its floodlit kill zones stretching away in either direction, interrupted only by Checkpoint Charlie. The border guards still stood on the east side, their weapons poised. Strangely, even as they held their fingers over the triggers, their interactions with the crowd seemed almost friendly.

Veniamin took up a position as close to the checkpoint as he dared. Mindful that Cousin Yermolov might be looking for him, he remained in shadows.

As soon as Ranulf hung up from speaking with Oily, he made his way the short distance to the main building at Stasi headquarters. He felt unsettled that there were so few officers around. Then again, he reasoned, the crowds required as many men as could be spared. The demonstration five days ago had been estimated at over a million people. This one was even larger.

He went to the rear of the building, where he started up a back stairwell. This was a private entry and exit for the director and senior staff. He did not expect to see anyone there, particularly not at this time of night or under the current circumstances. He climbed to the seventh floor to a small vestibule outside a door that was hidden inside the office. He stood listening to voices that came from inside. They were muted by the thick walls. *Yermolov and Klaus. Good thing they don't know about this private entrance.* He stood still, hoping to catch their conversation. Finally, he heard Yermolov ask, "Are you sure you've checked every component?"

"Yes. They're armed for remote triggering. The frequencies are set, and the fail-safe systems are on."

Yermolov clapped his hands together. "Well then, let's be on our way. You take one. I'll take the other. I have all three remotes."

Ranulf heard them leave the office through its main entrance at the far end of the hall. They waited there for an elevator. When the doors closed, Ranulf slipped through the hidden door into the office.

He could hardly believe his luck. The two duffle bags of money were still on the floor by the desk. He threw them over his shoulders and headed back into the vestibule, carefully closing the door behind him.

As he started down the stairs, the elevator arrived on the landing. He heard Klaus exclaim, "I can't believe we almost forgot five million dollars."

His heart thumping, Ranulf hurried down the stairs, careful to make no sound. As he reached the ground floor, gunfire exploded somewhere on the floors above him. He stopped to listen. He heard more shots and took off again at a faster pace. On the ground floor, he headed out the back exit and wound his way through darkness to his office.

* * *

Klaus rushed into Baumann's office. Seconds later, he burst back out to the elevator landing. "They're gone," he cried furiously. "The duffle bags. All the money. Gone."

Yermolov regarded him with amused calm. "How could they be gone? Only you and I were in the office."

"They're gone. Who was there when I moved the bags behind the desk?"

"You, me, Baumann, and Ranulf. But they haven't been back since they left." He watched the fury on Klaus' face. "Too late to do anything now. The plane should be ready for departure. Don't worry. As the Americans say, that's chump change. When we succeed, we'll have plenty of money. Let's go."

Klaus scowled but said no more. They got back on the elevator and headed down.

* * *

Johann Baumann sat in his overstuffed chair in the living room of his home. He had never referred to it as "his" house, understanding that he lived there at the will of the East German state and that it could be taken away any time that political winds changed. *And they're a cyclone now,* he thought ruefully.

The house was comfortable, even sumptuous, by Eastern Bloc standards. He had visited the West often enough to know what luxury looked like, although it was not an element he craved in his life. He approached eighty-two years of age. In his lifetime, he had participated in what some considered the worst of times for East Germany. For him, they had been the best of times.

Who does that fool Yermolov think he is, ordering me around? He smirked reflectively and took a sip of cognac from a crystal glass. *I helped organize Stalin's purges and transform this country into a Marxist-Leninist state. Yermolov never would have survived under Papa Joe. I flourished.*

He swirled his drink and chuckled, thinking about a conversation he had just had with KGB Chairman Nestor Murin a few minutes ago. Then, he laughed out loud, imagining Yermolov's surprise when Murin met his plane in Moscow. *We'll see who delivers a bullet personally to whom.* He laughed again. *With any luck, he'll press those remotes and blow that part of the world into oblivion.*

He mused that Yermolov's mistake lay in misperceiving the calamity taking place in East Germany, and in misjudging Baumann himself. *The West grew faster than we did. We had fewer and fewer options. He thought I was weak, that I hadn't recognized the change in history's course.*

He sneered. *I'm old, but that doesn't mean I'm dead.* He felt again the fury that had first come over him when Yermolov had usurped his authority. *And what the hell happened in that press conference tonight? No one saw that coming.*

He took his cognac and headed to a set of stairs hidden behind a wooden panel. At the bottom, he flipped on some lights and turned to a massive steel door. It was the entrance to his underground bomb shelter, hardened against a nuclear attack. He entered and then pushed a button, activating electric motors that clanked and pulled the door closed behind him with only a slight *thump*.

He looked around at the interior. It was comfortable and fully stocked with plenty of the provisions needed to survive for an extended time. "Take your best shot, Yermolov," he chuckled. "Who cares if the bombs go off or the Wall comes down." He looked around his bunker again. "It's time for me to disappear to my ranch in Argentina and live off my Swiss bank account. But tonight, I sleep."

* * *

Sofia watched through bleary eyes and a haze of pain as Collins worked the crowds. She felt increasing respect for him: he treated each person politely and interviewed them while walking alongside them. When he had finished with one person or group, he thanked them and then moved on to interview the next set of excited East Berliners. In this way, he kept progressing toward Checkpoint Charlie at a pace that eventually would put him, the team, and Wolfgang's family at the front of the crowd.

Nina kept a periodic check on Sofia's arm. The bleeding had stopped, but she dared not remove the tourniquet. Sofia's complexion had turned pallid and she was dangerously lightheaded. Her gait became staggered, one foot dragging after the other. Team members rotated to support her weight and prevent her being jostled by people in the crowd. Wolfgang positioned himself on her right. His family hardly spoke among themselves, their eyes fearful. They stayed close together within the moving perimeter.

Jeff and the remaining team kept wary eyes on the throng. So far, no hostile activity had been spotted. He hoped that Wolfgang's security chief had given up the pursuit. Of concern, however, was that the cameraman's bright lights marked their position within the crowd.

Careful to be friendly, in keeping with the surrounding mood, the team jostled people when needed to keep up with Collins. All around them, people ambled along good-naturedly, smiling, laughing, clapping each other on the shoulders, and reacting with goodwill to inadvertent jarring from others around them. Occasionally, those who were less patient groused, but they seemed to be few and far between.

Despite her weakened state, Sofia worried about Atcho. He had the most critical part in this overall mission. Failure would be horrific. She shuddered at visions of flaming mushroom clouds consuming this crowd of over a million souls.

Collins forged ahead as best he could, keeping his cameraman and Sofia's team in tow while taking care not to annoy those he interviewed. Fortunately, most people spoke with him eagerly. His main question, broadcast live, went along the lines of, "What do you think of tonight's events?"

The responses were as varied as the people walking with him. The common theme was incredulity.

"It's hard to believe it's really happening."

"We have family on the other side waiting for us. We haven't seen them in twenty-eight years. I was a small child then."

"I'm in my mid-twenties. The Wall has been there my entire life. I want to see it crumble."

"Can you believe we can cross into West Berlin or any place in Germany, and no soldiers will point machine guns at us, or shoot us, or send hungry dogs after us? I'm speechless."

At last, Collins saw Checkpoint Charlie ahead in the distance. His pulse raced. He turned toward Sofia, and his heart dropped. She looked as though she might pass out. Her teammates continued their diligent care. There was nothing he could do to help her; he walked gamely on.

Finally, two hours after setting out from Alexanderplatz, the entire group approached within a hundred feet of the last obstacles separating them from West Berlin. There in front of the barriers stood the line of border guards and Stasi officers with automatic weapons pointed toward the crowd. People had ceased forward movement. Instead they milled about in front of the checkpoint. Jeff paused the team.

* * *

Collins continued forward and stopped short of the line of border guards. Behind him, the jubilant tone of the crowd changed to one of frustration, then anger as they encountered the sentries blocking further advance.

"You can't stop us," a woman shouted. "We have the right to unimpeded travel."

Others joined in with epithets, demanding passage. An unearthly quiet settled in. It rolled back along the streets to the crowd's furthest extremities, more than a million people waiting in breathless silence to know their common destiny.

The soldiers felt the tension. In response, they set their jaws, gripped their weapons tighter, and kept them trained on the crowd.

Collins directed his cameraman to focus on the line of guards, then at the people waiting to cross the border. "Get lots of close-ups."

When the camera was set, Collins broadcast his report. "I'm live at Checkpoint Charlie," he narrated, "where history is being written as I speak. Behind me," he signaled for the cameraman to zero in on the American guard shack, "is the iconic Checkpoint Charlie, scene of so many breathtaking escapes from East Germany. This is where Soviet and US Army tanks faced off in 1961 when the city was partitioned. Fear of nuclear war then was palpable." The camera swung to another angle. "There you see the East German border guards with their machine guns pointing at the people. Their mission since 1961 has been to make sure that citizens stay on this side of the border.

"In front of me," the camera swiveled toward the crowd, "it looks like all of East Berlin has turned out to exercise their newly recognized right to free entry into West Berlin. Two hours ago, Wolfgang Sacher of the East German politburo promised exactly that. The world wants to know how long it will take for that promise to be kept. Or, will the East German regime order its troops to shoot these people?

"A few minutes ago, this crowd was cheering. Now, they face the same machine guns used in deadly force against family members, friends, and neighbors over decades to keep them from escaping. The big question is, will that now change? I'll keep you posted as the night progresses."

Almost as soon as Collins signed off, his radio vibrated.

"Good report," Burly told him. "Now look around. Find a particular man. You might recognize him. He was in the room when you came back into our quarters the other day." He described Ivan. "As a last resort, ask Sofia to spot him. She knows him."

"Won't be necessary. I see him."

Ivan had made himself plainly visible, looking very official while watching the crowd from a position near the barriers in front of the guards.

"Good," Burly said. "Keep the cameras trained on him. History will be written permanently in the next few minutes."

"I understand, but listen: Sofia is in a bad way. She needs emergency medical attention."

"Do as I say, and she'll be in an ambulance within the next fifteen minutes."

Collins directed his cameraman per Burly's instructions. He watched as Ivan reached into his pocket and put a radio to his ear.

* * *

As Ivan spoke with Burly, he looked across at Collins. "I see him."

"Good. He'll record the entire event. Get to the head honcho of the border guard there. Throw your KGB weight around. Get that border open."

Ivan had to laugh. "I can do that. While I'm at it, should I build an ark and limit entrance to two at a time?"

Burly chuckled. "Good to see you didn't lose your sense of humor. Just do it."

"Roger. Out." Ivan shook his head at the irony of ironies that he of all people was about to take this initiative. He, Ivan Chekov, former Soviet spy, a defector, was here in East Berlin taking the last action that would erase the border between the two Germanys and open a gateway to the Soviet empire.

He approached the nearest guard. "Take me to the Stasi officer in charge."

The guard looked uncertain. Ivan showed his KGB ID. The soldier came to attention and escorted him to an officer at the center of the checkpoint.

"Why are these barriers still closed?" Ivan demanded. He presented his credentials. "The politburo ordered them to be opened"

The man eyed him cautiously. "I received word about new travel regulations, but no order to open the checkpoint. I can't act on the basis of a press release."

Ivan drew himself up to his full height. He pulled his shoulders back and brought his mouth close to the officer's ear. "Do you think the East German politburo would dare to act without the Kremlin's mandate?" he growled. "By order of General Secretary Gorbachev, I command you to enforce his directive." He glanced toward the crowd. Collins' camera and spotlight were aimed directly at him.

Ivan turned to make his face less visible. "Look at that camera. It's aimed at you." He stepped closer. The vapor of Ivan's breath in the cold air deflected into the man's face. "The world is watching."

The officer took no action. He gazed over the crowd, then at his men, and then into Ivan's grim face. "I have no orders."

Ivan's lips curled around his next words. "If you would like to explain to Mr. Gorbachev why your judgment is superior to his, I can arrange that." His eyes bored into the officer's face. They swept appraisingly down his uniform and then back up to meet the man's uncertain expression. "You're Stasi. You know what happens if you go against Soviet Party orders. You've seen the inside of a Stasi prison. That could be you." He looked again at the expectant crowd. "Tell your guards to stand down." He enunciated his next words slowly. "That is an order." He leaned in, his eyes mere inches from the officer's. "Let the people go." His tone was threatening. "Do it now."

The officer looked over Ivan's shoulder. Collins and the cameraman stood a few feet away, broadcasting his picture. Behind them, the massive throng stretched along Friedrichstrasse as far as he could see. He felt the urgency of their intent bearing down on the spot where he stood.

Ivan gestured toward the barriers. The officer snapped to. "Lift the barriers," he shouted to his men. He hurried to raise the one closest to him.

Border guards, immigration control, and Stasi officers alike stared in bewilderment. "Do it," he yelled, his tone harsh and bitter. "Now."

One by one, the guards lowered their weapons. They moved out of the way and lifted the barrier arms, the last obstacle to West Berlin.

A hush fell over the crowd. The Stasi officer stood aside and waved the people through.

36

Shortly before Wolfgang made his announcement, Atcho watched the crowd blocking his progress anxiously. *We're trying to save them, and they're slowing us down.*

"We're going to play hell getting anywhere to do anything, *Atcho*." Horton emphasized the nickname in his Texas drawl. He chuckled. "Ya see, I can break habits. It takes effort. Where does that handle come from?"

"Handle?"

"That's Texan for 'nickname.' Where did you get it?"

"It's a long story, Major Horton."

"We got time."

The throngs of pedestrians filling the streets had brought headway in the olive-drab sedan to a crawl. More than half an hour had passed since Chad had evaded the truck at the old building. They were only halfway to their destination, and the crowd became thicker by the minute.

Suddenly, the sound of loud cheering started somewhere ahead and rolled past them in a thundering wave. People danced in the streets and hugged each other. Horton told Chad to halt. He and Atcho emerged from the vehicle.

Horton nudged a man walking by. "What's going on?" he asked in fluent German.

Atcho stared at him, astonished.

Horton returned his look, deadpan. "What? My wife's German. We have to communicate." He turned back to the man and they conversed for a moment.

"Well, I'll be," he said, turning back to Atcho. "The German politburo guy—you know that Wolfgang Sacher? He just announced that East Germans were free to travel anywhere through any crossing point, including here in Berlin. Effective immediately." He put his hands on his hips, dumbfounded. "The little lady did it."

"Yeah, she did it," Atcho breathed. "And now we'd better do our part, or —" He left the thought unstated.

"All right, sir. Let's go." Horton started to clamber back into the vehicle and then stopped. "Atcho, we ain't gonna get there in time this way. If that guy, Yermolov, is doing what we think he's doing, he's not going to wait. Especially since that announcement."

"You're right." Atcho had already discarded the Army shirt he had been wearing. In doing so, he dropped his radio, unnoticed, on the floor in the back of the sedan. "I'll go the rest of the way on foot." While he spoke, Horton removed his own shirt. "What are you doing, Major?"

"Ya know, that ain't real friendly of you making me call you 'Atcho,' and meanwhile, you keep calling me 'Major Horton.' The name's 'Joe.'" He grinned. He had loosened his belt, and now stood in the shadow of the car between the two open doors. He reached down and untied his boots. "By the way, you never told me where the name 'Atcho' came from." He reached below his seat and pulled out a pair of civilian trousers, a shirt, and running shoes.

Atcho watched. "You're not coming with me, Joe. I'll do this alone."

"Like hell you will. Do you know your way there? How do you think these people will react when you ask for directions to Stasi headquarters? My job is to watch your six. You think I'm going to make lieutenant-colonel by not doing my job?" He looked up at the sky in mock indignation. "Like I'll ever get another promotion. But don't get the idea that you can order me *not* to do my job."

He dressed while he spoke, and when finished, he pulled out his pistol and checked it as if to make a point. "Check yours, sir." He returned the pistol to its holster and looped it on his belt. Then he stood, hands on hips, eye to eye with Atcho. "Are you going to tell me how you got that name?" He belted out his trademark laugh.

Atcho had to chuckle. He pulled his pistol out of his belt and checked it. "There's nothing to it, Joe. My father's name was Arturo. He was a colonel in the US Army during World War II. Some people had difficulty with the pronunciation, so it morphed into Atcho. It became my code name in Cuba during the invasion."

Horton glanced at him while tucking in his shirt. "Geez, sir. That wasn't so hard." He ducked his head into the sedan and called across to Chad. "Listen, you hoof it back to post as fast as possible." Then he leaned in farther and grabbed the driver by his arm. "Pay close attention. I got an order for you. Stay more than a mile away from the embassy." He looked Chad in the eye to make sure he understood. "If you're not safely home in an hour, take cover. Heavy cover. Get into a building with some concrete. Got it?"

Chad's eyes narrowed. He nodded. When Horton turned around, Atcho had already started down the street.

"If you're coming with me," Atcho called back, "stop talking and let's go."

Horton cussed under his breath, grinned, and hurried to catch up. They pushed through the crowd, darting around people who were slower. The sedan fell far behind.

"You never did tell me, Atcho. Why do you think Yermolov is at the Stasi headquarters?"

"Has to be. He's obviously exercising influence over the Stasi. They have the bombs. To move them through East Germany, he had to have Stasi help. Baumann's the last of the hard-liners. He still has an organization to run and political masters to answer to. With all this stuff taking place the last few weeks, he had to have stayed close to his command and control center. Yermolov will stick close to him." He gave Horton a sideways look. "Besides, Burly received a back-channel report from the Soviets that Yermolov had been spotted there. If they get to him first, they'll take him down." He grinned. "See, I can be subtle too."

Horton looked at Atcho with mock disgust. "An' here I thought you was bein' brilliant," he huffed through rapid breaths. "Good to have some confirmation that we're on the right track. What about the bombs?"

"Veniamin crossed the border less than twenty-four hours ago. Yermolov and his guys haven't had much time to do anything with them. No one on the eastern side expected Wolfgang's announcement tonight. With any luck, the bombs won't be activated yet, and they'll be with Yermolov when we catch up to him."

Horton mock-rolled his eyes. "Yeah, that'd be great. What about Klaus, the guy who's supposed to plant them?"

"Yermolov will control the bombs tightly. He'll give them to Klaus as he needs to. If they use remotes like last year, Yermolov will keep possession of them. I'm pretty sure that when we find Yermolov, we'll find the bombs."

Horton thought about that. "What if you're wrong?"

"Don't ask."

Twenty minutes later, they stood across the square from Stasi headquarters. While catching their breaths, they observed the building.

It was seven stories tall, light in color, longer than a city block, and boxy. Strangely, lights were on in many offices, but few people seemed to be inside. "They must have sent every last man out on crowd control," Horton observed. "Nobody's home."

"Or a lot of Stasi officers are hightailing it for cover. They could have a lot to answer for. A bunch of them are probably *in* the crowd heading toward the crossing points. Let's get closer."

They moved through the mass and approached the main entrance. It was shielded from sight by an awning that stretched across a driveway with a half wall and trellis along the front and sides.

Atcho felt for the radio to inform Burly that they were going in. To his chagrin, he could not find it. "I think I dropped the radio," he told Horton.

"Criminy, you mean we're going in there without commo? No one even knows where we are."

"Looks that way. Where's your radio?"

Horton put on his best exasperated look. "In the car where it's supposed to be. I ain't got one of them fancy-fangled handheld ones. You gotta have pull to get one of those." He shot one of his characteristic searching-for-sanity looks at the skies. "Oh well, it's like that time in Afghanistan. Did I ever tell you that story?"

Atcho grimaced. "Joe, do we have time for that now?"

Horton grinned. "Nah but remind me to tell it to ya later. It's a good one."

They drew their pistols and moved into the shadows on either side of the entrance. From that vantage, they could see into the lobby. One lone officer sat at a desk barring the way to the rest of the building.

Atcho put his weapon back in its holster, rounded the corner, and entered.

Horton joined him and walked straight to the desk. "Where is everyone?" he demanded harshly in German. The Stasi officer was young, probably newly added to the force and still in training. *He drew the short straw on duty tonight. Lucky him.*

Atcho glanced at Horton. Gone were the habitual half smile and twinkling eyes. The major looked as stern and forceful as anyone Atcho had ever met.

"I asked where everyone is," Horton bellowed. "Come to attention when I speak to you."

The young officer leaped to his feet. "Everyone left," he stuttered. "Only a few people are upstairs."

"Why are you still here?"

"Sir, I'm on duty."

Horton glowered. "You are relieved for dereliction of duty. Report to your superior tomorrow that you failed to come to attention when General Hortz entered the building."

The officer looked crushed. He fixed his eyes straight ahead as though he were afraid to move. "Before you go," Horton continued, "tell me how to get to Director Baumann's office. I will have a few words with him about the deplorable lack of discipline I see here tonight. No wonder the country is coming apart."

"His office is on the seventh floor, but he left a little while ago." The officer looked toward a bank of two elevators. "Perhaps one of his staff members can advise you. Some people are still in his offices on the seventh floor. Shall I call?"

"No," Horton replied. "We'll go up. Do those elevators work?"

The officer nodded.

"Good. Now go." He softened his voice. "Maybe I'll put in a good word for you."

The young officer scurried into the night. As soon as he had gone, Horton explained in a whisper what had happened. "You wanna ride up to the director's office?"

By way of responding, Atcho walked to the elevator and punched the button. From the shaft behind the doors, they heard mechanical groans and clanking as the car descended. A minute later, they rode it up.

Even before the doors opened, they heard voices. One of them Atcho recognized; a voice he would never forget. Yermolov.

"...When we succeed, we'll have plenty of money. Let's go."

Atcho jerked his pistol from its holster and bolted out of the elevator.

Yermolov was stepping into the second elevator. He saw Atcho, but his momentum carried him into the car.

Atcho opened fire and kept shooting until the magazine was empty. The bullets entered the second elevator, opening a pattern of tightly packed holes on the opposite wall. Atcho slapped in another magazine.

The doors started to close. Yermolov appeared in the space between them and returned fire, but the angle was too shallow. Bullets whizzed by Atcho. The doors closed. The elevator moaned and clanked and began its descent.

"The stairs," Horton yelled. He pointed.

"He didn't see you," Atcho called as they raced to the stairwell. "Go to the bottom floor. Get in the dark hall across from the orderly's desk. I'll herd them to you."

When they reached the sixth floor, Horton continued down while Atcho stopped. As the elevator light switched to number six, Atcho fired into the door. The elevator continued. Atcho repeated his action at each level until it passed the second floor. He expected that the sound of guns would bring others into the foyer, but the building was strangely, eerily empty. He raced to the bottom floor and positioned himself behind a heavy column.

The elevator arrived, and the doors opened. A fusillade of gunshots and smoke exploded from the interior. Bullets split the air, broke windows, and ricocheted off of walls. Then all was quiet.

"Come out," Atcho called. "You can't escape."

Silence.

"Come out, Yermolov. You're done." To make his point, Atcho fired into the middle of the elevator's ceiling.

Seconds ticked by. Then Yermolov called out. "Hold your fire, Atcho. I'm coming out."

"Throw out your gun."

A pistol flew out, clattering to the ground. Yermolov emerged, his right hand held in the air. In his left hand, he carried a suitcase.

* * *

Through a haze of excruciating pain, Sofia watched, mesmerized, as the crowd started moving forward again through Checkpoint Charlie. Despite all the planning, the careful organization and execution that had gone in to bring about this moment, the fact of it happening almost overwhelmed her.

A team member on her left carried much of her weight with an arm under her shoulder. Careful not to bump the wound, Wolfgang supported her right side with his arm around her waist. She was grateful for his paternal attention.

He had recovered his faculties as he moved with the surging crowd, but he clearly felt at a loss to fathom the full impact. He told her repeatedly, "I can't believe this is happening."

Ahead, Collins came into view, his bright camera lights creating a glow around him. Wolfgang's scarf had fallen away, revealing his face. As he stepped into the light, people recognized him and began cheering, "Sacher, Sacher, Sacher." Wolfgang waved, but quickly sought the safety of darkness. He was too late.

A man stepped inside the moving security perimeter. He shoved a pistol into Wolfgang's chest. His former security chief. "Wolfgang Sacher, you are under arrest for treason and other high crimes against the state."

Sofia moaned as Wolfgang froze, jarring her arm. Her adrenaline surged. The rest of the team and Wolfgang's family stood still. A group of uniformed policemen formed a ring around them.

"You will come with me," the bodyguard said. "You and your family."

Wolfgang released his hold on Sofia. He looked over the crowd. "For the love of God, man. Can't you see what is happening?" He waved his hand toward Checkpoint Charlie. "The gates are open. We are free. Let us go."

The security chief smirked. "There is no God in East Germany. This is your doing. Soon the gates will close, and you'll answer for your crimes. Because of you, many will die tonight. I have my orders."

Wolfgang's shoulders slumped. He turned around slowly to look at Sofia. "Thank you," he murmured. "At least we got a lot of people out. I hope your family is among them. I hope your Atcho is safe, and that your arm heals quickly." Then he looked into the fearful eyes of his family.

The team member who had supported Sofia's left side had let go as well and stepped away. Sofia stood on wobbly legs, trying to gauge the nature and direction of the threat, chagrined at her limited ability to respond.

Sensing the tension, the crowd diverged, opening a wide gap around them. Amber streetlights delineated the opposing forces, an East German police perimeter surrounding the inner circle of Sofia's team, now with weapons drawn. At the center were Wolfgang's family and Sofia.

The security chief grabbed Wolfgang's shoulder. "Let's go."

Sofia summoned every physical and mental reserve left to her. She struck, kicking the security chief's pistol away. Another kick caught him on the side of the head, knocking him to the ground.

Sofia's scream of agony tore the night. She fell in a heap.

Jeff's team leaped at their closest opponents. After a brief skirmish, the fight was over, almost as quickly as it had begun. The highly trained team subdued and disarmed the policemen—all except the security chief, who rolled and came to his feet, reaching for his pistol. He grabbed it and took deadly aim at Wolfgang.

The loud report of a gunshot split the air. The crowd fell further away. The security chief gaped at Wolfgang in disbelief. Then he slumped to the ground as blood bubbled from his chest.

Nina crouched by him holding her gun. Smoke rose from the barrel.

The man clung to life, each breath a bloody gurgle.

"You said we wouldn't live out the night," Nina said. "We did." Her eyes did not blink. "You didn't." She took his pistol from his hand and returned her own to its holster.

The man rolled to his side, his eyes staring into nowhere.

Wolfgang knelt beside Sofia and lifted her. Jeff walked over to help, but Wolfgang motioned him away. "I'll carry her." He faced the policemen grouped together under the team's guard. "Go home," he said. He indicated the crowd with his chin. "Go home before these people figure out what they can do to you." He nodded at Jeff. "Let's go." He set out again toward Checkpoint Charlie, carrying Sofia.

They went by Ivan, who stood not far from the Stasi Wartburg that had brought him there. He had posted himself by the barriers as if holding back the East German guards. He nodded, grim-faced, as they passed. They traversed the wide expanse of the kill zone, through Checkpoint Charlie, into West Berlin.

37

Ranulf fought his way through the crowds to return to his office. When he arrived, Oily was waiting for him, lounging in one of the chairs in front of his massive desk. Ranulf tossed the two duffle bags into a corner and took his seat.

Oily peered at the bags. "What's in there?"

Ranulf thought rapidly. He heaved a sigh. "Documents that Baumann no longer wants in his office. He's worried about what the next few days will bring." His eyes widened in false indignation. "Can you believe the Wall is open? What does that mean for us?" He regretted telling Oily to come by his office. Once again, he had been impulsive, intending to share his idea but not the money. "This has been a crazy night."

Oily leaned his chair back, his face expressionless. "What's your idea?"

Ranulf spoke eagerly. "With our hit squads, we built an organization that delivers a unique service." He did not mention that the idea had come from Yermolov. He smirked. "Speaking like a capitalist, we can expand our market in the West. I understand the demand for what we do is high there." He laughed. "The checkpoints are open. We can all go through. We don't even need papers."

Oily did not share his mirth. "You said you'd pay us tonight."

Ranulf nodded, attempting sincerity. "The money will be here tomorrow. I'll pay."

Oily allowed his chair to drop forward with a loud thud. The door swung open. Two men entered, pistols drawn. They aimed at Ranulf.

Fear crossed Ranulf's face. "What are you doing?"

Oily ignored him. He gestured to one of the men. "See what's in those bags."

The man stepped forward, opened one of the bags, and looked inside. He chortled and lifted out several stacks of wrapped bills. He set them on Ranulf's desk and looked in the other bag. "Same stuff here. Quite a haul."

Oily stood, glassy eyes on Ranulf. "You lied to me." He stepped over to peer inside one of the bags. "One thing you never understood. This was never 'our' organization. It was mine, and these are my men."

Ranulf's eyes widened in sudden terror. Before he could protest, Oily nodded. The two thugs shot into Ranulf's chest. He dropped, lifeless.

Without missing a beat, the man by the duffle bags turned his pistol and put two bullets each into his erstwhile companion and Oily. They went down. He checked their pulses. None. "You never had an organization either," he scoffed at Oily's limp figure. "We were never your men. Like everyone else in East Germany, we just survived." He threw the bags over his shoulder. Five minutes later, he blended into the crowd, headed to the nearest checkpoint.

* * *

Collins stood watching in disbelief as East Berliners continued to stream past. Their numbers had swelled as word spread that the borders were open. Ivan stood a short distance away.

Collins was not sure why Ivan remained, but the former KGB officer seemed intent on exerting his illusory authority over the guards to ensure they did not attempt to reverse course.

A face coming toward the checkpoint caught Collins' attention. It belonged to a man he knew, one he had interviewed outside Paris nearly a year earlier and had followed desperately through the West German side of the Helmstedt–Marienborn crossing less than twenty-four hours ago. *Seems like a century.*

Veniamin walked straight toward him. He looked frantic. "Please, Mr. Collins. The bombs. My family. I must speak to you."

"Yes, yes. Of course. I remember you from last year. I'm glad you found me."

"I saw you interviewing people. You must help."

They spoke for several minutes; their heads close together. Abruptly, Collins swung around. "Come with me." He led Veniamin to Ivan and repeated what Veniamin had told him.

As he listened, Ivan's lips hardened into a thin line. "Get in that vehicle." He pointed to the Stasi Wartburg.

Veniamin whirled to Collins in abject fear. "Where is he taking me?"

"Don't worry," Collins said calmly. "He knows what he's doing. He'll help."

Meanwhile, Ivan strode toward the Stasi supervisor. "I'm taking that car into West Berlin. I'll bring it back tomorrow. Any objection?" His tone was only slightly menacing.

The officer stared at him, and then at the car. He shrugged in resignation. "No. All border crossings are open." He ordered his subordinates to let the car pass.

Forty minutes later, Ivan parked the Wartburg in front of the Berlin Brigade headquarters and escorted Veniamin into the building.

38

Atcho stepped from behind the column in the lobby. Only twenty feet separated him and Yermolov. "Set the suitcases down."

Yermolov complied. He lifted both hands in the air. "Atcho," he crooned. "I knew that was your voice. I'd know it anywhere." He smirked as he wiped blood from his eyes. "That wasn't very nice, shooting into the elevator. After all we've meant to each other? The ricochets could have killed us. One of your bullets grazed me."

He looked down at his suitcase and then back at Atcho. "I'm going to pick up my suitcase. Then, I'm going to walk out of here.

"Before you shoot me, you should see what's in my left hand." He held high a black rectangular object. "This is a remote to one of my bombs, like the one I had last year. Do you see my thumb pressed on the single button?"

He held his hand out, palm up. His thumb held one end of the device wedged against his forefinger. "One punch, and it's all over for anyone within a mile of your embassy."

Atcho stared at the device. Horton remained silent in the shadows of the hall.

"You walk around with that in your hand?" Atcho's voice dripped sarcasm. "Sure. No chance you'd bump into something and set it off accidentally."

"Your appearance prompted me to use it. It's so easy. My cousin made it. The button is double action. I push and hold it down at least five seconds to arm it, and then push further down to detonate. It requires fifteen pounds of pressure for the second push. Would you like to try me?" He grinned, enjoying the repartee.

"How do you disarm it?"

Yermolov laughed. "Your clearance isn't high enough to know that. We're safely out of the blast radius, if you're wondering." He chuckled. "Are you calculating whether a bullet can get to me before I push the button?" He sighed. "Atcho, we've been together so long. Cuba, Washington, Siberia. Remember the Azores? I was a little hungover then." He sighed again. "Parting will be such sweet sorrow."

Atcho remembered vividly when Yermolov had driven into the night with his four-year-old daughter. Memories coursed through his mind of the long recovery after being beaten nearly to death on Yermolov's order. Then the loneliness and despair of nineteen years in prison and seven years of manipulation as a sleeper agent. The freezing cold chase through Siberia. He tried always to blot those recollections from his mind, but they surfaced sometimes, along with a rush of unbridled emotion. He had no time for them now.

"It ends tonight."

Yermolov turned his head slowly to the side. "Shoot me right here." He pointed to his temple. "My muscles will freeze. I won't be able to detonate the bomb." His face darkened. "But if you miss, I promise you, there will be a mile-wide hole in Berlin where your embassy is now." He mocked, "Never bring a gun to a nuclear fight." He glowered. "Drop it."

Atcho did not move.

Yermolov shifted his feet impatiently. "Atcho, I have a plane to catch. Klaus too. You remember Klaus? He wants to rip out your throat. Klaus, come greet your brother's killer."

Klaus emerged from the elevator, his face contorted with hatred. He carried a suitcase identical to Yermolov's. With his right hand, he aimed a pistol toward Atcho. "Can I kill him now? He won't dare shoot in this direction."

Atcho ducked behind the column. "Major Horton," he called. "If that man twitches, shoot him. Make it count."

Yermolov looked around and fixed his gaze on the dark hall behind Atcho. "You brought someone with you," he taunted. "How clever."

"You killed my brother," Klaus called in a savage growl that welled from the depths of his being. "I will kill you."

Suddenly, he dropped to the floor, rolled, and fired three rounds into the dark hall behind Atcho. He rolled again, firing at Atcho and hitting the column.

Two shots exploded from behind Atcho. Two bullets ripped into Klaus' right shoulder. He dropped the gun, howling, his joint destroyed. A dull thud sounded in the hall, but no more gunfire. Klaus struggled to his feet, grabbed the suitcase with his good arm, and ran through the entrance. He left his pistol on the floor.

Yermolov had not moved. He lifted his hand in front of his face with a look of stunned realization. He had pushed the detonation button on the remote, an involuntary reaction to the sudden burst of shots.

Atcho dove from behind the column to a new position next to a concrete wall. He fired the pistol on his way down, aiming for the center of Yermolov's chest. Given the speed of events, he had no idea where the bullets hit. He loaded a new magazine. Then, he braced for a massive explosion.

His options were limited. The best he could do was lie flat on his stomach against the wall that protected him from the direction of the expected blast. He covered his head with his arms. When he looked up, Yermolov still stood but teetered on his feet.

Seconds passed. No explosion. No distant roar. No vibrations or shattering glass. No heat waves. Yermolov was in the same place, but he had slumped to his knees and sat back on his haunches. Blood poured from his lower abdomen.

From the front door, Klaus bellowed, his voice agonized. "This isn't over, Atcho. I promise you, it isn't over."

Atcho fired off a couple of shots toward him and heard running footsteps. He scrambled to his feet and hurried to the entrance. Klaus was gone, leaving a trail of blood.

"You all right, Horton?" Atcho called, looking into the dark hall. No answer.

Atcho stood in front of Yermolov, covering him with his pistol. The rogue general looked down vacantly at his own hand. His thumb still squeezed the button on the remote. His other hand pressed against his stomach. He pulled it away slightly to look at it. The flow of blood increased, welling out over his palm.

Atcho looked closer. Yermolov held another remote. Atcho had no idea when or how it got there. He knew only that his nemesis, so close to death, remained a threat.

Yermolov raised his head, his eyes already bleary. "I guess it doesn't hurt to bring a gun to a nuclear fight after all." He gave a sickly laugh that ended in a groan of pain. He looked at the second remote. "Oh well, if I gotta go, I should take as many with me as I can." Coughing, he looked back up at Atcho. "This one detonates Klaus' bomb. He can't have gone far. We can all go together." He pressed the button.

Atcho resigned himself to eternity.

Nothing. Yermolov looked at the remote, confused. "Huh, that's two out of three. I'll have to speak to Cousin Veniamin. I should get a refund." He looked up at Atcho with a wan smile. "Aren't you going to save me now? That's the humanitarian thing to do. Then you can bring me to justice."

Atcho squatted in front of him. "You're beyond help. My orders are to stay with you until there is no pulse." He called back into the hall again. "Major Horton, are you OK?" No answer.

The rogue general chuckled, and then groaned. "I won't keep you." His eyes had receded into their sockets. A pool of blood encircled him. "So, Atcho, our long years together come to an end." His words slurred. "This time for real." His lower legs had splayed apart so that his thighs settled between them. He shot Atcho one last baleful glance, then his head dropped forward. He sat there upright, held in precarious balance by gravity, a solitary dead figure.

39

Atcho ran into the hall. Horton lay prone diagonally across the floor.

Atcho saw no wounds on the major's back, but blood pooled under his legs. Atcho felt for a pulse. He turned Horton over and checked his breathing. It was regular, but bleeding from his right leg was steady. Judging by the color, a bullet must have struck an artery.

Atcho tore off his own belt, made a quick tourniquet around Horton's wounded leg, and tightened it. Then he crossed Horton's feet and elevated them against the wall.

A figure darted into the lobby. Atcho ducked and peered through the dim light. Chad crouched in the foyer.

"Over here," Atcho called.

Horton awoke, groggy. He looked around. "If this is heaven," he groaned, "take me to that other place." He looked at the tourniquet on his leg and then back at Atcho. "One thing is certain. You got a lot to learn about puttin' on a tourniquet. An' do you have a clue how uncomfortable lyin' on the floor in this position is, with my feet up like that?" He spotted Chad. "What the hell are you doing here? I gave you an order."

Chad stood over him. "Major Horton, meaning no disrespect, shut up. You taught me never to leave one of our guys behind." He grinned. "Much as I hate to claim you, you're one of ours."

Horton glared at him, his jaw tightening, the characteristic mischief returning to his eyes. "You know I could bring you up on charges?" He looked at his leg again. "The least you could do is fix that tourniquet." He pointed at Atcho. "That guy don't know the first thing about putting one on. Good thing you happened by."

Atcho pulled himself to his feet and hurried back into the lobby. Yermolov still sat in deathly repose. Atcho felt for a pulse. *None.* He checked for breathing. *None.* Then he pulled the remotes from Yermolov's hands and patted the body down until he found the third one. He put all three in his pocket and picked up the remaining suitcase.

* * *

Sofia's eyes opened in slits. Everything she saw was blurred. She tried to turn but the motion produced sharp pain. She moaned and slid her eyes wearily to the right. Her arm was heavily bandaged.

Burly leaned over her, his face somber. "Take it easy. You're in the Army emergency room. Your arm took a serious shot. The doc patched an artery."

Sofia tried to speak. Her words came out in hoarse gasps. "Atcho? My family? Wolfgang?"

"Wolfgang's family made it through in great shape, thanks to you. He carried you out of East Berlin. Your family's fine. They're at the embassy. The worst that could happen to them now is that they spend some time in that bomb shelter. I promised to get you on the phone to them as soon as you're strong enough."

"And Atcho? Where's Atcho?"

Burly grimaced. "We lost contact," he said slowly. "We don't know where he is."

Sofia stared. She took a deep breath against a chaotic lurch of emotion. "Give me a few minutes. Coffee would help. I'll call my cousin. Where's the phone?" It was on a side table. Burly dialed the number and pressed the receiver to her ear. She held it with the hand of her healthy arm, and he left the room.

"Miriam, is that really you?" She spoke almost in a whisper, choking back tears. "How are Uncle and Auntie?"

They spoke for a few minutes, switching between English and German.

"We saw TV reports," Miriam said. "People are dancing on top of the Wall. They're using sledgehammers and picks to tear it down by the Brandenburg Gate. Can you believe it? The border guards are just standing around. They don't know what to do.

"Mom and Dad are watching. They're determined to walk through that gate as soon as it clears."

"Make certain it's safe," Sofia murmured. *The bombs are still out there.* "I'll come to meet you. Call me before you head over."

Miriam's voice suddenly took on a note of concern. "The team that helped us was incredible. They carried Mom and Dad, and our son. My husband carried our daughter. Everyone's worried about your husband. They want to help him, but they don't know where he is. Do you know?"

Sofia's throat constricted. "No," she rasped. She murmured goodbye and hung up, burying her head in the crook of her good arm.

* * *

Back in the car, Atcho found his radio on the floor and called Burly.

"Where've you been? We've—"

"I dropped my radio," Atcho interrupted. "Horton's wounded. We're taking him to the embassy. That's the fastest place we can get to. Also, I've got one of these suitcases. Something failed. Yermolov tried to detonate but it didn't work. What should I do with it?"

"Only one?"

"Klaus got away with one. The third one must be someplace at the embassy."

The radio was silent a moment. "All right. Take it on into the embassy. It'll be all right. I'll explain later. What about—?"

"Tell General Marsh, mission accomplished. Yermolov has no pulse."

"You're sure?"

"Checked, double-checked, and triple-checked. He won't bother us again. How about our people? Everyone OK?"

An interval passed before Burly responded. "Everybody's fine. Sofia's arm took a bullet, but she's out of danger."

Atcho felt like an abyss had opened beneath him. "Are you sure?" His voice caught.

"I'm sure. Don't come this way tonight. It'll take hours. Go to the embassy. Sofia's asleep now, under heavy sedation. Get some rest. We'll see you tomorrow."

Atcho leaned back in the front seat, all his thoughts and emotion concentrated on Sofia. He pictured their first meeting all those years ago at the Swiss Embassy in Havana. He had been a dirty, smelly political prisoner just released from Castro's dungeons. She had been there on assignment at the US Interests Section.

She had seen a noble man whose face bore the sorrow of a life destroyed by totalitarian thugs. He had seen a beautiful woman who had gone out of her way to be kind. Berlin was the third covert operation they had worked together. *We came so close to losing each other, again.*

Lying propped along the back seat in the half-light, Horton sensed Atcho's change of mood. "Hey, sir. Next time we do this, would you mind standing maybe two feet to your right?" He chuckled. "I'd have had a clear shot, but I had to shoot past your buttocks, an' if you don't know what that word means, I'll tell ya."

Atcho turned around in the front seat. "Out of curiosity, *Joe*," he emphasized the major's name with a trace of mock sarcasm, "how did you end up unconscious? You hadn't lost that much blood when I got to you. The pressure of the floor slowed the bleeding until I turned you over."

"Thanks a lot," Horton remarked, wearing his most serious face. He could not hold the expression and broke into laughter. Then he groaned from a jab of pain. "That was the damndest thing. The bullet hit. I got off two shots and dove for cover. I forgot it was a narrow hall. I guess my head hit the wall and I knocked myself out."

Atcho could only shake his head.

* * *

As soon as Burly finished speaking with Atcho, he turned to the others in the room. With him were Ivan, Veniamin, the two generals, and the intelligence and operations officers. Burly looked at Marsh and arched his eyebrows.

"I heard," Marsh said. "Next time you see Atcho, give him an attaboy for me. Same for you, Ivan, and everyone else on those teams. I'll get my adjutant to develop appropriate recognition. That reporter, Collins, too. Let's get back to business."

Veniamin sat across from them at the conference table. He was much less frantic than when he had arrived, but still showed some anxiety.

"Let's go through this again more slowly," Burly told him. "I need to understand the part about the bombs. You told me they wouldn't detonate. Why not?"

"I'll explain, but what about my family? Can you please make sure they are protected? Those are bad men."

"We alerted the French government. They put a watch on your family. If everything checks out about the bombs, the US government will provide greater protection and even move you, if you like."

"Yes. Please. The arms dealers know what I can do. They will never leave me alone. They'll keep threatening my family."

"Tell me again why the bombs didn't work. You said they were viable."

Veniamin sighed. "I had two wiring systems. One was a dummy. The other was hidden inside the dummy. The hidden line supplied electricity, but only enough to test positive for individual components and the overall system. The battery was large enough, but the hidden system stepped the current down to a fraction of what was needed to detonate the bomb.

"I was worried when Yermolov had two nuclear engineers inspect them. If they had looked any deeper, they would have seen what I did. But they were so scared..."

Burly scratched the back of his neck. "So, are they real bombs?"

"Yes."

"But they can't be set off?"

"They *can* be set off, but they would have to be completely rewired."

Burly contemplated that. "What about the fail-safe system?"

Veniamin grinned in spite of his nervousness. "That was always a fake. It was never active, even when I set the switches. But who was going to try it?" The others around the table exchanged relieved glances and raised their eyebrows.

"Did I hear Atcho say that he was bringing one in?" Marsh asked.

"That's right," Burly replied.

A knock on the door interrupted the discussion. A soldier stuck his head in and addressed the intelligence officer. "Sorry to break in, sir. You told me to go over that Stasi car with a fine-toothed comb for intel before we give it back."

"Right. Anything worthwhile?"

"I'm not sure. I thought I'd better show you this. It was in the trunk." He held up a suitcase.

"That's one of mine," Veniamin burst out. "Yermolov sent Klaus to plant it at the embassy. Now I can show you."

Ivan groaned audibly. "That was in the trunk?"

"Yes, sir," the soldier replied.

Ivan slapped his hand to his forehead. "And I brought it here. I even had to hotwire the car. Klaus must have had the key."

When the soldier left, General Marsh sidled up next to Burly. "You know what this means?"

Burly looked grim. "Yes, General. There's a Chechen terrorist out there with a violent history. He detests both the US and the Soviet Union. In particular, he hates Atcho. And he has a viable nuclear bomb."

EPILOGUE

Dawn burst over Berlin, turning the skies the color of flame. Collins had remained all night at his position on the border at Checkpoint Charlie watching the human drama unfold. People kept coming. On crossing into West Berlin, some dropped down and kissed the ground.

Many stopped at the museum. They gazed through the plate-glass window in wonder at the photos of successful escapes—and tragic deaths. Quiet grief over those who had not made it all the way across followed recognition of people and scenes remembered. East Berliners filed in and out and went to reacquaint themselves with old friends and family and learn what their new reality meant to their lives.

Collins interviewed hundreds throughout the night, beaming his live reports to a breathless world. Some people did not care to be interviewed, but the vast majority waved and called to him when they saw him with his cameraman and bright lights. However, he had been unable to see what was happening along other parts of the Wall.

One man passed by, whom, at first, Collins barely noticed. He had a medium build and wore a thickly padded jacket, and his dark hair was unkempt. He seemed to make a beeline toward Collins and his cameraman. As he approached, he waved and called to them. "Thank you, America. I love America. I am going to America."

Collins smiled and waved back. "Would you like to speak to the camera?" The man grinned and kept walking. He seemed to be alone. Watching him go, Collins wondered what life the man had come from and what life he would now lead.

The reporter watched until the man disappeared into the crowd. Nothing about him distinguished him from any other East German, except that he carried two duffle bags, one slung over each shoulder. *Maybe his life's possessions.*

When Collins turned back to the east, another man caught his attention. He seemed to avoid not only the camera, but the lights themselves. He was nondescript except that he looked to be in remarkable physical shape. He walked rapidly compared to the rest of the crowd. However, his expression showed that he was trying to hide extreme pain.

He shot Collins a contemptuous look. Then his pain seemed to surge. He stopped and set down a suitcase. Oblivious to Collins' curious scrutiny, he reached inside his jacket and nursed his right shoulder. It looked heavily bandaged. Then he picked up the suitcase again, recommenced his trek, and disappeared into the crowd.

Collins sighed. *Another new beginning.* The radio in his pocket vibrated. He put it to his ear.

"All's well that ends well," Burly told him. "No more bomb threat. We have Veniamin here. Everyone got out safely. History is sealed. Good job."

Collins thanked him. "What about Yermolov?"

"Gone. Permanently. Listen, a tip for you. People on both sides of the Wall are tearing it down all through the city, including at Brandenburg Gate. You might want to get over there. I think you'll see something personally gratifying."

Collins grabbed his cameraman. Together they walked along next to the Wall, toward the iconic monument. They broadcast live video of everyday citizens taking picks and hammers to the hated partition, chiseling holes through it, beating the reinforcing steel into useless fragments. More intrepid people brought ladders, climbed the Wall, and proceeded to take it down from the top. In some places, whole sections had been knocked down and lay in what had been, only a few hours ago, the kill zone.

Finally, they arrived at the west side of the Brandenburg Gate. They gaped at what they saw. Berliners on both sides had brought the Wall down to half its height along the length of the monument. In a few places, it had been hammered to the ground. People streamed through. On the opposite side, East German border guards and police mingled with East and West Berliners, smiling and laughing.

Collins spotted Burly, Sofia, and Ivan standing together in the middle of the parking lot on the west side of the Gate, observing the crowds moving through. Sofia's right arm was bandaged and in a sling. He started toward them.

Later, when Collins spoke by phone with Jakes, his editor was ecstatic. "Great reporting, Tony. You scooped your competition again."

Collins' thoughts went to his part in the averted global calamity. "Believe me, Jakes, the achievements of the last twenty-four hours are not mine."

* * *

Sofia observed the magnificent Brandenburg Gate, the most iconic site in all of Germany, East or West. It was now a symbol of unity. Despite the years of poor maintenance under the East German regime, it stood proud and tall, complete with its Quadriga, the stately statue of four horses abreast pulling a chariot with a winged Victory Angel holding a Roman-style banner. Although it had not originally been intended as a triumphal arch, Napoleon had first used it for that purpose after defeating Germany.

This morning, it served as a fitting tribute to the indomitable spirit of the East German people. They had defeated the totalitarian regime that had subjugated them for forty-four years. *For them, World War II ended last night.*

Sofia felt weak. She had cleaned up as best she could, but her sunken eyes over dark circles and pallid skin gave away her exhaustion. The doctors had objected to her going out with insufficient rest, but she had stubbornly refused to stay in bed. "My husband and my family are coming through that gate. Try to stop me."

An hour earlier, Sofia's cousin Miriam had called. "Mom and Dad are rested. They insist on walking through the Gate." Her voice was full of excitement. "The whole team is coming with us—Rafael, Juan, Fernando, and Pepe. Atcho is here with us too. We love them all."

Sofia's eyes moistened. "I can't wait to see you." She choked back joyous tears.

"Oh, and there's this other man." Miriam laughed. "Major Horton? He is so funny. He told Atcho," she dropped her voice into a husky imitation of Horton, "'You ain't takin' that trek without me, sir.'" She brought her tone back to normal. "His leg got shot. He's on crutches, but he won't stay down."

Sofia had to laugh. "I'll see you soon. We're leaving now."

* * *

Burly nudged Sofia. "There they are." He pointed. Ivan also followed where he indicated.

They recognized Rafael, Juan, Fernando, and Pepe, escorting her uncle and aunt. The old coupled walked with their canes under the Brandenburg canopy. Next to them, Miriam held her son's hand, and her husband carried the little girl.

Sofia looked past them, searching deeper. Major Horton hobbled along on crutches, obviously in pain but struggling to keep up.

Her heart leaped. Atcho attended to Horton, which seemed to exasperate the major. The two were engaged in an animated exchange. Sofia smiled. *I've never seen Atcho be so expressive.*

* * *

Off to one side, Collins spotted the two converging groups. He edged closer. His cameraman lifted his equipment to shoot video. Collins waved him off. "Let them have their private moment. They've earned it."

"I can film it. They can have it as a keepsake. If they don't want it, we'll toss it."

"Good idea." Collins started to turn back, then hesitated. "Great job last night."

* * *

Sofia pushed through the crowd. When she was close enough, she waved and called to Miriam. They ran to each other and clung together, sobbing, replicating countless similar poignant scenes played out throughout the city.

Miriam's mother and father caught up to them. Tears streaming, Sofia embraced them. "I knew this day had to come," she breathed. "I never gave up hope." Miriam and her family joined around them while the rest held back.

After several minutes, Sofia felt something push against her shoulder. She ignored it, but it persisted. Finally, she turned.

Horton leaned on one of his crutches, grinning. He had used the other one to prod her.

His face morphed to deadpan. He cocked his head, rolled his eyes toward Atcho standing next to him, and broke into an involuntary laugh. "Hey, someone else would like some attention." Atcho shook his head in humorous disbelief at the effrontery.

Horton looked up at the Brandenburg Gate towering over them. Then he scanned the multitude of reuniting friends and family. His chest swelled with exaggerated contentment. "Well, you did it," he told Sofia. "You pulled it off. Little lady." He gave a solemn half bow.

Sofia had stepped close to Atcho. She whirled and gave Horton a look of mock indignation. "*I* did it? Anyone else?"

Horton bobbed his head back and forth, his face sheepish. "Well, I helped a little. Nice of you to mention it."

Sofia laughed. "Anyone else?" she said again.

Horton glanced around at Atcho. "You mean him? He's the reason we got in this fix in the first place. If he weren't so damned ornery..." He peered deliberately at the sling on Sofia's arm, and then pointed at his own leg. "Look who's wearing the bandages. You and me."

"What about Burly? Or Wolfgang? Or Ivan and Rafael? The others?"

"Why hell, all Wolfgang did was read from a slip of paper. Prob'ly a sticky note. Burly sat in the office drinking coffee the whole time. As for Ivan, he strutted around shoving that KGB ID in people's faces like a peacock showin' off its tail feathers." He gestured at the remaining members of the team. "All those others was here for a Sunday after-church walk."

"What about the German people—all of them?"

Horton brought a forefinger under his chin as if in thought. "Okay," he said with a grudging tone, "I'll give ya that one. Maybe they had a bit to do with it." He tossed his head, glared at her in mock seriousness, and pointed at the gaping break where the Wall had been. "But I'll tell you, ma'am, if it hadn't been for you and me, that Wall would still be right there."

He felt a hand grasping his shoulder. Atcho stepped between him and Sofia, giving his back to the major.

Horton put on his most indignant face and spoke in his best petulant voice. "Well, I'm offended—" He leaned on his crutches, grinning.

Atcho wrapped his arms around Sofia and glanced over his shoulder. "Joe. Shut up."

FAHRENHEIT KUWAIT

As the Soviet Union crumbles, its nuclear stockpiles are compromised. For one terrorist, it's the opportunity of a lifetime.

He is a terrorist mastermind, and a mystery to Western intelligence.

But he's no mystery to Atcho.

The two men have a score to settle with one another—and in a global game of cat and mouse, only one will prevail.

Armed with a weapon of mass destruction and fueled by his hatred of the West, the terrorist intends to kill as many people as possible...unless Atcho finds him first.

If Atcho succeeds, he will prevent a nuclear attack.

But if he fails, no force in the world will be able to stop his enemy.

Get your copy today at
severnriverbooks.com

ACKNOWLEDGMENTS

Writing thrillers full of twists and turns is not difficult—doing so against a backdrop of known historical events is much tougher. The outcome is known. To tell a rapidly paced story that entertains the reader requires detailed research and insertion of elements to raise conflict and add suspense without altering the facts of history. Surprising readers without confusing them or insulting their knowledge of history or procedure is the real art. Then there are the characters.... I'm grateful to the Editors and Beta Readers of Vortex: Berlin for their guidance with the finer points of plot and character, and for their assistance in fighting my natural inclination toward typos: Jennifer McIntyre, Stephanie Parent, John Shephard, Mark Gillespie, Christian Jackson, Anita Paulsen, Margee Harwell, Al Fracker, Steve Collier, Jerry Warner and friends who cannot be named.

ABOUT THE AUTHOR

Lee Jackson is the Wall Street Journal bestselling author of The Reluctant Assassin series and the After Dunkirk series. He graduated from West Point and is a former Infantry Officer of the US Army. Lee deployed to Iraq and Afghanistan, splitting 38 months between them as a senior intelligence supervisor for the Department of the Army. Lee lives and works with his wife in Texas, and his novels are enjoyed by readers around the world.

Sign up for Lee Jackson's newsletter at
severnriverbooks.com
LeeJackson@SevernRiverBooks.com

Printed in the United States
by Baker & Taylor Publisher Services